Forbidden Speculation

edited by
Seth Crossman

Golden Acorn Press

Individual story copyrights appear at the end of the book.
Cover Art © 2007 Lee Kuruganti

A Golden Acorn Press Book
384 Markowitz Road
Parish, NY 13131

Printed in the United States of America

for those dreamers
and those who don't

The Insides

9 The Other Side
Greg Schwartz

11 With Mars in His Hand
Bosley Gravel

22 Certified Organic
Sara Genge

26 Five Dead Women
Lori Strongin

37 Bilroy Five
Michael Savastano

45 Something Sinister
Joseph Vadalma

49 Deep Waters
Manfred Gabriel

56 Love in the Time of the Serpent-King
Rachel Astruc

65 Dwarfblood
Berrien Henderson

79 Poetic License
Lindsey Duncan

93 Farewell Dinner
Jakob Drud

98 I Am Tellis Moore
L. Christopher DelGuercio

114 Inside of Me
James Steimle

126 Paper Cuts
Timalyne Frazier

129 The Treasure
Michael Davis

136 The Darkness of Truth
Steven Mathes

143 The Fate of the Crystal Eye
Barton Paul Levenson

Introduction

I was seventeen when I first traveled out of the country. I remember stepping off the plane in Shannon, Ireland to a light drizzle. It was six in the morning and I hadn't slept on the plane at all because of how stiff and uncomfortable it was trying to sleep in an upright chair. I had to use the bathroom and hadn't because of an unreasonable dread of airplane bathrooms. My backpack was heavy and there was an almost unbearable pressure on my bladder, but I still walked with a feeling of incredible anticipation—the same kind of feeling a king must have the day he is crowned or a bride on the morning of her wedding or Neil Armstrong had when he set foot on the moon. Something special was happening, was going to happen, and I was going to be part of it.

Every time I travel I have that hope, that excitement that makes my toes sweat. What will I see? What will I smell? What will I taste? Who will I meet? What will be around that corner? Is today the day my life changes forever? Is it going to be the kind of day that stories are made of?

While traveling is great, we can't do it all the time. But when we pick up a book, turn a page and start reading, we do travel. We travel to impossible places and times and become swash-buckling heroes and terrible villains and ordinary people with extraordinary lives. We live, we love, we laugh, we get lost in experiences we could never have a chance of living. That's what makes picking up a good book so addicting.

This is one of those books.

When I set out to collect the stories for this anthology, I knew that I wanted stories that pushed the limit, that made us think about the lives we live and how those lives might change if one or two "impossibles" suddenly became reality. I wanted stories with characters I loved or hated. I wanted stories that moved me. I wanted the anthology to be diverse at the same time a single theme ran through all the stories.

I knew what I was looking for. And I found it. The seventeen stories in this anthology were chosen from an overwhelming number of submissions. Each one speculates about crossing the line from what we consider acceptable conduct and reality to what is forbidden.

I hope you enjoy the journey.

Seth Crossman, December 2007

The Other Side
by Greg Schwartz

Greg Schwartz fixes copiers in Baltimore, Maryland while he patiently waits to win the lottery. His stories have appeared in Black Petals, Writer's Journal, Theatre of Decay, and Dark Jesters. He is the staff cartoonist for SP Quill Magazine and his chapbook of horror poems, "Bits and Pieces," is available from Spec House of Poetry.

This story pulls you into another world and leaves you there.

John stepped out of the shower and grabbed his towel. Melissa would be yelling soon, but there was no helping it. He needed the shower. It helped him relax before a long evening with the in-laws.

"John? You ready yet?" Her sweet voice floated under the door, right on cue.

"Coming, hon." He stood in front of the mirror and dried his hair. Then he wrapped the towel around his waist and reached for his toothbrush.

Movement in the mirror caught his eye. He spun around, looking for a spider on the wall. He hated spiders. But there was nothing—just the empty towel rod.

He turned back to the mirror and examined his stomach. He'd lost twenty pounds in the past three months, and it showed. He flexed his arms and smiled at his reflection.

Suddenly he cried out and leapt backwards, slamming against the towel rod. *His reflection had winked at him.*

John shook his head and rubbed at his eyes. His heart pounded against his ribcage. Cautiously he glanced at the mirror.

His reflection regarded him, arms crossed. It was grinning.

John felt the room start to spin. He grabbed the counter to steady himself. The world slowly lost focus, and John wondered if he was going blind. Then he blinked and everything came back into sharp relief. When he was able to let go of the counter, he looked back up at the mirror.

He thought back on all of the horror novels he'd read as a kid.

They all had one thing in common—*the vampire in the story never cast a reflection.* The mirror showed every aspect of the bathroom perfectly, minus the fact that he was standing right in the middle of it.

John splashed cold water on his face and closed his eyes. This was crazy. It must be stress. His mind was telling him to stop working so much.

Avoiding the mirror, he put his hand on the doorknob and turned.

The door didn't open.

John frowned. He turned the knob again and pulled, to no avail.

"Melissa," he called, rattling the knob, "the doorknob's busted on this side."

That's odd, he thought. His voice sounded strangely muted, like he was speaking into a blanket. He called his wife's name again with no response.

John saw something sparkle out of the corner of his eye. He turned and saw his wife in the mirror, wearing a long black dress and the diamond necklace he'd bought her for their anniversary. Standing next to her, calmly adjusting his tie, was John.

No, John thought, *that's not me*! His mind felt like a bowl of stirred jelly. *That can't be me—I'm standing here in a towel.*

The Melissa-reflection said something he couldn't quite catch, and the John-reflection laughed. Then they both walked out of the bathroom, out of sight.

"Melissa!" John shouted. He hammered on the mirror with his fists. It felt more like steel than like glass.

This isn't real, he told himself firmly. *What the hell is going on?*

He tried the door again. This time he braced one foot against the wall as he pulled, but the door didn't budge an inch. He put his face to the floor to peer under the door, and panic pounced on him like a starving tiger.

There was no gap under the door. The door and the tile floor met seamlessly, like conjoined twins. There was a shallow indentation running the length of the bottom of the door, which to the casual observer would appear to be a gap, but the door and the floor were one.

The air suddenly felt too heavy, and John had to struggle to catch his breath. He inspected the sides of the door with the same impossible result. The door was merely part of the wall, with only carved indentations to make it look like an actual door. John sank to the floor and tried to think.

On an impulse he grabbed the cabinet doors, expecting them to be fake as well. But they swung open easily, revealing an empty cabinet where there should have been extra rolls of toilet paper and various arcane feminine products.

He closed the cabinet with a sigh. Then he noticed the scratches.

They were carved into the wood near the bottom of the cabinet.

Harsh, angular letters formed two simple words.

MY TURN.

John screamed.

With Mars In His Hand
by Bosley Gravel

Bosley Gravel has published over a dozen short stories and poems in venues such as The Deepening, Bewildering Stories, Wanderings Magazine, and Insolent Rudder. He is finishing his second novel while the first one is circulating the world looking for a lucky publisher.
This is a story of love that crosses space and time, but can it cross death?

Two months ago Javi would never have guessed he'd be smuggling his beloved wife's corpse into a museum.

He blasted a third guard with his gun. The guard would live. Javi had seen too much death already to kill them without reason, but he wasn't going to let them stop him. The alarm was a rhythmic wild chirp that would have disoriented him if he hadn't expected it and worn a protective helmet.

Two more guards turned the corner, and with no hesitation in their hands they fired blue beams across the room. Javi flung himself behind the cryo-coffin as it gyrated wildly in the air like a log on water. He drew it down. Amiel, his beloved, was inside. He had to be gentle with her. All this would be for naught if they damaged her exquisite flesh.

"Javier Jelcor, we have been authorized by the state to take your life . . . but we'd rather take you alive." The voice was transmitted on all the channels, and Javi heard it through the speakers in his helmet.

"I don't want to do this . . . I knew Amiel . . . she was my friend."

Javi clenched his jaw, pressed a button on the coffin and let gravity hold it to the floor. The ship was in the next room. He knew because he'd grown up in this strange tribute to a more innocent time.

"Leave me be! I just want my grandfather's ship, and I'll be gone." he said into his helmet's mic.

"You're upset, Javi," the guard broadcasted. "That ship will never get off the ground!"

Javi's accomplice blasted the two guards in the back. He motioned to Javi, who already had the coffin floating in the air again.

The accomplice disappeared around the corner. Javi rushed to keep up—and there it was, the Negal Planet Hopper. The first fully functional, self sufficient, interplanetary, four man star-cruiser. He hoped the relic still flew. He needed it to . . . or . . . or nothing mattered anymore.

Javi's accomplice was already hacking the perimeter lasers—they were mostly for show anyway. The curators had long since removed the ship's heart, a synthetic crystal core. Javi hoped the one he had saved for some thirty years still had magic in it. The accomplice was through the first pathetic defense of the exhibit. He physically forced the door open after some crude fumbling.

The ship looked surprisingly like the flying saucers of the previous century's bad science fictions. But it was only a superficial resemblance—once the thing was airborne and the shields went up it would look as smooth and sleek as any modern craft. Granddad had built this prototype in his spare time. He stole minutes here and there, like a poet might compose a line or two, and what had resulted was many years ahead of his time.

"Javi, get over here! We have about ten minutes to get this erector set off the ground."

"Copy that." Javi squeezed the coffin through the door. He disappeared into the ship's hull, while his accomplice nervously guarded the ship.

* * *

The coffin was large enough to be a hindrance in the small cockpit, but they worked around it. Javi pulled off his mask. He was a handsome man, with a trim black beard and dark brown eyes barely visible by the sorrow tightening his eyelids. He bit down on his lower lip, and watched the small panel that split four ways, each pane, covering a quarter of the outside view of the ship. More guards were gathering, pointing their guns. A guard's voice came through his discarded helmet.

"Javier, please surrender yourself. Your service credits to the state will be considered. The ship can't fly. "

Javi didn't listen to them. He slid the crystal into place. His accomplice fiddled with some knobs, and the spaceship came alive with a quiet whurr. Outside the guards were scrambling, confused at the ring of rolling blue fire that built under the machine. The wooden mounts smoked and turned to ash and the ground blackened.

The accomplice spoke. "Is it a go?"

"Yes," Javi said. He turned on the space-barrier and pulled the throttle. They shot upwards, crashing through the ceiling, leaving the guards on the ground scrambling for cover, pointing and shaking their heads.

* * *

Aruno Rickle, the accomplice, took off his mask. He was, in a way, beautiful to Javi. Aruno was the twin brother of Amiel, Javi's wife. His eyes were pale china blue, as if God himself had flecked them with pieces of shattered planets, moons, whole ringed solar systems. His hair, like hers, hung in tight curls down the back of his neck. For a moment, Javi wished it was Aruno in that coffin instead of Amiel.

Aruno looked to the four consoles and watched the sphere of the earth become smaller and smaller. He shook his head and put it gently in his hands. They wouldn't be able to return to earth now.

"Another eighteen hours until Mars," Javi said, ignoring Aruno's quiet regret.

"The seeds?" Aruno asked.

"Got them, wouldn't be here if I didn't," Javi opened a pocket on his suit, and dug around and pulled out a plastic bag full of what appeared to be acorns. "Trees," he said, and handed them to Aruno.

"Do you think they will grow? You think she'll want them?"

"I don't know," Javi said, focusing on the controls. He didn't want to think about the possibility that she might not want them, that he might not have the price she demanded.

Aruno watched the view panel that pointed towards Mars. A faint red light among all the rest.

"You know the ship will only take two of us back?"

"Of course," Javi said with irritation. "I told *you* as much. It's too late to back out, and you know that, so sit down and shut up."

Aruno took no offense. Amiel had been the world to Javi, to him, and anyone who had met her.

* * *

The Negal Planet Hopper set down on Mars gracefully, all worked as designed. Aruno had been here once before, and he had hated it. In those days, before all the death had come on its pale horse, he had been a contractor. He had delivered supplies here. The place was haunted, he felt, not only by the thousands of Chinese who had died here four hundred and fifty years ago of plague and famine, but also by the ghosts of cult members that had been exiled here. The other spirits were older, much older.

He knew Mars was a graveyard, and he had come anyway.

Javi and Aruno waited in the air lock with their helmets on, as pistons hissed and vents closed and pressurized. They entered the welcome chamber. The room had not changed much from when it was built. Chinese writing dominated the signage, but they had worked tiny English letters into the information.

They removed their helmets once the needled gauge on the wall was pointing to a blue spot between two red zones and they felt the artificial gravity tugging at them.

"What you want?" a voice said, the creature springing from the shadows with surprisingly light steps—the ancient voice like old reeds rasping in the wind, and perhaps was once human. It's only garment, a silky cape, hung around its neck.

"Chino?" Javi asked.

The creature stood up. It had long smooth breasts, waxy brown like the rest of its body. Its face was covered with light white fuzz that matched its tightly tied pony tail. The false gravity had pulled its pot belly into the same shape as its breasts.

"I got a lot of names," it said, and stood up. It was female, Aruno decided, only because it lacked an appendage between its legs. "But call me what you will," she said.

"We've got seeds," Javi said.

"Seeds?" Chino said, and gurgled something in her throat and spat to the ground. "Get out!"

Javi held them up in the bag. Chino sniffed the air. "Infertile," she said simply.

She walked towards them, her eyes on the coffin.

"What is this box? Another smelly corpse?"

"Can you really raise the dead?" Aruno said.

"Pffft, pffft," Chino replied. "Not for seeds. For plants. Plants for my garden. No seeds."

"So you can?" Javi asked, his hands trembling.

"Maybe," she sniffed the air around the coffin. "You brought the plague, yes, you did."

"She died of it," Aruno said softly.

"Pfft. Pffft, no matter. Old Chino has lived here a long time. Ate a lot of meat. She isn't afraid of the plague."

"Will you help us?" Javi asked.

She thought for a moment. "No," Chino said finally.

Javi sighed deeply. "I'm sorry," he said, "But I'm a desperate man." He pulled his gun.

Chino grinned. "What you want? The pain?"

Aruno and Javi both fell to their knees, fingers pressed into their ears, yet they could still hear her.

"Stupid, stupid, stupid," she said.

Javi had long since dropped his weapon. She picked it up and pulled out the safety chip, she sniffed it once and then popped it into her mouth and gagged as she choked it down. It took them a moment to recover from whatever magic she had defended herself with. They shook the ringing from their heads and reamed their ears with their fingers trying to shake the confusion from their consciousness.

"Maybe," she said. "I have a good idea . . . you grow the seeds. Grow them in my garden. If plants are strong, I'll raise her up."

* * *

Aruno pulled Javi to a corner of the room.

"She's crazy," Aruno whispered.

"Oh yes, yes, I am!" Chino yelled. "No doubt on Mars."

Aruno glanced at her and back to Javi. "Javi, please. Be truthful to yourself. She can't raise the dead. She's just some crazy old woman, kept alive by God knows what kind of drugs and tech."

"I'm staying. These seeds will grow. I know it."

Aruno shook his head no, and held out his hand.

"She was my sister, and I want her back too."

"Take the ship, go to Venus. Amiel told me your parents' property is still available to you."

Javi looked at Chino who was mumbling to herself and measuring out lengths of air with her fingers.

"Take it or leave it," she said. "My garden wants me."

"Javi?"

"Go," Javi said.

Aruno nodded. Javi was a ruined man anyway, he'd be imprisoned on Earth, and he'd die of a broken heart if he came with him to Venus. They'd have to leave Amiel's corpse. There wasn't enough fuel for the three of them. Aruno was positive that if anyone could die from sorrow it would be Javi, and he didn't want to watch it happen.

"Thank you," Javi said, "For not making this—"

"Don't thank me—" Aruno said looking around. Chino had one leg propped against the wall. She scratched herself in a most unladylike fashion. "Thank yourself," he finished.

* * *

Chino's garden was huge, both in the size of the plot and the size of flora. For unknown reasons the plants grew to incredible sizes. The citizens of the garden varied, and came in all forms: tiger lilies the size of men, mushrooms the size of children, hibiscus hung their heavy heads like drunken men at a bar. Javi held the bobbing coffin behind him, as he took in the sights and smells of the garden. Fruit trees like apple, fig and pears accented the foliage. A great dome let in the light and huge machines pumped the air into the rest of the colony complex and return vents brought it back. Javi was struck by the beauty of the garden as well as the simplicity of the dome engineering. Chino had nearly solved the problem that had portended the ruin of the original colony. Food and air, at least for a few people, was being generated in a self sufficient cycle. In the center of the garden a large phallic fountain humidified the whole room.

Through the seemingly clear dome, Javi saw the Negal Planet Hopper rising up on a length of blue fire.

"When you get hungry, have some fruit," Chino said.

Javi looked around. "Where can I keep the cryo-coffin?"

"Put it with the others. Follow me." Chino led him down a path through the garden.

"Eat the fruit, but I say don't eat that one," she pointed. Javi glanced at it momentarily. It looked like nothing special to him.

"Why?"

"Nightmares," she said.

They cut off to the left on the path, and quickly came to hooded area. Dozens of cryo-coffins lay in disorder. Javi's eyes shone as he saw that, yes, some of them were empty. He recognized models that were well over seventy years old.

"Did you raise this many?"

"Many, many," she said.

A handful of the coffins were still sealed.

"What about these?"

"Can't raise 'em all," she said. "When they don't pay, I don't raise."

Javi parked Amiel's coffin. He pressed a button and the hood became translucent. He gazed upon her; finally the feeling that she was only asleep was warranted. The milky barrier between them blurred her image. Chino was licking her lips and looking over his shoulder.

"Good looking meat," she said shyly.

"She's my wife. Not food, you crazy bitch!"

Chino looked guilty. Her face twisted up in a look of deep personal hurt.

"I know about you," he said. "I've heard the stories. They say you were the only one left alive up here . . . your government hid the fact your colony was perishing of famine—and forced to extreme measures you did what no one ever should do . . . and where are all the 'followers.' Where are they now?"

"You'd eat them up too," she said scratching herself again. "Mister, Mister who never ate the dead. If you are hungry you do it too."

Javi shook his head angrily. "Look, Chino, this coffin has what amounts to a nuclear bomb inside it. I've been chipped with enough smart silicon to blow this thing up from across the planet with a simple hand gesture. It will take half of Mars with it, and I've got nothing to lose. If you try to tamper with it, I promise it will detonate. So don't fuck with me, or her."

Chino considered this for a moment. "Bah, you're telling me stories," she said. "Go plant your seeds." She whipped her robe around her and wandered off into the garden mumbling to herself in Chinese.

"Where do I plant them?" he yelled after her.

"Where ever, when ever," she said, and disappeared off into the jungle of plants.

* * *

He found a shovel and a bucket in a small makeshift shed and wandered the garden. A library of pleasant fragrances worked into his nose and his mouth. He could taste the nectar and pollen on the artificial breeze. Nothing like this existed on earth, he thought, or probably ever would. The flowers loomed with a strange anthropomorphic presence. Small mechanical bees buzzed, exchanging pollen and grooming the plants. Javi knew these were the expensive ones from the way their wings buzzed. These bees would have a hive somewhere, and it would be dripping with amber honey.

He passed the tree that Chino had told him to never eat from. Poison, he thought. What else could it be?

He had been searching for a patch of dirt, but everywhere seemed to be mulched with mounds of dead plants and leaves. He picked a spot and ran his shovel down on the earth, testing the firmness. An angry howl came from the dirt; Javi stepped back fearfully.

"Not here! Not here!" Chino pulled herself from the mulch.

"Where then?" Javi said, his voice a cross between anger and fear.

"I was sleeping a good sleep too. You watch out, you can only sleep when the ghosts let you," she said, shaking the loamy mulch from her wizened body. She picked the bits that still clung to her with thin fingers.

"Ghosts?"

"Mars is all ghosts," she said, "Nothing but ghosts of the living and the dead."

"Spare me the religion. Where should I plant these seeds?"

"Here is fine," she said, "Plant your seeds."

Javi scraped away at the ground.

"I'm going somewhere else to finish my nap." Chino said.

"Go then," he said.

He struck the dirt, and although he had no experience, his instinct told him he should till the soil, and so he did. He dug deep and turned the dirt back into the resulting hole, until it was smooth and silky. These seeds would grow, he promised himself. If he had to breath his own life into them, they would grow, and he would be with Amiel again. He pushed them six inches into the soil and covered them. He fetched water from the fountain and watered the seeds.

* * *

The dome grayed itself, for it was not truly transparent, but only mimicked the outside world. Like a great glass eye, it watched the universe and interpreted the results for those who lived under its protection. He made his way in the dusk to the pile of coffins, found a large one and removed the door and tore the lining from another. He set it down next to Amiel, climbed in and covered himself with the liner and tried to sleep. But his mind kept whispering a macabre plan of opening the coffin next to him and brushing his lips against Amiel's cool flesh, of holding her close and weeping. And what if Chino couldn't raise her?

Then Mars would have two more ghosts, he thought.

* * *

He dreamed of Golgotha, the place of bones, out on the barren red surface of Mars. The wind had whipped this rock into the shape of a skull, and the bones and skulls of a thousand people lay half crushed, piled up around it. Chino was perched on top, gnawing on fresh piece of bloody meat, holding it by a great chunk of bone. The blood dripped down her chin and her chest.

Then he could see the ghosts—so many it was if Mars was nothing more than the dead embodied. Trying to see Chino on her bone pile was like trying to see through tears, but the tears were souls, lost and angry. Where was Amiel's ghost in this mess? he thought frantically. Where in this mass of writhing angry spirits? Would Chino pick one at random and animate Amiel's perfect flesh with it?

He woke gasping in air; the dome was still dark. It took several minutes for him to calm himself down. He could see stars in the glass dome, and as he ran his eyes over them, he realized the view was forged; he saw mistakes in the constellations. For some reason he took comfort in this, and let himself drift back into sleep.

* * *

Gray streaked his once black hair, his ears drooped slightly on the sides of his head. The difference in his appearance was not subtle, but time is the one force man had never tamed, nor ever would. Time trumps all—as a child Javi had played the ancient game of paper, rock, scissors with his grandfather, and he thought now, of the great width, the length, the depth of the universe—time trumped them all. It trumped love, indifference, and soon, he hoped, it would trump greedy death.

He had braided his beard tightly and it still hung to his groin. He looked up at his tree, stroking the thick braid. He had built a small day camp here, but always returned at night to sleep next to Amiel's coffin. The clocks here were unpredictable, jumping ahead hours, even days. He had notched a stick when the dome would gray, but perhaps even that was not accurate. Per his morning ritual he made a notch and laid the stick with the other sixteen.

The tree was taller than him now, but as the flowers grew large the tree grew stunted as if some great force had equalized all the plants of this garden. He hadn't seen Chino for nearly two years, but this was not too strange. She came and went, perhaps burying herself deep in the loamy ground for months at a time. He had given up searching for her long ago. Wherever she went he could not find her or follow.

So he waited. When she appeared again he would force her to raise Amiel. It had been long enough—it had been long enough ten years ago. Chino had been right about the ghosts. They haunted every moment of his sleep, and sometimes when he was awake he would hear their murmurs . . . but never Amiel. Why not Amiel? Where was her ghost? What chance did Chino have when Amiel's soul still haunted the earth and not this ghoul infested chunk of rock?

"Chino!" he yelled, "It's time! I'm going to beat the wrinkles out of your stinking carcass if you don't show yourself."

No reply came, just the quiet buzz of the mechanical bees.

"Chino!"

Nothing.

* * *

For a month he stalked her in the forest of flowers. He'd often catch the tail of her robe just leaving his sight around a bend or a couple of footprints pressed into the mud. Sometimes she would cackle and he would follow the noise, but to no avail. Other days he'd beg and plead as he wandered the garden. Often he'd find her wastes buried like tiny corpses in shallow graves.

* * *

He found the beehive during one of his long searches. Indeed, it was dripping with honey. The hive was a tall structure, semi-organic, semi machine. The back side dripped unharvested honey.

He tapped the exposed buttons, a screen and an input device unfolded itself. He overrode the programming so the bees would not bother him. He poked his fingers into the dripping honey and pushed them to his mouth, and licked the sticky sweetness, savoring its richness.

"That's mine!" Chino said, appearing from behind a raspberry bush. Javi, not wasting a second, grabbed her by the throat. She instantly invaded his mind, bringing him to his knees, his huge hand pulling back as if he was being electrocuted.

"Rude! Eat my honey and try to snuff me. Rude! Rude!" she said and released him from her hold.

He stood up. "The tree is grown," he said, gasping for breath and massaging his hand. It felt like the muscle might have torn.

"Yes, promise is a promise," she said.

"So you'll do it?"

"If you leave my honey alone."

"I will," he said. "When?"

"Soon," she said. "Stars have to be just right."

"How long?" he asked.

"One week," she said.

"One week," he repeated back. "And if you don't. I'm blowing up Mars."

She looked him in the eyes and he hoped she could see the sincerity.

"Doesn't work sometimes," she said. "Sometimes the dead want to be dead."

"The tree is grown," he said, "and I have nothing more to live for."

"Why she so special?" Chino asked. "You can get a new wife."

"Because she was my universe. She was what all other beauty is judged by. She was perfect."

"Bah," Chino said, and licked her lips, "Never was anything perfect in this universe, except maybe my garden."

He shook his head. "You are wrong."

She shrugged.

* * *

The next week was agony to Javi, each second seemed to spasm for an eternity, but finally the time passed. Chino had come to him, her arms full of huge flowers. Her lips pulled back showing off teeth worn almost down to the gums. She inspected the tree somberly as she walked around it twice and then carefully retraced her steps.

"Come on, come on. I knew you could do it."

Javi followed her as she led the way to Amiel's soon to be living body. It only took minutes before they got to the coffin.

"Open it up," Chino said.

"You know this can only be done once? I can't seal it again."

Chino shrugged from behind her load of flowers. "Only need once," she said.

Javi typed a code on the keypad. The coffin seemed to gasp, almost like an infant's first breath. Chino shuddered as if she had caught a chill.

Amiel was the eye through which the universe beheld itself, thought Javi. He felt weak, as if he might faint from looking upon her perfection. Chino dumped her arm load of flowers into the coffin.

"Good looking," Chino said, licking her thin brown lips, and started organizing the flowers. It took a few moments, and when Chino was done, Amiel was fittingly wreathed in flowers, their beauty slight in contrast. Chino put two large daisies on her eyes.

"Is it working?" Javi asked.

"No," Chino said. "But I only started." She had a small length of branch and several of the fruit she had warned him about hung on the branch. They were small, perhaps no larger than the tip of his thumb.

"I thought they were poison?"

"No. The Fruit of Life. Only plant native to Mars. The first tree in my garden."

Chino pried open Amiel's mouth and pushed one in.

"Don't hurt her," Javi said.

"Oh, Mister Mister, she is still dead right now."

He clenched his jaw. "Raise her up."

Chino looked at him nervously. "Can you really blow up my garden?"

"Yes," he said.

"Oh," she said and lifted one of Amiel's perfect feet and examined the sole. She put her ear to it, listened for a moment, and put it back down gently in the coffin.

"The bells," Chino said. "Not with out the bells." She began patting herself down. Javi considered with disgust, where she might have stored any bells she might be carrying. But she came up empty handed.

She shook her head, "I'll be right back," she said.

"I expect you will." Javi looked as his watch. "In ten minutes, or you know what I'll do."

"Sure, sure," she said, and wandered off, not even in a hurry.

* * *

His watch read eight minutes, and he was beginning to curse under his breath. Another three minutes passed. He watched the third minute cycle by on his watch. Chino wandered back, her fingers now adorned with tiny bells that jingled as she came. She snapped her fingers at Javi.

"I'm late," she said. "Mars is still here."

"I gave you the benefit of the doubt."

"And yourself too," she said, jingling her hands at him.

"Get on with it," he said.

She showed him her gray tongue and rolled her ancient eyes. Amiel's beauty was still unreal to him as he watched Chino press her fingers into her cheeks, adjusting the fruit.

"I ate some, you know, a long time ago," she said. "And now I'll live forever. So will she. You are an old man, and she will be young forever."

"She deserves it," he said.

"Crazy man, nobody deserves it," she said and began her ceremony. Chino blew her own breath into Amiel's mouth, forcing the fruit deep. She massaged her throat, as Javi grimaced and finally turned away when she removed the bells from her hand and pushed her small fist down Amiel's throat, pushing the fruit deeper and deeper. She sang while she worked, something in Chinese. He turned back when he heard the bells go back on her fingers. She shook them over the corpse, still singing her haunting song.

Javi took one of Amiel's hands, and gazed at the daisies over her eyes. He prayed to a God he didn't even believe in. And in the end, it didn't seem to matter. Chino gave up, shaking her head.

"Can take a while, sometimes, or not at all."

Javi was weeping now, and when he regained himself he cursed Chino and chased her away by throwing handfuls of flowers from the blanket she had wreathed Amiel with. Chino scampered away cackling like a crow scolding an intruder. He crawled in the coffin and lay beside Amiel, his true love, his hand and hers together, wondering how it all had amounted to this . . . he squeezed gently, trying to remember the precise gesture that would activate the weapon in the coffin, trying to remember if it was even real or just something he had invented to scare Chino and deluded himself into believing.

His body grew weak with sorrow, and he lay watching the false sky turn dark, squeezing Amiel's hand, hoping to perhaps randomly trigger the bomb, end his life and shatter this graveyard like a rock under a sledge hammer . . . and where would the ghosts go, he thought? Not earth, it too was a graveyard now. He was sure it was full of its own restless dead. The plague had brought that final destiny. Venus? Too far, he thought. Working Amiel's hand in his, he squeezed with what he hoped was his last movement. But to his joy, Amiel squeezed back.

Certified Organic
by Sara Genge

Sara Genge is a medical student in Madrid, Spain. Her work has appeared in Strange Horizons, Helix SF, and OG's Speculative Fiction among others. She is a founding member and contributor of the Daily Cabal, a microfiction site.

This story is about a disabled woman who ponders love with the wrong kind of man.

The waiter lifted the metal beer kegs so that Una's wheelchair could pass. The bar reeked of tobacco, spilt alcohol and something acrid coming from the basement..

Nestor followed closely without touching her chair. It had taken Una several weeks of scolding to teach the government appointed robot not to help her with things she could handle herself, but he was getting better at not annoying her all the time.

They sat and she ordered a large beer, wondering how many it would take to get her from paraplegic to paralytic. She pulled out her PDA and started fooling around with graphics she needed to get done for work. She drank and worked fast, making a bet with herself that she'd get the job done before she was too drunk to do anything coherent. Nestor sat in petrified politeness, just another reminder that he was not human. She wasn't bitching; he was damn useful. If she got too drunk she could always ask him to synthesize her some analgesics. Speaking of which, would he obey orders for illegal medication? Una thought she'd been too good when she was whole and she'd gotten screwed all the same, proof that staying off drugs hadn't done her much good.

She was sitting in a wheelchair in a decrepit bar alone with a robot. What did she have to lose?

"Nestor, what are kids doing nowadays?"

His pupils contracted, a sure sign that he was focusing on her expression to try to understand the underlying meaning of her words. His eyes roamed her face, paying special attention to her eyes and mouth. When his face went blank, Una knew that he'd understood her.

Nestor clicked alive. "MDMA, cocaine, pot and some new synths. The usual," he said.

"State uses, doses and secondary effects," she ordered.

He did. She looked down at her beer. Maybe she was taking this angst thing too far? Her life was shit, but did she really want to risk it? Most of those drugs sounded nasty.

"Anything safer?" She asked.

Nestor turned to her with a hint of a smile. She hadn't known he could do that. By God, he even seemed to understand what was going on in her head. Did he know what she was thinking of doing? She shivered and hoped he wasn't as sophisticated as he let on.

"I can make something new, " he whispered, "something special, just for you."

"Shouldn't you be talking me out of this?" Una said.

"I'm here to serve," he answered.

She shut her eyes. Tears burnt behind her eyelids. She nodded hard, so that the robot would know it was an order.

Nestor dipped a finger into her Guinness.

"Is that it?" Una asked.

The robot nodded. Una smiled, put her PDA away and drank up.

There were lights. There was music. That's all she would remember the next day. Stink of sweat, specially intense since Una's wheelchair came up to the dancers' armpits, people rubbing against each other, most of them higher up than Una was. Bodies parted to let Una twirl, quickly learning that their limbs could not compete with a metalloplastic wheelchair. Nestor fluttered at the edge of her vision, keeping the thugs at bay, filtering the men into those who could approach her, and those he wouldn't let close. She didn't resent it, although she would have liked to meet that cold blue eyed guy. A boy, maybe eighteen, sat on her knees and tilted a glass to her lips, then jumped off and offered the same drink to some ten or twenty people.

They left before dawn. Nestor removed his jacket, which he had no use for anyway, and placed it on Una's shoulders. That's when she noticed that he had his own particular odor, something about the copper his body used instead of iron to carry oxygen. It was a neutral smell and marked him off as not human at first sniff.

She told him about it, more than anything because she knew she'd forget otherwise, and she was too lazy to get out her PDA.

"You've got a good sense of smell, for a human," he said.

She looked back surprised, and then realized that, of course, these beings would have the best sensory perception in the animal kingdom. If you were going to make something artificial, you might as well make it perfect.

"Does the smell bother you? I'm sure I can reprogram my biochemistry to something less offensive."

"Oh no, not at all. She dug her nose into the jacket. It's quite nice, actually." She looked up at him with an impish smile. The game came naturally to Una and she hadn't played it in a long time. She looked down, fake modesty, and wondered at the limits of his humanity. The drug clouded her judgement and she wondered if Nestor could transcend his nature and be a real companion.

"Are you still awake?" he whispered.

Una nodded.

"Then we should go to a place I know. I want to show you something," he said.

The first sniff told Una that the clients in this joint were mostly not human.

"Very illegal," Nestor whispered. "But I know I can trust you." His innocence was so endearing.

Of course it was illegal for a robot to go off alone, specially if the owner had given it an order to hibernate. Una was soon surrounded by what had been described by a savvy politician as "a waste of expensive batteries." Except for their scent, the things around her looked perfectly human. That is, until they came too close and the lack of wrinkles, imperfections, hell, even pores, gave them away. Still, they were remarkably well designed. Their skins ranged from Nordic whites to chocolate to blueish-black. She wondered vaguely why anyone would go to the trouble of making a robot's skin seem real but then another wave of whatever Nestor had given her washed through her system. The drug seemed to be a slow release chemical and as it took hold, she stopped looking at the pores and the unnatural perfection of them, and concentrated on dancing.

Several robots circled her. Nestor had seemed placid in the last joint, but here, he drove off the other artificials as if there were no tomorrow.

Una found this funny. She found everything funny. The robots, their coppery smell, the blue aseptic pee on the walls. Very funny. Everything funny.

She woke up at home with a tolerable hangover. Nestor lay beside her on the bed. She'd never seen him naked before.

"What happened?" she asked.

"What do you think happened?" he answered.

He helped her sit up. His eyes laughed back at her. She hardly remembered anything, not that it mattered, she thought ruefully, she wouldn't have felt much anyway, would she?

"I'm a certified organic robot," he said. "You knew I would adapt to please you, didn't you?"

She nodded, but she didn't really understand. Yes, she'd been told about the learn and adapt bit. She'd always thought that meant he'd learn from his mistakes and that she wouldn't have to repeat an order more than a couple of times. She hadn't expected him to seduce her.

"You're a weird little person, Una. You take some getting used to," Nestor said. "My brain is a thousand times faster than a human's and I almost burnt it out getting into your groove."

Una stared back at the being besides her. What was wrong with him? Was she still hallucinating? She closed her eyes, focusing inward for that drifting feeling you get in dreams. It wasn't there. Should she ask Nestor to pinch her? No, she didn't really care if this was real or not.

"Would you like to go out with me sometime?" she asked.

She saw his pupils contracting and decided to save him the extra computing time.

"Go out, as in a date," she continued.

"I thought you'd never ask," Nestor said and took her hand.

Una shivered: his skin was too smooth for a man.

"Do you need help getting into the shower?" he said

"No, help me into the chair and I'll manage."

He shook his head.

"I have to help you; I was programmed to help you." He picked her up and placed her on the chair.

"Leave it. Go robot yourself or something, I can handle!" she said.

"It's not about whether you can handle just fine or not, it's about whether I'm willing to let you get around or not." He seemed dead serious. This wasn't funny any more.

"Nestor, let me be," she said.

"No!"

"Nestor..."

"Fuck you, Una!" He seemed to be picking up all her bad habits. "I'm meant to help you and you've been fighting me from day one. What the fuck is your problem? Don't you realize I've been programmed to help? How do you think I feel if I can't help you?" Nestor said.

Una gasped. She hadn't bargained for this. Who did this machine think it was anyway? How dare it speak to her like that.

"No! And that's that." She felt vindictive and she made sure it showed in her voice. "But I've got to say, you surprised me back there. Never thought a day would come when a robot would surprise me," she said.

He leaned back on the bed and looked genuinely sad. What gave him the right to try and manipulate her like this? It was a pose, and he knew she knew it. A robot could not feel.

"I can't stand aside and watch you struggle to do even the most basic things. I'm meant to help you. That is my mission, it's the reason why I'm alive." He saw Una's look and corrected himself. "Or functioning or whatever you want to call it. I won't let you do this to yourself. I'll help you and that's final."

It stung. She did struggle. But she needed to have some control over her life. She knew cripples who let their robots carry them around like oversized sacks, but not her. She'd vowed she'd never go down that road.

"Nestor: erase temp archives of the last twenty-four hours".

He started to cry but then the command took hold and his face went blank.

"Nestor, I'm going to shower. Check the mail while I dress, OK?"

"Yes, Una," he answered in his best monotone.

The robot looked bewildered as he fumbled for his clothes and got out of her room. It was sad watching Nestor trying to make sense of the situation but not daring to ask her. What the hell, he didn't have a right to boss her. He was her property. She was perfectly entitled to do as she wished. If she couldn't remember last night, it was perfectly correct that he shouldn't either. It had been a mistake and she should forget it. Thank God she hadn't compounded it by going out with him. How pathetic was that anyway? Nothing good would ever come of that kind of relationship.

Una made her way to the bathroom, took off her clothes and drove her wheelchair under the shower. When the gentle pellets of water drummed on her skull, she started to cry.

Five Dead Women
by Lori T. Strongin

An English/Creative Writing honors graduate of the University of Colorado at Boulder and conference director of the Florida Writers Association, Lori Strongin currently works at Walt Disney World. She has been published in Tip o' the Tongue, Reflections of the Flatirons, Beneath the Harvest Moon, The Florida Palm, and the Florida Writer. She gets her ideas from an overactive imagination, lucid dreams, and many sleepless nights.

This story is about five women all linked to one man.

1

If not for the choking cloud of blue smoke filling the room, the scene might appear tranquil. A glass beaker, its liquid the color of death, sits among crumpled papers, open bottles and gray ashes. The thick liquid inside remains paralyzed, undisturbed by ripples or bubbles. A stirring rod, still smeared with the remnants of the concoction, lies abandoned on the counter. And a flask, a chip now marring the rim from the fall, is clutched in the fist of a woman, whose body preceded it to the floor.

Marie enters the room seconds after hearing the crash. Surveying the scene with wide eyes, she takes in the smoke, the lab equipment, the thick liquid, the glass rod, the flask, and lastly, the woman. The color of the liquid does not escape the intelligent six year old, nor does the fact that this woman has never mixed a formula wrong in her life.

The girl looks on a moment longer, the haze in her head slowly sharpening into shapes —a dark rider on a pale horse—that brings to mind a name she's never heard. Her mind clears and she forgets the word entirely, until the rider recedes and the drizzling rain outside turns the sky to stone.

When her father arrives home from work, Marie is sitting on the living room floor, stringing rubber stoppers together with careful precision.

"Mamá is dead," she tells him, glancing up from her work. The expected scene ensues: he drops his attaché case and runs to the kitchen, alternately shaking and cradling the corpse on the floor. Marie hears his sobs and again imagines the cloaked silhouette on the cream-colored horse to drown him out.

Monsieur Curie returns to the living room, his face sunken. "You always say things exactly as they are, don't you?" She nods, and he drops to his knees, collecting her in his arms. As he takes her upstairs, past the kitchen with its fading smoke and beakers the color of death, neither of them notice the battered old tome splayed open upon the counter top:

Le Morte d'Arthur.

2

Move on. Move on. Move on.

That's all anyone says to her anymore. Elizabeth Cady is sick of it. *I'll move on when I'm damned well ready to move on and not a second sooner.* And anyway, what's with society's obsession with "moving on?" What's wrong with just being depressed for awhile? *She was my teacher, my mentor, my friend, and I'm just supposed to forget all about her?* No chance.

The bottom of the glass looks awfully familiar to Elizabeth tonight, and she isn't the least bit sorry for it. She signals for yet another refill, ignoring the knowing nod from the bartender, with his greasy hair and hairy arms. He inhales a mushroom-shaped puff from his cigar as he serves the requested refill, blowing the steely smoke straight into Elizabeth's face.

When Elizabeth decided to try her hand at social activism, Annie helped her do it. Annie worked hard to get the government to change their unspoken rules; to allow women to be a part of this changing world. And Elizabeth nearly killed herself from exhaustion and stray trainee shrapnel, just to make Annie proud; went out of her way to prove herself so that McKinley and his lot of Republican cronies gave her the credit she deserved. None of the other trainees could believe she wasn't just there to land a husband, and Annie was always there with a stern pep talk...or a shot of whiskey, when it got to be too much.

The woman had been a great teacher in the art of refusing the advances of idiots who thought their pretty instructor just needed a date in order to loosen up. Lord, Elizabeth had lost count of the number of times Annie introduced a man's crotch to the pointy edges of her knee.

"Ah hell, Elizabeth," the former Wild West star would say, twisting some blockhead's arm around his back when he tried to pinch her bottom between classes, *"you're too nice with 'em. Got to show 'em they can't mess with us, yeah?"*

And Elizabeth would smile, wishing she had Annie Oakley's confidence.

They pushed through together, ignoring the whispers of *"dykes"* muttered under the breath of trainees who failed to secure a date with either of them. Elizabeth pushed aside that sabotaged rifle; Annie stayed silent over that missed promotion. And, most importantly, both kept doing their best to brush off centuries of prejudice that tried to tell them that women make bad sharpshooters.

And now, judging by the President's reaction to Annie's death, it was looking an awful lot like their efforts had been for nothing. Things were getting worse.

Elizabeth slams her flat palm on the bar and lets her head fall forward, raking her fingers through her hair until it hurts. *Move on*, they say, all the stupid men who want to forget that Annie ever existed; was never killed in a "train derailment."

She'll be next. Elizabeth knows that.

It's 1915. They can't legally stop a woman from speaking out, or helping to coach new snipers for the Army, but they sure as hell can do everything in their power to keep women silent and send them back to the abusive bastards waiting for them at home with an empty bottle and full trousers.

Either that, or they'll just make sure she's front and center in the line of fire during the next newspaper junket, just like Annie was. A woman killed in the limelight is still just another dead woman—and one less for all those men to have to worry about.

All things considered, it's pretty tough to *move on* when you're convinced you'll be next.

Hey," the bartender pipes up, gazing so intently she has to look away. He pours her another whiskey. "I've seen you in here before, right?"

Elizabeth rolls her eyes and stares at the wall, slumped over the bar with one hand still stuck in her brown hair.

"Yeah," he continues slowly, wagging his finger at her. "Your hair was different, but it was you. With your sister, right? That older woman—the pretty one."

Elizabeth sighs. "Yeah. So what?"

He narrows his eyes before forcing a chuckle. "Nothin.' Just thought you might want this back. She left it behind. Been waitin' to see if one of you'd come back for it." He reaches under the bar and pulls out a thick, dusty book, dropping it on the counter with a *thud*. "Had a peek; hope you don't mind." He leans forward and licks his lips, the whites of his eyes shot with red. "It's a smart lady that can understand this shit."

She doesn't notice his leering wink, because her eyes are glued to the large tome in front of her. *Le Morte d'Arthur*. Annie was reading this?

Elizabeth stares.

"Thought I'd find you here," a gentle voice calls, and Elizabeth turns to find a familiar journalist-cum-stalker looking at her with concern.

"Not now, Mr. Stanton," she begs, and curses when she slurs his name. She wants to get far away from him…from this bar…from everything. She rises abruptly from her stool and stumbles. He steadies her on unsteady legs, but she wrenches free and bolts for the door. Not a moment's peace in this world, she thinks. Never a moment's peace—away from this war, to think, to swallow a bottle of whiskey, or just to *grieve*.

Untouched atop the bar, the book watches her go.

3

"Miss Baker! Put that broom down this *instant*. It is not a weapon. Has it escaped your attention that this is a school corridor and the other children may be trying to learn?"

"But Sister Agatha, he was trying to steal my book! I was just…"

"No excuses, Miss Baker. I saw no evidence of Mr. Miller trying to steal anything from you. Detention, tonight at eight in my classroom."

"Please, Sister, I…"

"That is the end of the matter. Off you go now, or you shall be late for your next class."

Norma Jeane hurries off down the hall, her mouth a thin line and head bowed low. Sister Agatha watches her go; watches some of the other church wards usher her to their next class. Norma Jeane clutches the book tightly under one arm, careful to keep it separate from the others in her shoulder bag. Sister Agatha watches. Oh yes, she has been trying to figure it out for weeks now: what is it with that girl, and *that book?*

Norma Jeane arrives at Sister Agatha's office for her detention that evening without the book, and its absence shows. She looks as though she is missing a key piece of herself, like a finger, or a heart. "Sister," she says timidly, bowing her head a little.

"Sit down, Miss Baker," the old woman replies, gesturing towards a stiff office chair in front of her desk. She regards the girl for a moment, sizing up her discomfort, and vows to get to the bottom of it. "Now tell me, what is the problem between you and Mr. Miller where that book is concerned? I have seen you two arguing over it for weeks now." She gazes over her spectacles at the girl, fixing the brunette with an icy stare.

Norma Jeane, the nun notes with displeasure, does not miss a beat. "What book?" Her eyes are wide with feigned innocence...and fear.

The elderly woman removes her spectacles and glares at the girl until she cracks.

After a prolonged silence, Norma Jeane confesses. "Oh, fine. He's right, I took his book. I saw him making notes in the margins in class, and I...well..." She pauses a moment, her cheeks flushing.

"Yes?"

"Well, I really like English Lit, Sister, you know that. You encouraged me to enroll in the advanced class..."

"Yes, yes," Sister Agatha interrupts, waving her hand. "Get on with it, Miss Baker."

Norma Jeane swallows. "Right. Well, the two of us have always been top of the class, but I just...well, I've just been *dying* for a chance to get a leg up on him, you know? Just beat him outright for once."

Sister Agatha watches with interest as the girl's face darkens, as though she's revisiting a particularly nasty memory.

"I just wanted to wipe that smug little smirk off his face," Norma Jeane continues in an angry voice. "Show him that a girl can be just as smart as any boy."

"So you thought that getting a peek at his notes would help you beat him at his own game, did you?" Sister Agatha narrows her eyes at the girl, and Norma Jeane's shoulders sink.

"Yes, Sister. I suppose I did."

"And did those notes help you?"

"Um, a little, yes." Norma Jeane shifts uncomfortably in her chair.

Sister Agatha raises her eyebrows, suddenly wishing she was permitted to supervise detention with a nice glass of sacramental wine in one hand. "But?"

For a moment, Norma Jeane looks as though she wants nothing more than to tell Sister Agatha the secrets of the universe; to reveal that the earth is, in fact, flat as a board, and that she knows this because it says so in the margin notes of that book. But the look disappears as quickly as it came, and her expression closes off. "I'm sorry I took the book, Sister," she says instead, dropping her eyes. "You have no idea how sorry I am."

"Very well," Sister Agatha replies, clasping her hands on her desk. "You will return the book to Mr. Miller first thing tomorrow morning, and you will spend the rest of this evening working towards achieving high marks in English Literature *on your own*." She rises to scan her bookshelves for the volume she seeks. "Ah, here it is. Homer's *Odyssey*.You will read the first fifty pages of this book, and in two hours' time, I want a report on at least five similarities between Odysseus and Our Lord Jesus." She tosses the book at the girl. "Well? Get out some paper."

But Norma Jeane is shaking her head. "No, Sister, please. I can't give it back."

"I beg your pardon?"

"I'm sorry I took the book. I'm *very sorry* I took it, but I can't give it back. He...the book..." She pauses and takes a deep breath. "If he gets the book back, terrible things will happen."

Sister Agatha again raises an eyebrow. "Miss Baker, please. It has been a very long day, and your petty feud with Mr. Miller about grades is not one I care to waste any more of my time on. Now, open that book and get out some paper to take notes, so we can both be done with this and go to bed."

Norma Jeane reluctantly reaches for her bag and pulls out a crumpled piece of lined paper, but the aged nun notices that the girl's eyes are shining. "Sister, you don't understand. There's something wrong about that book. It feels... it *feels* strange."

"Miss Baker..."

"And he admitted it," Norma Jeane continues quickly. "I asked him... told him it made my fingers tingle... and he..."

Sister Agatha shoots her an impatient look.

"Please, Sister, you have to listen! He said that girls can't touch it. That bad things happen to girls who touch it. His mother told him..."

Oh, honestly. Sister Agatha sighs. So now the selfish boy was going to tell his classmate ghost stories in order to protect his precious grades? She should just get Sister Kennedy to fail the pair of them, to see if that teaches them a lesson about this ridiculous competitive streak they have. She furrows her brow. Perhaps she will ask Sister Kennedy to speak to the boy and make sure he's coping with his mother's recent death and adjustment to the children's home. She sighs again and looks up at the girl seated before her.

"Did you touch it, Miss Baker?"

"I...well yes, of course."

"And did anything bad happen to you?"

Norma Jeane's eyes drop to the floor. "No, Sister."

"Then I suggest you stop this rubbish and give Mr. Miller his book back, do you understand?"

She nods slowly, defeat etched on her face, and opens the new book. With a weary sigh, Sister Agatha watches the girl work, satisfied with her resolution to the children's dispute.

***

Later that night, alone in her bed, Norma Jeane pulls the book out from under her pillow and opens it with shaking hands. She runs a moistened finger over the tip of her bookmark pen, hoping there will be enough ink left for her purposes. She doesn't want to risk waking her dorm-mates.

Sitting cross-legged and smoothing the heavy book open across her lap, she hunches over the inside of the back cover and begins to scratch with her half-dry ballpoint, using her new self-proclaimed initials for the first time.

He's damned this book to kill women. DON'T TOUCH IT! Please, please, somebody help me.   *M.M. 05/44*

4

The deserted library smells like lost ambition.

Moldy curtains hang over grimy windows, as stacks upon stacks of leather bound books rot mournfully on the shelves. *Books are words,* Diana thinks as she reaches for another one, *and words transmit knowledge, and knowledge is power.* She nods to herself as she repeats that mantra, flipping through pages with increased frustration.

Well, if she has so much *power*, then why the bloody hell can't she find what she's looking for? Her sigh echoes against the hollow walls, as she leans back in her chair, rubbing her tired eyes. "Grace Kelly," she whispers, shaking her head, "where are you?"

She wasn't in any of the old *Evening Standard* archives, that was for sure. Nor was she in the *Harrow Times*, any of the books about royal lineage and marriage, or the *London Daily*. And she wasn't in any of the records in the *Sutton Guardian*, as Diana had suspected. Refusing to admit to Charles that she might have been mistaken about the rumors concerning Kelley's untimely death, Diana has to keep trying.

But so far, the only place Grace Kelly has turned up is in one old photograph, the shining starlet of America's Hollywood, lauded as lying under more actors than a nautical toilet.

Diana is just about to place the yellowed articles back in their drawer when she sees one last glimmer of hope in the back of the cabinet. The title beckons at her from the index card marking this paper's separation from its *respectable* counterparts, and even as she tries to ignore it, her curiosity gets the better of her. She reaches for the stack of tabloids dated the year of the princess' death. She grimaces as she hauls the dusty pages to a table, dropping them with a *thud* that reminds the newlywed only of wasted time.

She flips idly through one issue, two, then three, wrinkling her nose and puffing her cheeks at each increasingly ridiculous headline. Four issues... five... *This is just silly.* By the middle of the sixth issue, she is getting hungry, and her thoughts drift elsewhere. She carelessly flips past the page before her subconscious mind instructs her to turn back. She stares with wide blue eyes at the headline:

Prince Rainier Pays off St. Nicholas Cathedral?
Second cousin of widowed prince tells all!

In an exclusive interview with Christian Louis,
bastard-born cousin of widower Prince Rainier of Monaco,
The Daily Sun has learned that the Royal House has
offered St. Nicholas Cathedral one million francs in
return for silence on the haunted book issue. (See *The
Daily Sun* Issue 29 for full report).

Diana's brow wrinkles as she paws through the stack of perused papers beside
her, searching for Issue 29. She locates this 'haunted book article' in the front
index and, cursing herself for not paying closer attention, flips through the issue
only to find... that the article is not on that page. In its place is an advertisement
for Shanghai Cigarettes. She turns back to the first article in frustration.

The Royal House has refused to comment on Louis'
information, stating only that, "There are no 'haunted
books' at the Palais de Monaco, or at St. Nicholas, or
anywhere in the world, for that matter. The entire tale
was a fabrication of an overly-imaginative child."

BUT WAS IT?

"One night, she picked up a book to read to us and
just started screaming," Louis informs us. "She said
there was blood in it, and secret messages appeared on
the pages, and that it whispered to her! It told her
that any woman who touched it would die, and that she
should go back to where she came from."

After confessing her concerns with Father Jean-Luc,
Princess Grace was never heard to discuss the incident
again. It is unknown why the mystery has resurfaced now,
a full year after Princess Grace's unexpected death.

Repeated calls to the palace have gone unanswered.

Diana slams the archive binder shut, her palm connecting hard with the wood
of the library table. *Rubbish.* She should never have looked at this ridiculous
tabloid in the first place Here she is, wasting twenty minutes, when she could
have been searching *reputable* sources. Her mind volleys back and forth between
disregarding the article, and daring to take something from *The Daily Sun*
seriously. She can't *possibly* use such an article as evidence! Charles will laugh at
her. After all, she has never made a secret of her disdain for tabloids.

Any woman who touched it would die... she should go back where she came from...

Rising to place the bound pages back in their empty shelf, Diana notices something taking up the space: a deep crimson volume, tattered at the edges. She plucks it from the shelf, then jumps and drops it when she feels her fingers burn.

"What on earth..." she mutters, bending to pick it up from the floor. It landed awkwardly, with its middle pages ruffled and its back cover splayed wide open. Lifting it to the table, she notices a strange scratching in the upper right corner of the back cover.

He's damned this book to kill women. DON'T TOUCH IT! Please, please, somebody help me.   *M.M. 05/44*

She jerks her hands away from the book, the tingling in her fingers spreading like poison. But 1944? Princess Grace died long after that date. It doesn't make sense. *He's damned this book to kill women.* Who is *he*?

No, it's ludicrous. This cannot be the same book that "spoke" to Grace Kelly. The initials aren't even the same.

She returns her research materials to their shelves, then hovers over the book, thinking. She touches her thumbs to the tips of her fingers, shivering. There must be an explanation for this. There is *always* an explanation for things she doesn't understand. She simply needs to think some more and do more research tomorrow. Exiting the library, she heads for her new chambers, unconsciously clasping the book to her chest.

She suddenly realizes that the book holds terrifying possibilities, and if there *is* a way for it to hurt women who touch it... she is in trouble. She forces herself to breathe steadily. This is no time to panic. There will be an explanation; there always is. Logic has never failed her. It won't abandon her now.

Princess Diana reaches her rooms and pauses to catch her breath, determined to stay calm, and determined to resist the feeling of dread creeping up her spine.

Dear God, what have I done?

5

Babies and death. That's all she has left now.

She shrieks with laughter at the thought, then immediately regrets doing so because those awful women in white come running to restrain her again. She pulls uselessly at her wrists after the White Women have left, rubbing her skin raw on the bindings. It's an awful night, with howling wind and sweeping snow and tree branches that creak mournfully to her from outside the window. She doesn't have much time left.

But the White Women don't know that.

Well, wouldn't her brother just *love* to see her now. She almost laughs again, but bites her lip just in time. The bitter taste of blood fills her mouth, and she slackens her jaw. *Ow.* Everything *hurts* so much now. Everything she thinks, everything she does, everything she *is* just *hurts*. They think she'll claw the *thing* out herself, if they don't restrain her. *Wait*, they say. *It's not time yet.* As if they know anything about it.

The place is crawling with White Women who are going to rip her open any moment now. She asked them to; that's why she came here, to this awful place that smells like babies and tastes like death. Her brother would never come here. He must never know she was here. She shouldn't leave a trace, but she will. She has to. A baby with his father's name has a chance in life. A baby with his mother's name has nothing.

She will make sure her baby has his father's name.

The pain of a thousand pikes tears through her body, and she screams again.

"You are not in labor yet," a White Woman shouts when she bursts into the room. "There is *nothing* wrong with you. For the love of God, stop this screaming!"

She watches the White Woman leave again, slamming the door behind her. Stupid women; they never see anything they don't want to. There is *everything* wrong with her—everything that can't be seen or spoken of, but that doesn't mean it isn't there.

"Arthur," she whispers, her dry lips sticking together as they close around the last letter of his name. She sees him walk out of the wall, dressed in riding gear and as handsome as the day they joined. "Light a fire," she asks him. "It's so cold in here." But he glides past her, through her, then out the door, out to where the White Women sit, waiting to tear her open. "Get back here," she screams at him, then clamps her mouth shut again.

She holds her breath, waiting for the White Women to appear and reprimand her once more. *Be quiet*, she instructs herself sternly, her arms falling slack over her head, pulling against the limits of her restraints. *Be quiet and Arthur will return.*

But Arthur does not come back.

The White Women return soon enough, bringing her a tray of gray food. They untie her hands so that she can eat, and she sees an opportunity.

"Please," she whispers, "my book." She points to the small burlap sack lying open on the floor, against the back wall. Inside are two ragged frocks and a leather-bound journal. She loathes that journal, that book; it has caused her nothing but trouble. But she cannot let it go. It tells the story of his life, his loves, his victories. That book made Arthur love her.

The White Women give her an appraising look, then shrug. "Here." One tosses it onto the bed.

"No pens or pencils, though," the other warns. "No telling what you'd do with 'em, eh?" They leave her to her food. They think she is crazy.

Alone again, she pushes the food aside and sets the book on her lap. The cover is worn; the lettering on the title already faded. It's the sort of book that has always looked old, because it has existed forever. It is only words now; listed in the order they should be read. Nothing more. She runs her fingertips over the cover, feeling the cracks in the leather burn through her skin.

It is nothing now, but it could be so much more.

Thinking about the possibilities contained within those pages makes her think of Arthur, and thinking about Arthur makes her chest hurt and lips go numb. All she has ever known are men—feeding her, clothing her, beating her, screaming at her, raping her, hating her… and now kicking at her insides, so hard and so often that she begs for death every minute of every day. *He will be the worst*, she thinks, staring at her swollen belly under the book cover. *He will wound more than any of the others, for as long as he lives.*

The book stares at her, and suddenly she knows what to do. She knows what will help. She knows what will save the others like her. She will find a better place. She'll go first, and get it ready. She will make curtains, and plates of cheese, and the White Women won't be invited. She'll invite the others, and they will all live together on the other side, and leave the men here to hurt and wound and yell at each other.

She claps her hands as the idea takes hold, careful to bite her tongue to keep from crying out in excitement. Mother will be there, to look after her. She will introduce Mother to all the others, when they come. Mother will be so proud of her.

A hiss rises up in her throat as she gazes again at the closed book on her lap, running her fingers in lazy patterns over the cover. She has buried this language for so long that it doesn't come easily anymore, but after a moment of concentration, she remembers.

She flips through the pages, one by one, speaking to them in hushed, secret tones, flattening her palm over each one before turning to the next. When she reaches the page where Arthur's name appears for the first time, she pauses. Pointing her index finger to the page, she closes her eyes and begins to write with her fingertip. When she opens her empty eyes again, spiky blood-red letters run across the parchment in an angry line—

He is the Once and Future King. Within these pages lay his story as penned by his ever faithful sister, Morgaine le Fay.

She cackles softly to herself as she watches the letters sink into the page, forever disappearing from the view of mere mortals. This book will answer to no one now, and will pass through many hands, whose owners will never be quite sure how they had stumbled upon it, and will never know exactly what it can do. Nor will they ever understand *why* it can do it.

She continues turning the pages and whispering to herself in the Taliesin's language, sealing the magic inside the volume with every syllable. After fifteen minutes, it is done.

Staring at the back cover with unfocused eyes, she feels the pain rip through her body again, and she can't hold back the piercing scream that escapes her lips.

"Lady Morgaine, *really*. Your cries for attention are not going to…oh my good Lord. Someone, call for a healer! Dear God, Lady Morgaine, what have you done?"

The book falls to the floor with a sick *thud* as the White Women clamor around the bed.

You'll see, Arthur—just you wait, she thinks, her mind clouding with pain. *You'll see. You can hurt me, you can rape me, you can force me to bear your bastard child. I cannot stop you. I never could. I am not strong enough.*

"Lady Morgaine, breathe into the cloth, please. The healer is on his way; you need to relax…"

A man can still wound, as long as he lives. But I can make sure no one else will suffer because of you. I'm bringing them with me—all the other women. We're going to live somewhere without you, without any of you.

"I don't know what to do! Where is all this blood coming from?"

Any living man will always be free to wound, but a dead woman cannot be hurt.

As the blood and life and magic drain out of her, the last sound she hears is not the cry of baby Mordred, but her own mocking laughter.

A dead woman shall be free.

Bilroy Five
by Michael Savastano

By day Michael Savastano is an IT Administrator and by night a fiction author perfecting his craft. He has been writing for less than a year. This is his second publication.
This story is about two buddies and choices, hard choices.

The hardened red rocks of Bilroy Five turned to dust beneath Ridley Ryder's weighted boots. He spun to Becker Hurst. "You hear anything on your COM yet?"

"No. Why? Did you?"

"No, but you're the one who's supposed to have perfect hearing." The wind kicked up small pebbles that ticked off Ridley's face shield. His bulky white suit started to take on a burgundy tinge as the day wore on. "We're seven kilometers from Base One. The COM's range is better than that."

"Relax. There's probably a storm or something over Dunder. It'll pop back on after the interference is gone." Becker shifted the scanning device over to his left hand.

Ridley gazed back. The usually reddish sky had filled with a darkness that hovered over the small rocky crag the colonists had called Dunder Mountain. Base One was set in a flat plane below. Bilroy Five's landscape stretched for kilometers of nothingness. Just sand-filled horizons in every direction. An ominous feel came over him.

"My suit is getting hot," Becker said. "And I'm itching like crazy. I don't think my temp control is working."

"Don't get all fussy, now."

"Okay, well then maybe *you* should be the one lugging this thing around."

"Oh, no way. I carried it all day yesterday." The two men had scanned the area for the last seven hours. The Admins needed a new colony site that would begin the first stages of terra forming. And they wanted an answer by tomorrow. Ridley longed for the day when he could take off his helmet, feel a cool breeze on his cheek, and inhale non-toxic air. He knelt and shoved his fingers into the ground. "Whatcha think?"

"Well... the stability vector reading isn't too promising. It looks like they'd need seven-hundred meter posts to make the structure secure. And those atmospheric treatment factories can be a load on the crust's plates."

"So much for the rover's estimates. Some decent equipment would've been nice. The Admins aren't going to agree to use posts that big." Ridley mimicked them: "Make sure you use all of our resources in the most efficient way possible, thank you."

Becker grinned. "The next closest choice is beyond Rapshaw Crater. They're not going to want to run transporters between bases every day over a twenty-two kilometer stretch either."

"Whatever." Ridley raised his palm and sifted sand between his thick-fingered gloves. "Why hasn't Base sent out a transporter for us yet? Are they waiting to hear from us?"

"You're just hopin' they send out that cute red-haired driver."

"Hell yeah. Is she something else or what? Big green eyes, smile that makes your head spin. Rockin' bod."

"*And* she has the best job in the colony. Just drives people around in her climate controlled pod while guys like us sweat it out in the middle of nowhere."

"Yeah, no doubt how she got that gig. I bet ya that fat admin guy, Charlie, flew her out to the space station personally for the interview. A couple of bats from those eyelashes and I wouldn't be surprised if he offered up his job."

"What're sayin' Rid? A sweet young girl can't get a good job based on her credentials?"

"No, that's not what I'm saying at all. She's just beautiful. And I guess I would give her any job she wanted."

"Yeah, well, if she's the one who picks us up, you better say something. If you don't, I'll ask her out for you."

"Don't try to live vicariously through me just 'cause you're married..."

"Shut up." Becker threw his hands up in a threatening gesture.

"...with a kid."

A crackle fired over the COM. Ridley's shoulder jerked. "You hear that?"

"Yeah, shush for a second."

Another crackle and a high-pitched whine. Silence.

Both men tried to page Base One simultaneously.

Becker said, "Was that a person?"

"It sounded like someone yelling, but ended with like a..."

"Feedback?"

"Yeah, like that." Ridley made several more tries to contact Base One. "I can't get anything."

Becker asked, "So what do you want to do?"

"We could start walking back; follow the path the transporter takes. Maybe they'll spot us. We'll be able to get a read on the tire vibrations with the scanner from a couple miles away." The heat in his suit was rising; drips of sweat rolled from his temples onto his cheeks. The orange Bilroy sun, enlarged by the thick atmosphere, began to dig into the horizon. Even with his good friend within ten feet, he began to feel alone in this vast stretch of red dunes.

"Yeah, but that's a hike in these suits if no one comes."

"How much time will we have?"

"'Bout two hours of air, but only an hour of good temp control. That would be under ideal conditions. I don't know about you, but I'm not recycling enough water to keep myself hydrated in this suit." Becker examined his gauges.

"So give me the bottom line."

"We'd be climbing the dunes..."

"Bottom line..."

"Hour and a half to an hour and forty-five—tops."

Ridley reminded himself to draw normal consistent breaths. "Even without a call, the transporter should've been here forty minutes ago. Something's wrong. We're in a bad spot."

"Definitely in a spot. At two-point-five kilometers an hour it would take almost three hours. And that would be if we overexerted ourselves—which we shouldn't do."

"Don't panic. Let's just start walking."

The two began the trek toward Dunder Mountain. A gust of wind swooshed by. Ridley teetered on his shaking legs. "We wouldn't be in this situation if we could just take a small transporter out with us."

"And use a precious resource for only two people. Not likely."

Ridley coughed, unable to control his air intake.

Becker halted. "Come on now, buddy. I can hear you heaving. You're gonna use it up too fast."

Ridley scrunched over and cupped his kneecaps. The rigidity of the suit caused pain to shoot up through his hips. "I'm all right."

Ridley knew these suits well. As time went on, the suit would divert less power for cooling purposes. As long as the body's core temperature stayed under one-hundred and one degrees, the suit would let you boil. It was a measure to save power in case a user's temperature skyrocketed. The only reprieve was the half-inch of open space between the skin and the inside lining of the chest and back. Uncomfortable? Yes. Safe? Maybe.

Becker said, "If something happened at Base, Command would know. They'd deploy a shuttle right away from the space station."

"We would've seen it..." Ridley coughed, "ahem—land on the strip." He shook his head. Ridley could feel the muscles in his body clenching. *Just breathe.* "Where's Robin working today?"

"She's on Field Four, testing the hydroponics again."

Ridley could hear the shakiness in Becker's voice when he spoke of his wife. Also, Becker's daughter, Jo, was in the learning room on Field Two. His friend's worry permeated the space between them.

"Next time I see Robin, I'm gonna give her a big smooch, right on the kisser."

"Bull, you are."

Ridley smiled. "I think she's always liked me."

"That's funny. I think you mistake pity for affection. Tell you what; you can kiss Robin if I can kiss your redheaded transporter girl."

"Deal." *Now let's hope we get the chance.*

The next few minutes were silent. Ridley consumed himself with thoughts of his red-haired fantasy. At a time like this, his simple crush had ratcheted into a dire passion. He sucked a sip of water through his H2O stem. A drop rolled off his bottom lip which he caught by biting down. He could tell that his reserves were down. He hoped to urinate soon.

Conserve, damn it. Conserve.

He rubbed the itching stubble on his face along the inside lining of his helmet. With each step, the backside of his suit scraped and chafed the nape of his neck. It felt like a solarburn.

A crash sounded to Ripley's right. He whirled. The scanner was broken in three pieces and skewed behind Becker. Ridley wished he had something to smash. "Man, you really put that down."

"If a transporter rolls up on us now, I'll blame it on you."

"I know these guys can be pains-in-the-asses, but I think considering the circumstances—they'll understand."

Becker interrupted, "Yeah, but you weren't at the meeting last month when Dick Denkins explained how much it costs for every cubic inch of livable area on Bilroy and blah, blah, blah."

"Pisser on that." Another sharp pain dug into Ridley's neck. He winced.

"He went on and on about how this is a scouting operation and how it's not making any money..."

"Oh, that's crap. We're scouting to see if the company can make as much on Bilroy as they did on the Caldea colonies."

"It is a business after all."

Ripley looked ahead. Dunder Mountain grew larger in his view, but not fast enough. Becker was keeping a close eye on his gauges. Now and then, he could hear him gasp for oxygen. Water, air, and temperature. He knew Becker was doing the math in his head, but Ripley no longer had any intent to ask him questions. The news wouldn't be good. He wanted to trudge on until his body keeled over—nothing could stop him from that.

The sting in his neck stretched down into the area between his shoulder blades. He could feel sweat drip down his lower back and into the crack of his ass. It tickled him in an uncomfortable way. He didn't want to talk. The heat dried his tongue and throat to a crisp. But he had to keep his mind off the pain. "You know what I hate?"

"What's that?"

"When people call the money we use 'spacebucks'."

"What's so bad about that?" Becker swerved his head.

"It sounds like one of those old science fiction movies."

"No, they always said 'credits' in those movies. Besides, it's better than saying 'Nictonern Inc. Dollars'."

"Yeah, but I was thinking about 'Bilroy Bucks'."

"Okay. When we get back, we'll tell all hundred or so people that we're using that term."

The banter made Ridley feel normal again. He knew Becker well enough to say the same for him, but in the ten years he had known Becker, Ridley never remembered him giving in so easily. If he ever knew a fighter, it was Becker Hurst. "So that's it then. Bilroy Bucks."

* * *

Becker panted, "We've been walkin' for forty-five minutes. Not makin' good enough time. Both of us will die if they don't find us."

"Why even bring it up, ass hole? I plan to walk until I drop. I'll carry you if I need to."

"I have a good reason." Becker paused for a moment. "If we both keep going, we have no shot. But if one us takes the other's tank, they'll get back with a few minutes to spare."

Ridley's head snapped back. "No, no way. I can't do that."

"You can and you will."

"Then I volunteer to die."

"And so do I." Becker's voice grew louder in Ridley's helmet. "We've been friends a long time. We're gonna die friends. One of us before the other. We'll decide how it ends the way we always do."

Ridley's and Becker's lives came down to drawing straws. "This is too nuts. I can't believe you want to do this."

"According to the gauges, I figure we need to choose in about twenty minutes. If they don't find us in that time, we draw. Agreed?"

Ridley mustered a nod. The loser dies. The winner goes home with the guilt. Maybe the winner and loser should be switched. The short straw walks home.

The next few minutes flew by in a flash—like a snapshot in a moment of time. Ridley's pain never waned. Neither man spoke.

Becker stopped. "It's time."

Ridley kept on.

"Ridley."

He halted and bent his neck backwards. A grunt came from his throat, as he twisted around. He dragged his weighted boots through the red clay. The crosswinds in his face opposed him.

Becker held out his fist. Two strings, one black and the other green, hung over his knuckles. One would have a long tail, the other would have none.

Ridley reached out, unable to look into Becker's eyes, and said to himself, "green or black?" Green or black? Which one will accept the long walk? Which one will sit and savor a last few breaths?

Ridley had the black string between his fingers when a voice burst over the COM.

"Can anyone..." More crackling. "...me? Is anyone out there?" It was a female.

The two strings floated to the ground. "Yes. We're here. Is this Base One?" Becker's voiced grated. He grinned at Ridley.

"Ridley is that you? This is Louisa from Command at Base One."

Ridley said, "Yes, yes. I'm here. Oh, thank..."

She interrupted, "Listen, I may not have much time. We're in trouble here."

"What do you mean?"

"Catastrophic power failure all over the colony."

Becker said, "Is everyone okay?"

"I don't know. I..." Crackling. "...for four hours. All nine Fields shut down. I have no contact. I'm running the COM off reserves from an extra suit..."

Ridley cut in. "Where's the shuttle rescue from the space station?"

"Don't know. I have to assume either someone's asleep at the switch, or they have problems of their own. I think..." The COM cut out for three seconds. "...crazy electrical storm blew through here. All the transporter vehicles are dead. I have people wandering around in their suits out there. No one can get in or out of their fields."

Becker said, "What about the emergency suits?"

"I'm sure everyone's using them, but none of the doors will move. The techs are stuck in Field Seven. All the filters are down. Once people's suits are out of air, that's it."

"Ridley, I know you worked on the DL-5000 series cells on Caldea. Every one of them needs to be reset and configured. Can you get back here? Please tell me you can."

Ridley stuttered a faint whimper. His body trembled and chest constricted.

Becker said, "He'll be there."

* * *

Ridley dragged his red-stained boots through the sand. His body ached, soaked with sweat. His mind tried to detach the visions that were glued to his eyes. Two-hundred yards behind him, the body of his best friend lay lifeless. Only minutes before, Becker pulled face-to-face with Ridley, their glass face guards dinged together. He screamed, "Yes, you will go on! You will fix the problem and save my wife and child. Pull it together!"

Ridley reached the landing strip. His general disregard for the Admins had grown into a hostile hatred.

He yelled out, "Where the hell are you people?" His helmet vibrated. No echo in the vast canyon. No one could hear him.

He thought about all the time the colonists spent preparing for emergencies. Procedure? Protocol? Now, the last hope—one man—broken down, burning alive, and almost out of air.

Ridley started up the rocky crag. Fifty yards to the top, but it appeared taller than usual. Just over the peak he would see Base One. His gauge showed twenty minutes of air and the temperature control was useless. He had already sucked down the last of his own oxygen and was working on what should have been Becker's. Sand and rocks crumbled and rolled under his boots as he scrapped and clawed upwards.

He felt a surge of euphoria kick in. Too much. His pulse went up, breathing quickened, but he needed to reach deep for the strength to crawl up the crag. At the crest, he flattened his chest against the edge and peered over. It was dead. Strange to see such a typically active area frozen still. The three transporters were motionless between fields. People in suits, the size of bugs, huddled around the field units. He wondered if they were dead or alive. Some inched in slow movements. Others just looked like deflated bags.

He let the rocks break beneath him as he slid to the ground feet first. Grains of sand pinged off his face shield. The unbearable stuffy air of his own stink flooded into his nostrils. His gauge read twelve minutes. The trip took too long.

Ridley picked up the pace as he approached Command. A main console controlled the DL-5000s and thick wire ran the configurations out to the secondary power cells on each field. The transporters had their own power cells; someone needed to reset each one individually.

He looked up into the cabin of the first transporter he passed. He wished he hadn't. The redhead inside banged on the window. Her beautiful green eyes flashed panic. She spread the fingers of her right hand across the glass and appeared to mouth the words, "Five minutes." She pointed to her suit gauges.

Ridley peeled his eyes away. He left her there—likely a death sentence. It felt like a spear in his gut, but one-hundred and twenty-two others needed him. And most of all, he told himself, *keep the promise. Save Becker's family.*

The console board cover fell off as dug into the handle. He sucked in a deep breath —air constricted in his lungs. Not enough to draw from. The keyboard flipped out and landed in front of his face with a clunk; a monitor nestled above it with a blinking cursor. He searched his mind for the reset commands and carefully picked at each key with the tip of his right glove.

The config commands came next. Like remembering a foreign language he hadn't spoken in a few years. But it came back, even through his weary state. Bits and pieces at a time. He mis-typed. Back. Back. The screen ran question after question. He hit "y" over and over. Something went wrong. He didn't remember this. *How many questions!*

An obnoxious din sounded off beyond Dunder Mountain. The shuttle arrived.

He turned his attention back to the screen. Drowsiness set in his eyes. His breaths turned quick and short.

RELOADING... A blue background. The lights on the main console building lit up. All over Base One, windows flashed, air locks opened, and humming noises sounded. The COM in his helmet buzzed with human voices. Cries of joy, gasps, and names, all blared at once.

He stared back. A hover-car sped toward him from the shuttle area. Green suits crawled down Dunder. He wanted to scream—point to the transporters. *Save them. Save her.* Nothing escaped his lips.

He began to crawl toward the air lock. The darkness enveloped him. A man stood above him. He closed his eyes.

* * *

Three weeks after the incident and hours after the memorial service for Becker Hurst ended, Ridley sat alone and picked at a pasta dish. His appetite had yet to return to normal. He hadn't talked to Becker's wife since that fateful day when she broke down on the floor of Field Two before he had even whispered a word. They still had yet to share their loss privately. His remorse drew a wedge between them that only grew as time moved on.

A solar blast from the Bilroy Sun had caused the power loss on both the Admins' space station and the colony. Four people died on the station, including a man that saved the shuttle from destruction. The rescuers made it to all the transporters. Everyone on Base One survived, except for one.

The guilt bore down on him at times. Guilt for leaving his friend. Guilt for being alive. He wondered if it would dissipate after awhile. People presumed him a hero, but he didn't think it was deserved. He politely asked them to stop, and they did, for a few days. The Admins wanted him to speak at Becker's service. His words were few, but powerful. The chance to tell Becker's story to the people he sacrificed himself for quenched his shameful pains. He realized life would go on—even without Becker.

A hand lightly touched his shoulder. He dropped his fork and pasta sauce splattered over the table.

"Ridley?"

He swiveled his body. Robin's sad eyes gazed at him. Her forgiving look pulled him in and closed the gap between them immediately. His throat tightened, only allowing an inaudible gasp.

"You did the right thing."

Something Sinister
by Joe Vadalma

A retired technical writer at a major computer manufacturer, Joe Vadalma has always loved science fiction and fantasy. He has published a series of dark fantasy novels called The Morgaine Chronicles with Renaissance E Books, as well as the SF novels, Star Tower and The Bagod. Another book, The Book of Retslu, was published by Mundania Press.
The internet is a fantastic invention and your worst nightmare in this story.

A perfect stranger greeted me like an old friend. Not unusual, you say. It is if it happens several times in a single day. I'm not talking about the same person doing it over and over. Several strangers have said, "Hi, Harry," to me today. My name's not Harry. Who the hell is this Harry who looks so much like me? Is someone playing a practical joke? Am I on Candid Camera? I have a creepy feeling that something sinister is involved.

Today is Saturday. I've got the day off. I'm window shopping at the mall while my wife's at the ShopGood supermarket on the other side of the highway. The guy approaching me is a type I normally shun. He has a shaved head, a dozen rings on his ears, his lip and his eyebrow. His black T-shirt has pictures of demons and skulls and the name of a Goth band. He walks up, gives me a weird look and says, "Harry, you bastard, I'm really surprised to see you back in Springfield."

"Excuse me. You've mistaken me for someone else. This Harry guy must be my identical twin, because you're the fourth person to take me for him. Actually my name is Adam, Adam Townsend."

The guy gives me a smirking grin. "Sure. Adam Townsend. Is that the moniker you're using now, Harry? Don't bee-ess your old buddy." He sidles up to me, grabs my arm and whispers in my ear. His breath stinks from alcohol and something rotten. "If I was you Harry, I wouldn't stick around. You-know-who is looking for you. No alias is going to fool him."

I brush his arm away. "Look, I'm not Harry. And I don't know you. If someone's looking for this Harry character, it isn't me they want. Leave me alone."

He shrugs. As he walks away, he says, "I ain't bulling you, Dude. It ain't healthy for you to stick around." He slides a finger across his throat.

I don't like the sound of that. If I resemble this Harry so much, and this you-know-who person is after him, he might mistake me for him. Who knew what kind of trouble this Harry was in. I assume that he's as disreputable as the guy that accosted me. The idea that my double might be on a gangster's shit list makes me queasy. I'd better leave the mall before I run into you-know-who, whoever he is.

* * *

I've walked around ShopGood for at least an hour looking for Deb. She's not here. Our paths must have crossed. She's probably at the mall looking for me. After what that Goth character said, it gives me the creeps to even think about going back there. Deb has her car. I'll meet her at home.

* * *

This day started out crappy and is going down hill. I didn't watch my speed on the bypass. A cop has me stopped.

"License and registration," he's saying in that snotty cop manner.

I hand him the documents. His eyes are going from them to me. What the hell? He's drawing his pistol. "Step out of the car, please."

Jesus, what's got into him. "Hey, what's the idea?" I say. "I was only speeding a little. You ain't got any call to..."

"Just get out of the car." He keeps glancing at my license. "What's your name?"

"Adam Townsend." I open the car door and step out.

"Place your hands on the vehicle and spread your legs. That's right." As he's pats me down, he says, "Adam Townsend's the name on the license, but the picture doesn't look anything like you."

What the hell is he talking about? I reach for my license. "Let me see that."

The cop leaps back as though I'm going to grab his gun. Ow. Jesus, that hurt. I fall to my knees in pain from a shot in the kidneys with his nightstick. He's yanking me up by the collar and handcuffing me. "Don't try anything like that again," he yells.

I'm angry and confused. Why is this cop doing this? And why did he say that the picture on my license doesn't look like me? It was taken only five years ago. As I sit in the back of the patrol car, I wonder whether I'm having a nightmare. First, there were all those mistaken identities at the mall, that punk blathering on about somebody being after me and now this cop acting weird. I'm getting paranoid. I'm thinking conspiracy. But who and why? And why me?

* * *

The police book me, and I use my one phone call to call Deb. The phone rings until the answering machine picks up. Damn it, she's not home yet. Don't tell me she's still shopping! I leave a message. The cops put me in a stinking holding cell. I feel like shit. I wonder where this is leading. I hope Deb comes home soon.

* * *

I've been sitting in this rotten cell all day. They took away my watch, but it's dark out. A lawyer in a pinstripe suit just arrived. I'm surprised that Deb didn't call our family lawyer. This guy doesn't not look like any lawyer I'd hire.

"Did my wife send you? Is Deb waiting outside the cell area?"

"Wife, Harry? You married now?" His mustache is twitching. This guy is a shyster if I ever saw one. "Is that why you're back in Springfield?"

"You too?" I cry. "I'm not Harry, no matter how much I look like him."

"Have it your way. The cops said that you tried to pass yourself as somebody named Adam Townsend. But the fuzz who arrested you knows you from your previous arrests. Your rap sheet in this town is as long as my arm. Good thing they called me and not you-know-who. I got a judge to waive bail. If I were you, I'd hightail it out of Springfield and keep going. There's a hit out for you on account of what went down six months ago. In fact, I'm sticking my neck out. I should take you to you-know-who. But I've got a soft heart. I don't like to see guys wasted."

The things the shyster lawyer was saying made my blood run cold. I protest again that I'm not Harry. It's no use. The lawyer simply grins at me. Whoever this Harry was, he must be my identical twin. I'm happy, though, to be getting out of jail.

Deb's not in the station. As the lawyer and I walk out together, he warns me one more time. "Get out of Springfield tonight, Harry. Don't put it off. Your life's not worth a plugged nickel here."

I'm terrified, but I figure that you-know-who, or whoever he sends to kill Harry, wouldn't look for him in the suburb where I lived. It's middle class and quiet. Although I'm shaken and upset, I'm careful not to speed or disobey any traffic laws. I don't want another encounter with the police.

***

It's after ten. No lights are on in the house. That's strange. Jesus, don't tell me Deb went to bed? How could she knowing that I was in jail? Even if she didn't get my message, you'd think she'd be worrying where I was.

I'll try to wake her. What's going on? Inside our bedroom, I hear grunting and sighing. I'll switch on the lights. What the hell! A man and Deb are going at it. Deb screams as she spots me. She'd better. I've got murder in my heart. I'm going to beat the hell out of the guy. What in blue blazes? This must be a nightmare. He has my face. He's my identical twin.

"Oh my God, Adam, it's a burglar!" I hear Deb yell.

The man with my face reaches behind the pillow. Oh shit, he's got a gun. "Don't worry Deb, I'll take care him."

"You're not going to hurt him."

"Don't be silly. I'll take him downstairs and call the cops. Just stay in bed."

"Are you Harry?" I ask. I'm bewildered.

The man makes no reply. He waves the gun, indicating that I should leave the bedroom. I feel the weapon in my ribs, and we march downstairs. "Sit down."

"Are you going to call the police?" I ask. "What are you going to tell them? That the owner of this house broke in and disturbed you and the owner's wife having sex. Does Deb think you're me?"

He laughs. "Not only does she think I'm you, but I am you. Upstairs, you asked me whether I'm Harry. I was Harry. But not any more. Look in the mirror."

"What? What are you talking about?"

"Look in the mirror."

I gaze into the mirror above the mantle. A stranger stares back at me, a tough with a broken nose and a scar on his cheek.

"Jesus Christ, what the hell is going on? This is impossible. I've got a stranger's face, and you've got mine."

"Now you're catching on. I supposed you've heard of identity theft. Well, I've found a way to take it to the ultimate. From now on I'm you...Adam."

"How could you do something like that?"

"Witchcraft and the Internet. Last week you downloaded porn from my web site. My friends, who are witches and hackers, have created a new kind of virus. A magical virus that caused your computer to perform a spell that allowed my soul to possess your body, and sent your soul into my body. Not right away, of course. I had to find you in the mall first to complete the transfer. I was the first guy to call you Harry. Simple, huh. When this gets around, you're going to see a lot of people taking over the lives of jerks like you."

"No, it couldn't be," I cry. "It's not possible."

My double shrugs. "It is though. I tell you what I'm going to do. I'm going to let you run for it. Get in your car and drive off. I'll fire a couple of shots in the air. Then I'll call the police and report the car stolen. So I wouldn't stay in it long if I was you. Ha, ha. That's funny. I am you. Give me your wallet. I wouldn't want you to get arrested for credit card theft and posing as me. Ha, ha. Now get. Unless you want me to waste you right here. Believe me, I wouldn't blink an eye. I'd tell the cops that a burglar threatened me. Oh, and you'd better get out of Springfield. I'm pretty sure that a guy's got a hit out on me. He might mistake you for me." He laughs again.

* * *

I abandon the car in a supermarket parking lot. As I stand on the shoulder of the highway with my thumb out, tears run down my cheeks. I'm in a terrible hopeless situation. Harry has stolen my life, my beautiful Deb, my home, everything. What's worse, his life, now mine, isn't worth a plugged nickel. Someone, a you-know-who, who I don't know, is out to get Harry.

* * *

"Thanks for the ride, friend. Do you ever surf the net? If you do, my advice is to get good virus protection software and be very careful about what you download. Bad things can happen if you're not careful. Very bad things."

Although I try to hold back, a tear runs down my cheek.

Deep Waters
by Manfred Gabriel

Manfred Gabriel lives and writes in western Wisconsin with his wife, two daughters, and two very big, but very sweet mutts. His stories have appeared in Tales of the Unanticipated, Dred, and Not One of Us.
In this story a man struggles with how far he will go to save his marriage.

Thomas cuts the engine of the rented motorboat. It bobs anchorless in the middle of the cove. The light of the slowly setting sun dances on the lake like fireflies. Haven rises from the fore of the boat, kicks off her flip-flops, pulls off the T-shirt she wears over a new two-piece she bought especially for this occasion. She stretches, raising her arms above her head and arching her back. Stretch marks, faded with time, scar her waist. Her thighs are thick with cellulite. A varicose vein runs up her left leg like a river and its tributaries. Thomas longs to reach out, cup her breasts in his hands, kiss her long and deep. This is his wife, the mother of their two sons, the girl he fell in love with back in college over two decades ago.

"It's a little early to be going in," Thomas states.

Haven adjusts her bikini bottom, running an index finger along the elastic at the right thigh. Thomas crosses his legs to hide his erection.

"I'm just going for a little dip, to get used to the water." Haven dives in, form perfect. The lake barely ripples as it enfolds her. She swims beneath the water, a simple silhouette. In the deep, her imperfections disappear. Thomas sees only soft shoulders, a narrow waist, the curve of her hips, the taper of her legs.

Haven pops to the surface. "The lake's warm," she calls. She is treading water. Her arms move in and out from her body as if in flight; her legs kick like egg beaters. Beneath her, something shadows her movements. Thomas wants to believe it is a trick of the light, but he knows this isn't true. He blinks and it is gone. He shudders. His erection subsides.

"You should come out," Thomas says.

Haven frowns. "I'll come out when I'm ready."

Her tone nips at Thomas like a spider bite. Even though he fears what lurks beneath the surface, he knows better than to push the issue. This is the way she's been this past month—every comment suddenly a discussion, every discussion blown up into an argument, every argument teetering on the brink of her leaving and never coming back. In years past, it used to be this way for him, too, this sudden falling out of love. He used to believe that this was simply because time changes everything, even wedding vows that were heartfelt when they were said slowly become empty words. It has taken him a year, since their last trip to the lake, to admit to himself that it is because of something more sinister. That thing he glimpsed at the bottom of the lake, like a drug, lifting them high so that they crash that much faster and farther, keeping them coming back for more.

Haven eventually makes her way to the back of the boat, pulls herself up the ladder. Thomas greets her with a towel, tries to embrace her with it. She steps away from him, snatching the towel from his hands. She runs it over her legs, her torso, her arms, through her hair. She sits back, puts up her feet, water glistening off her skin.

Thomas goes to the boat's cooler, pours two vodka tonics from a tumbler into tall plastic cups. Haven takes one, sips it slowly. Thomas remains standing, gulps his down, pours a second. After drinking for time in silence, Haven motions for her husband to sit next to her. She is feeling much better, Thomas thinks. The anticipation of what's coming.

"To another year," Haven says. They toast. Their glasses barely touch. Thomas slumps in his seat, gaze distant. He looks out at the shoreline, tall trees, deep and green, spotted with clearings where grand houses stand, complete with private docks and lawns that roll to the shore.

"What's wrong?" Haven asks.

"I don't want to go in the water this time," Thomas replies.

Haven laughs. "You say this now, after all this time? We've been married over twenty years, haven't we? How many of our friends can say the same thing, the Simms, the Trotters, poor Jackie Wilson?"

"It's just not natural."

Haven gazes at Thomas in disbelief, but Thomas is watching the lake. Waves lap the side of the boat. What appears to be a woman floats just beneath the surface of the water, long legs, round breasts, arms out as if crucified. Her face is dark, her eyes deep caverns. He starts to point her out to Haven, but by then, the woman is already gone.

* * *

"It's okay." Dominica and Thomas sit naked on the edge of the bed, the sheets tossed, one of the pillows on the floor. The hotel's air conditioning hums, sending a ripple through the thick drapes that block out the otherwise sunny day.

Thomas rotates his wedding band on his finger—a plain gold band, simple as love itself. "It's just that—my wife."

Even though the woman told him her name was Dominica, Thomas knows better than to believe her. She puts an arm around him, strokes his shoulder. "I understand."

Thomas looks into Dominica's eyes. They are wide, deep, dark. He could fall into those eyes and be lost forever. It was those eyes that made him accept her invitation to come back to her room. They met at a breakfast reception during a conference and skipped the lectures they were both scheduled to attend. Talking in the hotel bar, she savored his every word, touched him on the knee as she laughed at his jokes. As they headed up in the elevator, her hand in his, he had almost convinced himself that this was Haven's doing, not his. She was the one who had lost interest in sex after the boys were born. She was the one who became all about play groups, then preschool, then little league. She was the one who had stopped calling him at work just to say hello, who never had time for him. He squeezes Dominica's hand and she smiles.

Dominica tries one last time, puts her hand between his legs. "It's my fault, too," he explains, as if Dominica knows what he has been thinking. He moves her hand away. "I've allowed my marriage to become so plain, so dull."

"People were never meant to be together forever. Meet, become attracted to each other, breed, move on to the next partner. Propagation of the species." Dominica straightens her blond hair. It is only now, up close, that Thomas notices it is tinted green as if from too much chlorine. "But society preaches monogamy. Before you know it, you're stuck."

"I love her."

Dominica rises, moves towards the desk at the other end of the room. Her walk is fluid, effortless. Her breasts are rounder, larger than Haven's, and for a moment, Thomas almost reconsiders. Dominica pulls a piece of hotel stationary from the drawer. "There are ways of holding on to passion, keep a relationship new. I'm going to give you something for both you and your wife. You know Lake Duprie? Well there's a cove..."

* * *

"It was you who first brought us here all those years ago," Haven says. "I thought you were crazy. You practically had to drag me."

"Wait until sunset," Dominica had instructed Thomas all those years ago. "Make love in the water." Out of desperation to save his marriage, he complied, somehow convincing his wife, despite her inherent prissiness, to go along with it as an anniversary present. They stepped off the boat, one after the other, meeting just beneath the surface. And once the fear of being caught, of not being able to perform, disappeared among wet kisses, their bodies became one in the water, flesh melded together so that it was impossible to tell where the one ended and the other began, and later, they lay on the boat's deck, naked, not caring who saw them. They were back, suddenly, to their first time, after dating for two weeks their final semester in college. Curled together on the sweat-soaked futon in Haven's studio apartment, both of them thinking they could never get enough of the other.

Until, day by day, week by week, month by month, Haven turned to her old routines, and Thomas, tired of trying to push her, touch her, be close to her, tired of rejection, receded into working past dinner time and watching B-movies late into the night. "It won't last," Dominica warned him. "You have to go back, year after year."

A pontoon boat drifts by slowly, overfilled with young people with trim bodies. They drink beer and a primal rhythm blares from their radio. The pontoon boat begins making a wide circle around the cove.

Thomas cannot help but watch the young women, no more than girls, dance on the boat's deck, clad in bikinis and skimpy one-pieces, strings clinging to bronzed skin. Bodies that put Haven's to shame. One of them smiles at Thomas, waves, as if Haven is not there. Thomas knows the type, a girl searching for the father she never had, more mature, more successful than the boys her own age, a man whose face has filled in over the years, become lined with strength, sharpened by confidence, a man who has grown round and fat and comfortable, a man who can take care of her.

Haven slaps Thomas hard on the arm.

"What's that for?" Thomas asks, rubbing his shoulder.

Haven crosses her arms. "For making this lake so necessary," she says.

* * *

"The other day on the way home from work, remember I told you I stopped by my Uncle Jack's." Thomas is trying to explain. The sun is almost below the horizon. He and Haven have been sitting silently at an impasse, Thomas considering ways to convince his wife to end this ritual, here and now. "He and Aunt Eloise are getting up into their eighties. Live in that same post-war ranch house. They still get around a bit. They have a nice garden. They asked about you."

Haven nods absently. He is telling her what she already knows, but Thomas feels he needs to tell her anyway. She hasn't seen them in years, even though they only live a few miles away. She always had an excuse when Thomas wanted to go and visit. Haven has an aversion to being reminded that she will get old. Thomas knows this is one of the reasons she has become dependent on the lake. She hopes renewing their love will keep her young.

"Anyway, they insisted on dinner. While we ate, I noticed how they spoke to one another, how they shared glances, how they knew what each other was going to say before they said it. How they joked at each other's foibles, how they kissed each other with genuine affection."

"This is crap. We both know why you don't want to get into the water." Haven nods to the pontoon, still visible in the distance. "Trade down to a younger model."

Thomas shakes his head. "It made me think. Relationships change. They grow. They evolve. They become different, but better. I want that."

"Let's say I do buy this. Your aunt and uncle are a different generation. They don't believe in divorce. They stay together when things get tough. Our relationship wouldn't grow. It would fall apart."

"Maybe that's true for our friends, your brothers, my sister. But it can be different for us. I won't say it will be easy. We're not dreamy kids anymore. We have over twenty years behind us. Trevor's away at school. Kyle will be soon, and at his age, he'd rather not hang with us, anyway. It's just us. We can move forward now, eyes open."

Haven turns away from Thomas, takes a long swallow of her drink. "I like the way it is afterwards," Haven says. "Waking up each morning like a giddy schoolgirl. Having that lump in my throat when I speak to you on the phone, having the pit in my stomach when you're away, making love each night like it was our first time. I'd miss that."

"I'd miss it, too," Thomas says. "I just can't help but think that if we got beyond that, there would be so much more. We're on instant replay."

Haven smiles. "But it's such a great song."

Thomas shakes his head. Reason is getting him nowhere. "We just can't do this anymore. We can't."

Haven's smile turns upside down. "This isn't about a visit to your Aunt and Uncle."

Thomas doesn't say a word. She is right. Going to see his Aunt and Uncle was only to affirm what he already knew. He debates whether or not to tell her what happened the last time they were here, but he knows she wouldn't believe it. It took him a year to believe it himself.

Something slaps the boat's hull. It rocks violently. Haven loses her balance. Thomas grabs her, steadies himself, keeps them both from falling in.

* * *

The pontoon boat has left the cove, heading back into the wide stretches of the lake, music trailing off as it disappears around a bend. Thomas sits at their boat's wheel, rolling his empty glass in his hand. Haven sits across from him on the boat's edge. The sun is no more than fingers of light stretching between the spires of the trees. Soon it will dip beneath the trees.

Haven bites her lip, looks anxiously at Thomas. Thomas avoids her gaze. She undoes her bikini top, moves to her husband, kneels at his feet, slips her hand under his bathing suit. She looks up at him, tilting her head slightly to let her hair fall upon her shoulder. Her lips form a lush pout.

"It won't work," Thomas says. "It's my life."

Haven pulls her hand away. "It's my life, too. You can't do this to us."

"I can. I will."

Haven rises, looms over her husband. "You can't be serious. You know what will happen if we head back now? You think we'll go on in marital bliss, like something out of Norman Rockwell, but you're wrong. It's going to get worse, not better. A few months from now, you're going to realize that there's nothing left worth salvaging between us. And that will be the end. Do you want to lose all we have?"

"You don't understand," Thomas replies, his voice soft, as if talking to a child.

Haven beats at him with her fists, scratches at him with her nails, screams in desperation.

At first, Thomas ignores Haven's blows. He outweighs her. She can do nothing to seriously hurt him. But as her nails begin to dig into him, Thomas begins to resist her. He grabs her wrists, pulls them back. He rises from his seat, pushing her towards the end of the boat. She struggles to break free. He manages to lock her arms against her body. She knees him, barely missing his crotch.

Thomas looks to the water. He knows that if they jump in, they're relationship will be renewed. All this will be forgotten. But it won't be real, has never been real. She must understand that, and in order to make her understand, he must make her see.

Haven manages to get her right hand free, slaps Thomas hard on the cheek. It burns, and his head snaps back. Thomas grabs her arm, spins her around, shoves her down to the edge of the boat so that her head is dangling over the bow, inches from the waves. He holds her head still, so that she is staring face down into the water.

"Look!" he shouts. "Would you just look!"

Thomas keeps a firm hold on Haven, all his weight pinning her so that she can't break free. The edge of the boat digs under her rib cage, making it hard for her to breathe. One of his hands is holding her by the hair, forcing her to stare into the water.

Something is rising from the lake's bottom—a woman, shapely, seductive. But as it moves towards them, it changes. A hundred tendrils flail from her body, which has become soft and round. Haven struggles. She screams. Thomas clamps a hand over her mouth.

"I first saw it last year just as we were coming up out of the water," Thomas explains through gritted teeth, shoving Haven's head closer to the water. The waves lap her nose. "It slips between us as we make love. That's how it feeds. It does not bring us eternal love. Instead, it devours our memories, makes us forget, start all over. We can't move ahead if each year we fall back."

The creature draws near, rising out of the water to meet Haven. Thomas does not let go. Haven can only watch as the creature rises nearer the surface. The tendrils, like a thousand strands of seaweed, brush her face. She shudders, shuts her eyes. The tentacles dissipate.

Haven's body relaxes. Thomas releases his grip, falls back. Haven picks herself up, stares at him. Her whole body is shaking. Thomas pours her another drink, but she doesn't take it. He sets it down in a cup holder at her left elbow and starts to tell her about the night in the hotel room with Dominica. He relates the story without explanation, without excuses.

"Was that the closest you've ever come to cheating?" Haven asks, her face as expressionless as a department store mannequin's.

At last, Thomas feels he can be honest. "I never even came near as close as that night."

"And you didn't? You couldn't?"

Thomas nods, and Haven's face brightens. This is not what he expected. He expected swearing, he expected threats, he expected hate. "You're not angry?"

Haven shakes her head. "All this time, I thought you had cheated. Not with Dominica, I didn't know about her, but with someone, maybe many someones. I had convinced myself that it was only because of the lake that you stopped. But you never cheated. I see that now." She pauses and looks at him. "You truly do love me. I didn't need the lake to keep you faithful." Her eyes well up with tears, distorting her face, making it look old. Thomas sees her then, not as she is, but as she will be as they move beyond middle age together, more distinguished, stronger, wiser, without illusion. It will be a beautiful face, he tells himself.

Thomas sits next to Haven. He puts his arm around her, lets his hand settle on her bare breast. She puts her head on his shoulder. Haven drifts into a light sleep. The air grows cool, the moon shines bright, fireflies dance. Thomas takes his arm from around her shoulder. He goes to the boat's wheel, moves to turn the key in the ignition and start the engine.

Haven picks her head up, opening her eyes as the engine roars to life.

"What now?"

Thomas shrugs, his hand on the throttle. "We'll just have to see."

Haven moves towards Thomas. She takes his hand off the throttle. "We can't just leave."

"Why not? We've faced it."

"You faced it a year ago. I faced it this evening. But *we* haven't faced anything. If we don't, our marriage *will* fall apart. We'll begin to resent the fact that we allowed ourselves to be fooled all these years. Or that we didn't allow each other to keep being fooled."

Thomas turns so that the moon casts a shadow on his face, so that Haven cannot see the fear in his eyes. He has spent the past year convincing himself that he would not enter the lake. He has woken up in cold sweats, with nightmares still swimming in his head about what awaits at its bottom if he were to go in again.

But at the same time, he knows Haven is right. The thing in the water will try to feed on them no doubt, but in the past, they have always been apart and needed it to bring them together. This time they are already one. He pushes thought of trying to perform in the water aside. It doesn't matter. It's their minds, their hearts, not their bodies that need to be entwined. He knew when they came out here, this was what needed to be done. All he needed was for Haven to give him a push. She is stronger than him, and he wonders why he has not relied on that strength before. He pulls off his shirt, slips out of his trunks. He wraps his arms around Haven, bringing her towards him. This time, he is unembarrassed by the erection that presses against her flesh. Haven slides out of her bikini bottoms as he runs a hand from her breasts down her stomach and across her legs.

Their lips brush together. Haven pushes off of him, diving into the lake. Thomas stands on the boat's edge as she treads water. Her face wet and dappled with moonlight, her hair floating on the lake's surface like a halo.

"Well," she says. "Are you coming in?"

Love in the Time of the Serpent-King
by Rachel Astruc

Rachel Astruc is an Irish-Mauritian writer currently based in Australia. She has been writing speculative fiction for about a year, appearing in Andromeda Spaceways Inflight Magazine, Fusion Fragment, Strange Horizons, and Visible Ink among others. Two of her stories have been nominated for the 2007 Aurealis Award.

This story tells of one man's extraordinary life, love, and loss.

I am four, maybe five, when the deev first visits me.

I'm sitting behind our house, drawing pictures in the sand with a stick. Save for the neighbor's chickens, I am completely alone. My mother is at the market with my sisters; my father and brothers are soldiers and have not been home for many months. As the youngest son of eight, I am used to entertaining myself. The chickens, a dozen scraggy, mad-eyed things, cluck and peck around me, occasionally walking through my pictures. I lean forward to shoo them away, and when I look up, there is a woman standing over me.

She is naked save for a necklace of green stones around her neck. Her skin is the color of ochre and her body casts no shadow across the ground. Ridges of bone protrude from her ribs and back like the spines of a dragon. Her hair is as long my mother's and shimmers like gold when the light touches it. But it's her eyes that I like best. Her iris are black, ringed within and without by a thin line of orange.

She is the strangest thing I have ever seen, and I think she is beautiful. I bow my head, as my mother has taught me to, and introduce myself.

"I am Rahaeb Reyad."

The woman smiles, a thin, tense smile, as if she's not certain what to do with me. It is not a friendly smile—her teeth are needle-thin and jagged like the dried piranha-fish the Nubians sell. "I am Jahazan Deev," she says, "and there is a new war coming, child."

I frown. I am only four, maybe five, and the word war lacks context for me. I know my father and brothers fight in it, and that people are killed in it, and that soldiers go to it, and that it can eat cities and devour men, women and children alike. But then, so does the desert, and I have no fear of sand. "Where is it coming from?" I ask.

"The deev have fought against the peri for many years. That is the old war, of old grudges long forgotten. But this new war is that of your kind, your mortal ilk. You have brought it to us. You have brought us to this."

"Can't we take it away again?"

She is about to reply but a rumbling thunder-sound interrupts her, and the sand between my fingers stirs. In the distance I hear shouts, growing louder, and foreign, guttural noises like the roaring of a wild animal. I get to my feet and move to turn my head, but Jahazan catches my chin and forces me too look at her, into her strange black-and-orange eyes.

"Come walk with me, Rahaeb Reyad," she says.

"But I—"

"Don't turn around." She takes my hand and entwines our fingers. Her smile is encouraging and perhaps genuine. I smell dust and fire and sulphur and blood; I hear the sound of stone cracking and a woman's shrill scream. The sand around us jumps and shifts as the earth itself pulses with what I know now is war. I think of my mother and my sisters; I don't want to turn around. Jahazan kisses my forehead. "Let's go," she whispers.

She leads me from my village. I hold her hand as tight as I can, until it hurts so much I have to cry.

* * *

I am fourteen, maybe fifteen, when the devil-deev Ahriman curses King Zohak with two black serpents that sprout from his shoulders.

They are huge venomous beasts that crave only the flesh of mortal men. Every time they are cut down they grow back instantly, and no doctor or witch or holy man in New Persia can cure the King of them. So King Zohak—now known as the Serpent-King—decrees that every day he will feed his snakes two of his own subjects to sate their hunger.

When the soldiers come to take me to the palace I am not surprised. I'm a pauper, an orphan; I am a lost thing in the world. I barely remember my old village, my dead mother and sisters, my father and brothers lost in the war against the deev. No one will lament my death; no one will notice my disappearance. At fourteen, maybe fifteen, I'm both realistic and apathetic. I let them chain me in a cell to await the serpents' whim.

It is dark there, beneath the palace, and as cool as a desert night. I am not alone in the cell. There are other men, perhaps a dozen of them, all equally poor, all equally lost. They talk in whispers to each other about their lives, their hopes, and their hatred for the Serpent-King, Ahriman's mortal puppet, a man who killed his father and may yet live to kill New Persia itself, the land once called the Kingdom of Light.

It is small wonder that the peri, the fair fairy-kind, have turned their backs on us.

When night falls the men sleep huddled together for warmth. I sit apart, staring at the ceiling, remembering the moon. If it weren't for Zohak and his serpent curse, I would be going to war in a few years, the mark of New Persia emblazoned on my shield. I'm a poor swordsman, clumsy and inelegant when I play with other boys; I suspect I would be an early casualty on the battlefield. But none of that matters now. I cover my face with my hands, and when I rub my eyes, Jahazan Deev is there.

This time she has come in the form of a giant black dog with great leathery wings like a bat. Silver tusks extend from her cheeks and a ridge of horn protrudes from her brow. Her fur is sleek and gleams blue in the dim lantern light of the cell, as bright as the armoury of the peri. But I know her instantly by her black-and-orange eyes, which gaze at me with urgency.

"Jahazan Deev," I whisper.

"Rahaeb Reyad."

"This time the deev brought the war to us," I say, going to her. "This is Ahriman's work."

"You mistake a battle for a war," the deev replies, "and mortal corruption for deev trickery. In this war we are now allies beneath Zohak."

"I'm not a child any more. I know the deev have no allies—only puppets." I touch her fur and find black scales beneath it, like those of the Serpent-King's snakes. "Why are you doing this?" I ask.

She lays her tusked head on the ground and I climb onto her back, curling my fingers around the horns of bone that jutt from her ribs. My doomed cell-mates do not stir. The deev spreads her great wings and around us the cell walls and ceiling melt away. Above us I see a hole in the palace roof and through it stars.

"Come with me, Rahaeb Reyad," says Jahazan, "and don't look back."

We fly out of the prison cell and sail through the night-sky. I cling to the deev's back and close my eyes.

* * *

When I am twenty-five, maybe twenty-six, I go to war.

I wear the mark of New Persia and the rough, dark clothes of a soldier, and I walk with my company across the desert. Under the rule of the Serpent-King, we do not hunt the deev, as my father and brothers did. The deev are the Serpent-King's new councillors, their evil suggestions his law. Instead we seek out those who would oppose Zohak, who would challenge the wickedness he has brought to New Persia. We bring insurgents to justice; we halt rebellions. Our new war is against ourselves.

I have become a fine swordsman. My feet are quick and light and my arms are strong. It is a long time since I have fought a man and lost. Although I am young, already the name Rahaeb Reyad is known to the people of New Persia. There are many stories told of my escape from the Serpent-King's prison and the destruction of my childhood village. In some circles it is rumored that I have deev magic about me. Perhaps they are right, and a lingering trace of Jahazan remains on my skin like perfume, protecting me from harm.

One day my company and I destroy a village in Ramadar. We have been told by the Serpent-King's men that there are rebels hiding in the village. We come down upon the place with all the might of an avenging deev. When we have killed all those who would oppose us, we set fire to their houses and let their animals loose into the desert.

At the back of a burnt out house I find a woman with a small child in her arms, her face creased with fear. It is my duty to kill them both, to erase all witnesses of the Serpent-King's treachery. But I find I cannot do it. The scene reminds me too much of the day twenty, maybe twenty-one, years ago, when the deev Jahazan saved my life.

"I am Rehaeb Reyad," I say, sheathing my sword. "You should go."

The mother scoops up the child in her arms and runs away into the desert, her feet making little impression on the shifting sands. I fall to my knees and hold my shoulders, bracing myself for tears of mourning that never come. Night falls and my company, failing to find me amongst the village's wreckage, numbers me amongst the dead. They leave Ramadar without me.

When I wake the next morning, Jahazan is at my side.

This time she has taken the appearance of a girl, no different from any girl I ever met in New Persia, save for her strange eyes and her smile that's neither kind nor cruel. She is not beautiful; she is not even unique, but her very presence trembles my soul. As soon as I say her name she is upon me, sitting on my chest, holding my shoulders to the earth.

"I won't be your puppet, Jahazan Deev," I tell her.

The deev tilts her head. "If I wanted you to be my puppet, Rahaeb Reyad, I would curse you until you had no choice, until you were as will-less and cruel as the Serpent-King. Until you had ears only for my truths, my twisted deev lies."

I think of the rumors circulating about my past. "People call me a deev-kin, sometimes."

"Underneath they see that you have the heart of a deev. You are the child who walked from the destruction of his village without looking back. You are the boy who escaped from prison without a thought for the man who would take his place. You are the man who has killed so many, by sword and by fire; you are a scourge of New Persia. Of course they call you a deev. You are hardly human."

"Yesterday I spared a woman's life."

"We deev can be weak too, sometimes."

"Did you do this to me?" I cry, my hand on her throat. "Did you make me like you?"

The deev laughs. "I only told you not to look. I was never your puppeteer."

She is a deev in the skin of a girl, like I am a deev in the skin of a boy. We roll together in the sand, in the ruins of the village I helped raize.

* * *

For two months, maybe three, we are together.

We fly to the mountains of Mazandaran, where the wild deev live. There, in the caves and crevasses, we fight and feed and copulate like beasts. When the old war comes to us—the peri soldiers, with their feeble hearts filled with pity and love—we attack them mercilessly, sending them fleeing through the rocks like scared rabbits. When the new war comes to us we go down to the battle and fight, sometimes siding with the Serpent-King's men, sometimes with the rebels.

One day we walk along the cliffs to a place where the peri sometimes come, to soothe their aches of war. It is a tranquil pool amidst the barren rocks, fringed by flowers and soft grasses, like the lush veldts the Nubians speak of. Tall trees provide a thick canopy through which the sun cannot penetrate. Fair fragrances, so sweet that they make Jahazan spit and retch, lie heavy in the air. It is a paradise.

The deev and I, we hide amongst the trees with our sharp teeth and sharp blades.

We have not been waiting long before peri passes us, on the way to the pool. He is delicate and beautiful and bare-headed, with thick curly hair as dark as Jahazan's eyes. At his side he carries a sword, beneath his arm a shield with the mark of light upon it. He kneels by the waterside, gathering water in his hands to splash his face.

As he bends to drink we come up behind him, and while Jahazan skewers his heart, I cut off his head with a single blow of my sword. His body tumbles forward and the water swallows it. Lilies bloom where his blood was spilt, the ends of their petals stained a deep purple.

"We killed a peri in a holy place, Rahaeb Rayed," says Jahazan, laughing. "Now you are as damned as I."

She wants me to be horrified, but it's not horror I feel but the sensation inside me of something coming apart. Of being stripped, of being broken. The smell of the peri's blood is pungent as poison. It is the smell of holy things, of heaven and purity and the cleansing of sin. It is the smell of warmth and family and home. It smells like waking up on a new morning in a village far away, my mother singing in the kitchen, my sisters laughing as they play.

I realize that I've been lost for a very long time.

"We shouldn't have done this," I say, turning away.

"We did it so easily," says Jahazan. "What's the life of a fairy to us? We could do it ag—"

"No. No."

"What is it?" But she has realized now how the peri's blood has ruined me, has ruined the deev-thing she made of me. "You did it!" she screams, and her voice is the voice of thunder. "Why did you do it? Why are you here?"

I think: because you can't fight a war without having something to fight for. Because mortals don't do it for vague, intangible notions like loyalty and patriotism but for real things, for things they can touch, like flowers in their garden, like the smile on a child's face, like the lover they left behind. Because all battles start and finish in the heart. Because opposites attract.

There are the right answers, answers she would have stayed to hear. But what I say changes everything, irrevocably.

"Jahazan," I whisper, "I'm in love."

* * *

I am thirty, maybe thirty-one, when I hear of her capture.

The peri army brought her down in the desert. They came for her like an arrow seeks its target and beat her to the door of hell. When she grovelled at their feet, they bound her with chains of truth that burnt channels through her flesh. When she wept and screamed, they dragged her through the rubble of every village she helped destroy, across the grave of every man she murdered, and along the palace steps of the Serpent-King, son of their ally, now their foe. When she was exhausted, half-dead, they took her back to their court in Jinnistan and tied her there like a dog, a warning to those who would flaunt their immorality.

The peri are creatures of love and light, but it's easy to forget that they are soldiers, too. Their grievances are deeper than those we mortals suffer.

The morning I hear of Jahazan's capture, I pack food and water in a satchel, sharpen my sword, and set off into the desert. I do not know where Jinnistan is, or if the beautiful cities of the peri are even accessible by mortals, but I have heard that the Arabs believe it lies above the deev's mountains, in the clouds that halo the highest peaks. It is a good a place to start looking as any other.

I wander the rocks of Mazandaran for many days. Sometimes I see the Serpent-King's armies patrolling the valleys below; most of the time I see no one. When I run out of food, I hunt wild ibex and pick bitter narud grasses, those flowerless green needles that grow even in the winter months. Thoughts of Jahazan keep me warm during the cold New Persian nights. I dream of her anger, her cruelty and her lust, the things that brought us together, the things that tore us apart.

One night I find a peri-child captured in a trap I had laid for the ibex. It is a little girl with hair like sand and eyes of emerald. When I approach her she drops to all fours and throws dirt and stones at me, her face set in a bestial snarl. It's laughable to think such a pathetic effort could deter a beast like me. I dismiss her little missiles with a wave of my hand; I kneel beside her on the ground.

"I am Rahaeb Reyad, and I do not want to hurt you. I need only information. How do I get to Jinnistan?"

The fairy girl sneers. "Tribute."

I let her loose.

At day break I go hunting for larger prey. The deev Ennaza suns itself daily on a cliff nearby, its rippling, scaly flanks a common sight as I walk through these parts of Mazandaran. It is a dragon-deev, a great green lizard that stalks the peri who stray from the mountain paths, devouring them whole. I find it lumbering along a slope towards its favourite sunspot. Spines like sabres ripple in a frill about its stout neck; and its face is as piggish as a boar. The stench of death exudes from its flesh like some foul perfume.

Without hesitation I leap upon its back, my hands finding easy purchase on its scales. Ennaza howls with rage as I clamber toward its head, riding out the dragon's bucking in the same way a horseman tames a wild stallion. As I cling to Ennaza's spiny neck, it turns and fixes me with a huge, golden eye—and I see recognition there, in that cruel lizard brain.

"I know you," it screams. "You are Rahaeb Reyad, Jahazan's lover. What do you want from me?"

"Tribute."

I cut its head from its shoulders and leave its body spasming on the slope. With my still-bleeding trophy in hand I walk to the top of the mountains, to the place where the clouds touch the earth.

"I am Rahaeb Reyad," I shout to the sky. "Peri of Jinnistan, let me pass!"

Darkness comes then, and lightness too. Then before me the gates of the peri's city appear, gleaming like Nubian gold, and as I watch they swing inward, to reveal a paradise that burns my heart.

* * *

In this paradise, maybe heaven, I am set upon by the peri.

They strip my sword from me and take all my clothes save my daujin, the loose cloth that preserves my modesty. They cut my hair and pluck away my eyelashes and beard. Across my bare chest they paint the letters ANDJIAH in Ennaza's blood; in their language this word is a slur that means the killer of brothers. Then they bind my hands and feet to a pole and carry me like a dead pig through the beautiful jewelled streets of Jinnistan.

So many peri come to see my passing! They run from their homes and their shops to stare at me, as if I were some visiting royalty. Peri youths point and jeer and throw stones; their elders simply shake their heads, as if I represent a great failure to them. Small children hide their heads in their mothers' skirts, while soldiers touch their hands to their swords reflexively, remembering past battles and my war-worn blade.

The peri take me to the palace in Amberabad, where their Queen Hasshana rules. In the palace's stately courtroom, they chain my battered body to a ring in the floor. Stunned, silent, I stand there in wonderment. The court's walls are alive with flowering vines, and sweet birds sit upon their buds. Its floor is a mosaic of jewels: ruby, emerald, and others more lovely that I have never seen before, perhaps mined from the lands of the Nubians or the Egyptians. And the ceiling of the court opens up to the clouds, which are charmed by their peri magics to form a perfect dome.

I begin to weep. I have not wept since childhood and without practice the act is awkward to me. I weep shamefully, then, hiding my face in my hands. About me the peri jeer, their pretty faces contorted to reflect the ugliness of deev-beast that lies within me.

"Let him alone."

It is a clear voice, a woman's voice, but a voice more lovely than any I've ever heard before. I raise my head and Queen Hasshana is standing over me.

"I know why you are here," she says, taking my chin in her hand. "It is written all over your face—your eyes are dark with shame. You came to plead for the deev's life. Isn't that right?"

She is tiny, beautiful, with eyes that shine like a fire in the desert. I want to possess her, the way I once possessed Jahazan, the way the deev once possessed me. In her hands Hasshana holds one end of a golden cord, looped around her wrist like the leash of a pig or goat. The other end of the cord vanishes through the open door behind her.

"So you are the deev-kin." She pushes me away and her peri-courtiers laugh. "Not mortal, not deev, but a bastard thing that belongs nowhere, to no one. You are worse than the deev, because you were once a true mortal—you made a choice to be like this. By rights I should kill you where you stand; your presence pollutes this holy place. What makes you think your pleas will mean anything to me?"

"Perhaps because you are curious."

"Curious of what?"

"Curious of why I made that choice."

Hasshana smiles. "Love in the time of the Serpent-King," she says. "Who knows why any mortal makes a choice these days? If Ahriman himself whispered words of evil in your ear I would not be surprised. But come—you are here, and

I suppose I can listen to you for a short time. Tell me why I should let your lover go."

"She can be good, Queen," I say. "Five years ago Jahazan came to me in a village I had destroyed. I was weak, I was broken. There, I might have taken my own life. She showed compassion then—she came to care for me."

The Queen shakes her head. "She came to lead you astray. She encouraged your immorality. She fed you lies of bloodlust and sex. How many innocents have died because she 'cared' enough to let your evil loose in New Persia? You know as well as I do that a man who saves the devil will not find honour in heaven."

"What about in the Serpent-King's palace, then? She showed compassion; she saved my life so—"

"So another would die in your place. Did you know that the man who replaced you was a child of ten, son of the last general to stand against the Serpent-King's cruelty? A child who died screaming his father's name. His death weighed hardest on the people of New Persia, for it was only then that they understood even the strongest were powerless against Zohak." Hasshana's fingers loop about the cord, as deft as any weaver. "Why reward the man who saves the fool, only to kill the king. You are wasting my time, Rahaeb Reyad."

"One last, please," I say, pressing my forehead to the pretty stones at her feet. "From the time before I was made cruel, when I was still innocent of war. Jahazan took me from my village when it was destroyed by the deev armies, and brought me to safety. She had nothing to gain from my life in those days. She saw only a small child in a burning city and knew—"

"Compassion? Weakness, I would say," Hasshana sneers.

"I thought only the deev believed those two words were interchangeable."

The Queen stares at me for a long moment.

"I am Rahaeb Reyad, a mortal man," I say. "And she loved me. From that day, in the burning village, she loved me."

Her frown deepens, and I know then that she believes me. "Jahazan will not harm another being again, whether you take her or not," she says. "We have tamed her; we cut the devilment from her. Now she is like a boar without its tusks, a snake without its fangs. It would be safer for her to stay with us. We could give her peace, here; we could give her purity. And there are many in New Persia who remember her cruelty—"

"Please," I say.

Slowly she unbinds the golden cord from around her wrist and passes it to me. In my hands I feel it flex and tug slightly—there is a creature tied to the other end. Jahazan.

"She will never care for you again," says Hasshana, turning away. "You saved her life but in doing so proved yourself weak as any mortal. She could not tolerate that in a lover. She will wish you dead."

"I know," I whisper.

"You must lead her through Amberabad and Jinnistan," says the Queen. "While you hold that cord in your hand, you must not look back. Not until you are back in the land of mortals can you set her free. Now go, Rahaeb Reyad. Leave Jinnistan and never return—this place is not for your deev-kind."

* * *

I am thirty, maybe thirty-one, when I walk through paradise with my deev-lover on a leash.

Through the jewelled city of Amberabad, where the streets are lined with foreign sea-shells and the houses are painted with blue enamel. Through the crowds of peri, who are no longer staring at me but at the broken deev dangling from the golden cord. Through Jinnistan, the heaven of fairies, and to the great gates that gleam like Nubian gold.

On the threshold I stand and stare down at the lands of mortals, the war-torn world of the Serpent King. And as I step out the cord behind me tugs, just once,

"Rahaeb Reyad."

"Jahazan?"

"Look at me," she says softly, and then screams it: "Look at me!"

How can I refuse her? Even as the Queen's warning rings in my ears, I turn around.

She is naked as she was when I first met her, save for that necklace of green stones around her neck. Her skin is still the colour of ochre, but her body casts a shadow now, a darkness on the sparkling Jinnistan street. She is human-shaped, but her iris are as they always were, ringed within and without by a thin line of orange. Yet they lack the fire they once had, that cruel passion. Queen Hasshana was right: they have cut the devilment from her, as sharply as husking wheat, and left only a shell. A weak deev like Jahazan would die in the kingdom of the Serpent-King.

And I realise with a suddenness that this is what was meant to happen; that Queen Hasshana never intended to let Jahazan go, only to teach me a lesson: that the only way to go forwards is to look back, for your future depends on everything that lies behind you.

I raise my hands to her: "Jahazan—"

But then the gates close and there are only clouds, and I am on top of the mountains of Mazandaran with a light snow falling.

Dwarfblood
by Berrien C. Henderson

*Berrien C. Henderson splits his time among family, work, writing, and mar-
tial arts. Undaunted by rising postage rates and a growing collection of rejection
slips, he writes at night and teaches during the day because bill collectors expect
to get paid.*

*This tale introduces us to a gem that is much more than a simple stone and
the lives that are changed by touching it.*

Days before his daughter's sixteenth birthday, Jax Jannson encountered an awful
dilemma. The child, of course, needed—demanded—a striking, memorable gift.
Among the Province's wealthiest merchants, Jax Jannson knew exactly what his
daughter wanted and how to procure it, although the price was steep.

It would be the rarest of gems (of course, for a nearly sixteen-year-old girl!). It
must be a dwarfblood ruby with its speck of argent-fire winking in plump five-carat
depths. Only three such gems were said to exist. The other two had vanished, along
with their owners, behind whispers of thievery and murder. Cursed gems, they
said. Nevertheless, Amber Elayn wanted one from her capable, wealthy merchant
father.

"Nothing else?" he asked days before the party.

"I've never asked for jewelry before," said Amber Elayn with a touch of exas-
peration. Both she and her mother looked at Jax with pleading, unblinking eyes.

"Well, you and your mother certainly managed to acquire enough of it," he
rebutted.

His wife said, "Not another word, if you know what side your bread is buttered
on."

Jax ran his hands through his salt and pepper hair, sure to acquire more gray in
the next few days. He heaved a sighed.

They were implacable, brows furrowed and lips pressed thin.

"There are only three dwarfblood rubies."

"Amber Elayn," said her mother, "leave us a moment, child."

Flipping her copper locks, the girl flashed a wicked, impish grin at her father.
"Thank you, Mother. And Father?"

"Yes."

She smiled and rushed up to peck his cheek. "Thank you for your generosity."
Then, stifling a laugh, she left the room.

Jax pursed his lips and wrinkled his nose.

"Smell something disagreeable?" said his wife.

"Residue of spent money. Lots of it."

"She could have asked for a stable of horses," said his wife.

"Horses are an honorable, intelligent gift," replied Jax.

"But jewelry doesn't eat."

"Only away at one's purse."

Jax's wife sipped some wine. He had taken great care of her over the years while building a respectable business from fur and timber ventures—had become the third wealthiest merchant in the Province and she the third richest merchant wife in the Province.

"Well, I suppose you'll just have to sell a few more fur pallets to make up for it," she said.

"I work hard enough to provide for you and my daughter. She has an excellent tutor and the beginnings of a good head for business," said Jax.

"Don't you think with your connections you could find a dwarfblood ruby? She'd be the envy of the Province," she prodded.

"Envy's not my concern. What about the curse?" eased Jax.

"Curse?" Her laugh was rich velvet. "The only curse you'll get is the one flung out of her mouth if she doesn't get one."

"She's my child. Not my foreman," he said. "Besides, it's too much too soon."

"In three days it will be too late."

"And if I don't?"

Her eyes became smoldering slits. "The shipping season keeps your side of the bed cold at night."

The audacity! Jax clenched his teeth. "Indeed it does."

"I'm sure Amber Elayn will be delighted."

* * *

He faulted himself for the false securities of believing financial stability would negate his not being at home. He had to take a hard look at the consequences of buying his way through a family life. His wife had been there at the start of his career, coming from nothing to something, servants tending the house now instead of her doing a day's work in the home while Amber Elayn had, through no fault of her own, known nothing but comfort. She was Jax's only child, his happiness. She knew what the word "no" meant, yet he was certain she would have a hard time accepting that on her sixteenth birthday.

A dwarfblood ruby? Jax shook his head.

When had she and her mother hatched such a dazzlingly bold and ridiculous idea? How many years had Amber Elayn harbored and waited and plotted before broaching the subject?

Jax's head hurt.

He had three days until his daughter's birthday and five until he set off for another voyage.

He also considered a cold bed that might not be so cold when he returned.

He could handle such innuendo. Maybe she had already done something. It would be only fair; there was, after all, more across the sea than his trading endeavors.

Jax had an inroad. There was always a person who knew a person who . . .

There was only one place he could go.

Low Town.

* * *

Jax walked the long road from his home to town, where the cobblestones gleamed from falling dew while songs drifted out of alehouses. Walking instead of riding gave him extra time to think. He paused to give some coin to an urchin who offered to sell him a handkerchief. Jax took it from the gnarled fellow and palmed a silver mark in his hand. At least selling handkerchiefs was better than begging outright.

"Many thanks," said the urchin. Light bled from out of a window near them and splashed across the man's hooded head. Jax saw only a knobby nose and dark eyes.

"Just trying to help," said Jax.

"It's good cloth, from the Fardeep Mountains."

Jax hummed as he inspected his none-too-well embroidered purchase.

"You look like a man who's searching for something," said the urchin.

"Always on the lookout for a good deal," said Jax. He squeezed the cloth. "Like this. Thank you."

"No, thank *you*," said the gnarled man. He cocked his head askance to scrutinize Jax. "You don't normally haunt Low Town's streets."

Jax laughed. "What makes you say that?"

With a wolfish grin, the stunted fellow said, "Your hands are quite clean, sir. Good nails."

Taken aback, Jax said, "A man can have clean hands despite his work."

"Certain work wants dirt's stain, and many hands get dirty this hour in Low Town," said the man.

"Don't they, though," parried Jax as the other's eyes glittered.

"Surely," he agreed.

Jax said, "Well, good luck with your business, sir."

"Be careful," offered the gnarled man, "that your generosity doesn't blind you."

"I'll do my best," said Jax, turning on his heel.

* * *

Jax needed aid from a man of certain resources—a night-worker betimes. Jax had not asked too many questions of his informant; sometimes that was for the best. In the shadows of these buildings lurked who knew how many cutthroats, and it wasn't the slinking, shifty-eyed folk he did see that bothered him: only the ones he couldn't see. Here on the west side of Low Town, anything could happen—a toss up between opportunity and avarice.

He found an alley and followed slick cobblestones down an unusually long path, then turned around and saw that he was only twenty yards from the street. The alley's end lay a good fifty yards ahead; Jax saw a doorway with a sign hanging over the lintel: Curiosities and Such.

As Jax continued walking, a wave of vertigo gripped him. He shook his head, then marched while having the distinct sensation of the cobblestones stretching beneath his feet. His equilibrium canted, and he shook his head again. Turning around, he went back to the street, which failed to recede the way the doorway had. He cursed under his breath at the magic affecting the alley.

He stopped, then turned around. If it was glamour, then he intended to circumvent it.

"Hello? Master Gwynyn?" His voice echoed against stone and wood. People passed behind him in the night.

Jax bent down and picked up a rock. He threw it as hard as he could. The rock arced high, falling with a scraping clatter against the cobblestones and bouncing until it thunked against the wood. The door creaked open. Someone stood silhouetted against the interior light bleeding out.

"Who calls?" searched a piping voice.

"Jax Jannson. Tobe of Hoffsetting referred you," said Jax. The names were code.

"Not many know old Tobe of Hoffsetting," returned the piping voice. "Only his friends."

Jax smiled. "An acquaintance, actually."

"Come then."

Jax stepped forward but didn't feel the rush of vertigo on his way to the door of Curiosities and Such. He loomed over the proprietor, who stood little more than chest high to Jax.

"Hope the glamour-gate didn't make you too sick," said Gwynyn. "Helps keep riff raff away."

"Just a bit dizzy," replied Jax.

The little man squinted as he looked Jax up and down. "Usually makes folks vomit. What's your profession?"

"Merchant."

"Over land?"

"Overseas."

"Ahhh," said Gwynyn. "That makes sense. Sea-worthy legs."

Jax smiled.

"Come," said Gwynyn. "As long as the door's open, so's the charm. Who knows what skulkers are about?"

Jax shut the door behind them and felt a shiver slither against his back as the warding reset. Lantern light cast a soft glow about a room littered with novelties and trinkets along with one terribly thin shop owner. Jax believed he might lose sight of Gwynyn if the man turned sideways.

Supposedly, though, this master procurer of oddities knew his material better than any imports expert.

Overlarge, midnight black avian eyes, searching for the odd and useful, blinked at Jax. This was the second time in his life he had seen a *Sidhe*. They could be . . . exacting creatures—stealers of babies, godlings of word-magic and thing-glamour.

As if sensing Jax's thoughts, Gwynyn nodded his head and flashed a smile full of pointy teeth.

The man cleared his throat and fiddled with his coat as if he felt out of place amid shelves full of vials of light and ceremonial drakefang daggers and color-shifting silks and petrified giant skulls. There was a fist-sized stone with a card relating that the rock had fallen from the sky—a thunderstone of old. He even saw hen's teeth ("The rarest of rarities in the explored world!" proclaimed its card).

Quite an array of expensive revenue, Jax thought, savoring it all with his merchant's eyes.

Across the room in a glass-fronted cabinet, under heavy lock, came intermittent chattering, muffled yelps, and incensed curses from a bottle imp (clearly an illegal thing). Free, an imp could run roughshod over a city until the local militia could fetter it—only then with the help of a handful of mages.

Gwynyn flashed another forestalling smile. "Security precaution."

"Security precaution?"

"In case of trespass," said Gwynyn.

"But you've got the glamour-ward," offered Jax, thinking it a bit paranoid on the *Sidhe's* behalf to keep a bottle imp for protection.

Gwynyn's eyes slitted and gave him a reptilian appearance. "Master Jannson, my folk are quite powerful, but there are thieves who would see such a store plundered for various reasons, the least of which is monetary. Nevertheless, let's continue."

"Indeed."

Jax followed and found himself in a spacious study filled with floor-to-ceiling bookshelves. A massive mahogany desk huddled center-room with squat leather chairs and a fat vault behind. As they sat, Gwynyn produced a ring of keys, each of which he snicked and turned in rapid succession in the vault's locks. The man couldn't see the vault's contents because of the *Sidhe*, who turned and grinned toothily.

The dwarfblood ruby's throbbing glow bathed Gwynyn and took away Jax's breath. Reverentially, Gwynyn set the dwarfblood ruby on one corner of the desk and with a practiced gesture said, "There it is."

"How did you come across it?" posed Jax.

"Surely you can appreciate the value of a source's anonymity. A trade secret, if you will." He chuckled. "My folk place a high price on secrecy." The *Sidhe's* teeth gleamed.

"Speaking of price," said Jax, his fingers drumming on one knee.

Gwynyn rubbed a thin, bony index finger on his chin. "A moment."

He began writing on a small slip of paper with a quill pen.

The *Sidhe* waved for Jax to scoot his chair forward, and Gwynyn slid the paper to him.

"My price," said Gwynyn.

Jax studied the figure. His face betrayed no emotion in the few seconds he considered fulfilling Amber Elayn's wish would take approximately three months of aggressive trading to cover. Actually, *re*cover, as Jax already had a cheque to write the *Sidhe*.

"Is the sum agreeable, Master Jannson?"

Jax clucked his tongue and said, "Neither agreeable nor disagreeable, Gwynyn."

"These things do not pay for themselves, and the trials associated with acquiring merchandise add to the cost."

"Oh, I understand wholly," said Jax. "As a fellow trader, of course."

Gwynyn smiled as he offered the quill pen to Jax, who produced the cheque. "You may take this to the Greater Provincial Trust."

He handed it over and rose from his chair, and Gwynyn shook his hand. The *Sidhe* dropped the dwarfblood ruby in a leather pouch and gave it and a letter of authenticity. With a touch of concern, he proffered the man a small vial.

"Free of charge, Master Jannson," said the Sidhe.

"I don't understand," he said.

"Insurance, if you will. It should protect you from any spell—a double-shift potion, returning twofold upon the sender the spell invoked upon you."

"Why would I need such a thing?"

"A dwarfblood ruby can't stay secret from thieves of any ilk for long," said Gwynyn.

Jax studied the purplish liquid in the vial, then tucked it in his vest pocket. "Many thanks." Gwynyn nodded. "I appreciate your time and resources, Gwynyn."

"I hope your daughter likes it," said the *Sidhe*. "Though I could only imagine the wheedling it took to get you here." He chuckled.

Jax heaved a sigh. "Women."

Gwynyn escorted Jax to the door. Silent now as they parted, both preoccupied with the same thought: such a hefty sum for such a small thing.

The *Sidhe* watched Jax exit the alley before shutting the door so as not to disrupt Jax's equilibrium by resetting the glamour-gate. He smoothed the cheque in the palm of his hand and grinned at his good fortune. A nice sum indeed.

As Gwynyn returned to his study, a gust of wind squeezed into the threshold a trice before the door closed and kept it open but a hair's breadth. An inky shadow spilled down the alley and slithered into the cracked door. This shadow-not-shadow resolved itself into its natural form.

Now stood the matter of the bottle imp, which began mewling and rattling the entire curio cabinet. The intruder cast a small nut in the imp's direction; it bounced, struck the cabinet, and wrapped the whole piece of furniture in the silence of a thousand midnights. The irksome imp gesticulated rudely, and its mouth worked soundlessly.

The thief continued.

"Stop," came Gwynyn's slicing whisper.

The thief froze, aware of some earthy scent barely veiled under the conflicting candles' scents. He silently cursed his inattentiveness. He inhaled deeply, sorting through the aromas to focus on the earthy one, its signature redolent. His lips tightened. He had been bested by one who knew charms from birth.

"I knew there was glamour about," he said. "Not some *Sidhe* adept."

"I'm a proprietor first," said Gwynyn. He muttered under his breath, and a spell washed over the thief but to no effect.

"You're slippery," said Gwynyn.

"I've always preferred greasy," replied the other. From the folds of his cloak, he produced a long-bladed dagger and a tiny pyramid. Each side had symbols etched on it: earth, air, water, wind, spirit.

Gwynyn's face betrayed little consternation at this man with a charm-defiant.

The *Sidhe* slipped twin stiletto daggers from his shirtsleeves. Magic wouldn't work now, but perhaps steel would.

The thief returned the charm-defiant to his cloak, then gestured with his dagger.

"Tell me why, first," said Gwynyn.

"That man earlier bought something, something of mine."

"Of yours?"

"She is very dear to me," said the other, his eyes flashing, "and I intend to rescue her."

"Nothing personal." Gwynyn shrugged. "Just business."

He pursed his lips, and a breeze blew out the candles in the room. In the darkness clashed flesh and blades, grunts and bellows. The bottle imp went wild in its silent prison. A clatter of items bumped off a table. Something cracked underfoot. Curses.

Soon was no sound, save the soft noise of the cloaked figure leaving and limping down the alleyway.

The *Sidhe* had been a worthy opponent, thought the thief, who grumbled to himself as he placed a handkerchief on his cut rib cage. He wasn't as mad about losing blood as he was about dropping and stepping on his charm-defiant in the fight. Those were difficult items to replace and could otherwise be handy in a tight spot.

* * *

The crisp night air invigorated Jax on his walk home. His hand eased into his jacket pocket where the dwarfblood ruby lay. Amber Elayn would be thrilled, his wife would no longer vex him, and he could focus on business matters.

Light from his manor shone from a mile away and welcomed him as he rounded a bend in the road. He had two days until Amber Elayn's birthday party, with the most difficult part done.

Still, an insinuating thought percolated in his thoughts.

"Trading keeps your side of the bed cold at night."

After nearly twenty years he could never remember something so frosty leaving his wife's mouth. He sighed, his breath pluming in the starlight and the sharp smiling slit of the crescent moon.

Jax thought he might be better off slipping into the guest chambers and spending the rest of the night there, so he followed the hedgerow around the property until he came to a side entrance. Some of the servants chattered idly as they finished the night's scullery duties; voices and laughter drifted on the night. Horses snorted in the stable, and the hostler talked in low, soothing tones. Jax loathed leaving when the shipping season would open. How irksome—his love of home and family cornered by innuendo and an extravagant gift!

Slipping into the guesthouse, he heard a door shut and noticed a shadow on a servant's path, someone going home to one of the bungalows on that end of the property.

Once inside, Jax tidied up the guest bed and entered the large closet between the master bedroom and the guest bedroom. He could enter without accessing the bedroom, and Jax didn't want to disturb her sleep.

Getting some nightclothes, he heard his wife stirring next door. Jax decided to let her know he was home safe and entered their chamber.

She was fussing with her nightgown and rearranging the covers—always a messy bedmate. One tiny candle cast a lonely yellow glow in the room. When the door shut behind Jax, the sound made her jump.

"Back again so soon?" she asked, turning around with a bright smile.

"Feels more like hours," said Jax.

Her eyes widened, and the smile maintained. "Oh, it seemed so soon."

"Deep night and long trips fool us sometimes," he said. "Look."

He showed her the dwarfblood ruby. Its depths pulsed like a miniature heart-beat and amplified the soft candlelight in the bedroom. Jax's wife gasped.

"You didn't!" she said, hurrying forward. Her eyes locked on the ruby while her hands hovered like two birds anticipating a place to light.

Jax patted his empty vest pocket. "I helped expand the wealth of a *Sidhe* merchant by no small degree."

The ruby's sparkle dashed and darted across her face as if she were under the surface of a red-faced pond. Jax let her hold the gem, which she rolled from palm to palm.

"Only three like it," she whispered. Her eyes flashed. "What of the rumors?"

"Just that," he said though his left hand went absently to his vest pocket.

"Our daughter shall have this one and be well-pleased, I'm sure."

"I should hope so," laughed Jax. "I don't think that *Sidhe* tradesman had a return policy posted."

He took the dwarfblood ruby back from his wife and put it in their armoire. Behind his hand he stifled quite a yawn. His wife raised an eyebrow.

"Some trip to Low Town," she said.

Jax shook his head. "No, just fatigue for haggling and getting this gem." He shut and locked the armoire, then put on his nightclothes.

His wife said, "Come to bed, dear."

After he buttoned up the last few buttons on his nightshirt, he turned around to blow out that one lonely candle. Quickly his wife took a moment to fluff his pillow. "You've earned some rest," she said, brushing off a few strands of red hair from the pillow.

* * *

The party came quicker than Jax had anticipated. Like ants parading food, caterers scurried to and from the kitchen. A table burdened with gifts stood in one corner of the room. Guests lounged and mingled in small groups throughout. Jax was proud of how Amber Elayn carried herself—floating like a hostess from person to person and thanking each for their attendance and making proper small talk. He cringed. Sixteen already! But she was beautiful and capable, spoiled only in the privacy of her mother and father's company.

Her mother's voice was a tad more noticeable, her laugh more pronounced after a few glasses of wine. She plucked one with a beaming, practiced smile from a waiter hurrying off to restock his tray.

Everyone gathered around Amber Elayn as she opened boxes of dresses and jewelry. Jax waited until she was done with the last gift on the table before offering her the drawstring pouch. *The* last gift. As Amber Elayn opened the pouch, a small reddish light leaked from it. Gasps and whispers rippled through the room as the guests nudged closer.

"Father, you found one!" said Amber Elayn. Her eyes had almost glazed with fascination at the five-carat ruby, its center twinkling. She rushed over and gave Jax a tremendous hug. "Thank you, oh thank you!"

"You're quite welcome, Amber Elayn."

"Is that actually one of them?" asked a guest.

"Yes," said Jax. He watched his daughter cradle the gift.

"It must have cost a small fortune."

"Something close, I assure you. And none too close to the new shipping year." He drank some more wine and thanked the smiling red-haired waiter.

"Good wine," Jax said.

"The best, sir," he replied.

Jax noticed the boy lingered at his wife's circle of conversation. A guest beside Jax glanced quickly that way.

"Well, I enjoyed the party. I must make a round of good-byes and go," he said.

"Thank you for coming," said Jax.

"Always." He took a few steps, then turned. "The house just isn't the same when you're gone. You really should be home more often."

"Should I?"

The man offered a tight smile. "Maybe you should let your assistants take over more of the operations. You've earned it," said the man.

Jax yawned. "My apologies. I had a late night last night."

"Fretting over ledgers, no doubt?"

He laughed. "Too true. Too true."

The man looked around at the thinning crowd. "A most delightful party."

"Thank you," said Jax. He looked at the great clock: few hours yet until midnight and quite late for a girl's party. The day tugged at him in little nips.

At his wife's behest the house servants were helping put away the gifts. She fluttered around like a bird while Amber Elayn ritualistically inspected each of the gifts again. Jax noticed how closely the girl clutched the dwarfblood ruby in her hand and felt a twinge of pride at his success in obtaining the rare gem.

Amber Elayn approached Jax and hugged him. She said, "Father, you outdid yourself."

"Oh, I don't know about that," said Jax. "Just make me a promise."

"What's that?"

"That you'll keep it locked away tightly tonight and only wear it under the supervision of several well-armed men."

Amber Elayn laughed. "I'll hand-pick the most strapping men I can find."

"You won't have to look hard, dear."

"Father!"

He hid a sudden yawn behind his hand. "Good-night, Amber Elayn. I would walk you to your bedchamber, but I think a sixteen-year-old lady is quite capable of finding her way," he said with a bit of heart-tug at her having grown-up almost overnight. Had it really been sixteen trading seasons? He measured life by sailing to sea each year. Maybe it *was* time to let some associates handle operations for him. Take a break. Maybe.

Amber Elayn said, "I think my father would still find time to walk me there, nevertheless."

He smiled. "True."

While his wife busied servants and caterers with the cleanup, Jax and Amber Elayn eased out of the room. "I'll be right back to escort you to bed as well," he said to his wife. She flashed him a grin.

"Promise?"

"Perhaps."

Coolly, she watched him leave.

The walk through the hallway gave Jax time to appreciate wealth of family. Even if his wife had guilted him about his business, at least his daughter showed some guile and interest in it.

She said, "When will I get a chance to help?"

"I don't know if you're ready," he said.

She stiffened beside him. "What's that supposed to mean?"

"You have plenty of opportunities many young women don't. Then a young man will ask for your time, then your hand," said Jax.

Amber Elayn said, "In the mean time, I want to try my hands at other opportunities."

"Like?"

"Like shipping."

"Too many rough men."

"You're not a rough man."

It was Jax's turn to bristle. "By that you mean?"

"That shrewdness and lewdness are entirely different things."

Despite himself, he smiled. Oh, she was a clever one. "It's late."

"You want to dodge my arguments," she said.

Jax feigned injury, grabbing his heart. "No. Just to consider them over a good night's sleep."

Her eyes sparkled, and she held up the dwarfblood ruby; a soft scarlet glow cast a patina on their faces. "If I didn't know better, I'd say you were trying to bow out gracefully because you realize your daughter batted her eyes in the right place at the right time to get just the right birthday gift." Oh, the sheer wickedness of her grin!

Jax surrendered. "Good-night, Amber Elayn."

"Good-night, Father."

"Lock that ruby up," he said. "It's expensive."

"Anyone foolish enough to try stealing it would have a long night of it," she quipped.

Chuckling, Jax shook his head. "I bet there's a dagger under your pillow this very moment, Miss Long-Night-Of-It," he said.

Amber Elayn raised an eyebrow. "I'll never tell."

He put his index finger to his lips. "Shhh."

She winked and shut the door.

* * *

Jax slipped off his boots and pattered around in his sock feet, feeling the cool stone floor and wiggling his toes. The bedroom door opened and closed softly.

"You're coming to bed early," he said over his shoulder.

Turning, he saw a short man standing there. A hot flash rippled through Jax. The man was stocky, squat with bulging shoulders and overlong arms—a dwarf.

His dark eyes glittered, and his knobby nose stood out from a pockmarked face Jax recalled seeing before but couldn't quite place.

"Who in the nine hells do you think you are?" said Jax, going for his dagger. "How did you make it this far?"

"I'm persuasive," said the dwarf, easing onto the balls of his feet. He sprinted across the room and jammed Jax's knife hand before he had half-unsheathed his dagger. Then the dwarf twisted Jax's arm, tucked his knees, corkscrewing down, then pumping back up. He pulled Jax's arm in a tight arc and flung him. Jax crashed to the floor, rolled a few feet, then regained his footing.

"Most would have stayed down," huffed the dwarf.

"I've been in a few scrapes," spat Jax. He noted those dark eyes and that caricature nose. "*Do* I know you?"

Nodding, the dwarf said, "Low Town. The handkerchief peddler. One never knows what kind of thing-glamour is floating around. You could be tracked."

Jax thought a moment. He was certainly no mage-adept, just a merchant. He considered the small lump in his vest pocket.

"You want money? Safe passage?" said Jax.

The dwarf said, "You have something quite dear to me."

"I've never dealt with you beyond the handkerchief purchase and this squabble."

"I'm here for my daughter." The dwarf drilled him with those obsidian eyes.

Jax said, "I don't have any dwarfish servants, nor otherwise employ dwarfish folk."

"A purchase several nights ago. The *Sidhe*. The ruby."

"Well, I bought 'her' squarely," said Jax.

"I'm not referencing a ship. Why do you think the ruby pulses like a heart?"

"I don't understand."

"My family feuded with another powerful family years ago." His eyes became ebony spear tips. "I cast a spell on three of its members and erased all knowledge of and ability for magic from those three. It wasn't taken well." His fists clenched to whiteness. "Their vengeance was swift and decisive. My three daughters were kidnapped and shape-changed." His face contorted with the memory.

Jax went cold. Thoughts of Amber Elayn's safety fluttered Jax's heart. "I can rectify this," he said. "You'll have the ruby and be on your way without one word to the authorities."

The dwarf sneered. "I can only get my daughter back if I substitute another's essence in the ruby to balance the curse."

Jax's mind tumbled. "That's why the stories claim the owners were murdered," he whispered.

"No, just converted to replace my two other daughters. I know where you're keeping the ruby." His eyes slitted.

Jax felt a bloom of white-hot fury. "You won't take my daughter." He held the dagger in a low guard position.

"Sacrificing yourself would do," parried the dwarf.

"I was born at night," said Jax. "But not last night."

"Damned fool! I've crossed oceans for my children's return. This is the last stop on a six-year journey, and you'll not forestall me."

Jax circled until he stood between him and the door. "You'll have a long night of it," said Jax.

He inverted the dagger; with the blade down, he could get in many more cuts.

The dwarf pulled his long-bladed knife and noted Jax's grip. "You're no stranger to blades. We should have a good time."

He came forward, muttering under his breath.

A wave of lethargy washed over Jax. Although Jax's body moved like syrup, his wits didn't, and a hand struggled to his vest pocket.

The dwarf closed and slashed. Jax tried to fade back and block up, but already the word-magic oozed through him like eldritch poison. His arm suffered a gash, and he grunted as the dwarf closed. Jax's other hand crept out of the vest pocket. He freed the tiny vial. Jax did a slow-motion toss at the dwarf, who tried to back away. As soon as the vial left Jax's hand, it was free of the dwarf's spell, and the little bottle shattered at the dwarf's feet.

"No!" he cried, a drop splattering his boot tip. He tried to charge, then froze. His face contorted as he strained against invisible hands.

The wave of lethargy left Jax. "Double-shift potion. Apparently a good investment."

The dwarf strained, "Bastard. Won't . . . last long."

"Oh, I know. You won't have my daughter. I'll drop you off—bound, of course—with ruby in hand, and you can figure out what to do from there."

The dwarf smoldered as Jax plucked the knife from his grip. "You . . . don't . . . understand. Must be . . . from . . . your family."

"Just the ruby."

Suddenly the dwarf's eyes twinkled with inspiration. "Hard bargain. But . . . this room."

"What about it?" said Jax.

"Youth . . . red hair."

"Yes. At the party earlier tonight."

"A . . . regular visitor."

"Perhaps. We host many parties. Even when—"

"You're . . . at sea." A slow grin spread across the dwarf's face.

Jax shook as his ire blossomed—right under his nose! He couldn't decide if he were mad with himself for not noticing or at his wife for her callous audacity. Jax would have to leave soon—and no telling what decadence would occur while he was away.

"Talk before the spell wears off or we have to fight again."

"Have . . . idea," wheezed the dwarf.

Jax listened. The terms were hard.

"Two birds. One stone." He stared at his own dagger in Jax's hand. "Promise not . . . to harm . . . daughter. Word-bond." He suddenly relaxed as the spell ebbed. "I appeal to you as a father."

Jax pursed his lips. What was he thinking? He had, for all intent and purposes, just saved his daughter's life. But what of the dwarf's proposal? What kind of man did that make him, even to entertain the idea? And if it were to replace a heart, a personality, in the dwarfblood ruby, well, would it really—

"A man may go to dark lengths for the sake of his child," the dwarf said.

Jax smiled bitterly. "You will have the ruby. Just wait until—"

"I know how to make it look," finished the dwarf.

"Not a trace," committed Jax.

The dwarf grinned, holding out a hand. "My knife?"

* * *

To Jax, this particular trip at sea felt longer than four months and was plagued initially with bad weather and later with bad news. While tidying up deals before the return trip, a dispatch had arrived.

Urgently, Jax opened it, sealed in wax with the family crest.

The note read:

Father,

Please return immediately. During one of Mother's fetes, a young man stole some jewelry, including the dwarfblood ruby, and Mother has left us. In my jewelry box I found a short note from her. She wrote simply, 'My comfort now comes from another. My heart is in a better place.' Father, please hurry home. Please.

With patience and

love,

Amber Elayn

Jax crumpled the letter and cast it on the deck of his ship. The wind caught the balled up paper and batted it around and away from Jax as deckhands hoisted sail. A caustic swell of ambivalence burned Jax's chest as he gripped the railing and looked out to sea. Another gust buffeted the ship.

What have I given up, and what gained? he thought bitterly.

On Jax's lips was salt. He wiped his face before turning to his helmsman.

"Go," he said, patting the helmsman's shoulder while walking to the prow and looking to the horizon, toward home and his daughter.

Poetic License
by Lindsey Duncan

Lindsey Duncan is a life-long writer and professional Celtic harp performer who feels that music and language are inextricably linked. She lives and performs in Cincinnati, Ohio and is a student at Indiana University working on a self-designed major. She has been published several times, including in OG's Speculative Fiction.

In a school that doesn't really exist, where fictional characters learn their roles and hone their craft, someone has been murdered—for real.

By the time I reached the scene, the body of Sebastian Argyll, lead professor in the poetry department, had begun to fade into the never-happened from which he had come. I snapped pictures, took measurements, and cursed the lack of mystery students when one was needed. Most of them were out on a tour of real-world strip clubs for Settings and Scene 206, a part of the course that not coincidentally had a high level of professorial oversight. I had no such background. I had dropped out of the historicals genre twelve years ago when the Academy filled its quota of fictive Queen Elizabeths, both I and II.

Sebastian was a reedy man with defiantly unthinned hair and a real passion for his work, despite its position as the dregs of the Literary Academy. While some of its students might go on to inspire sonnets and great works, most ended up in the undemanding position of a bit of doggerel, fleeting fame but easy permanence in the real world. Sebastian, though...if every student lived up to his standards, the world would have walked and breathed iambic pentameter.

I headed up to the dean's office with a set expression. I had taken over from the last security chief three years ago and never had a murder before. For all of us—people who were never born because of history's many unexpected turns, or who died too soon—the only existence left was training to become a fictional character, or serving those who were. The acceptance, or at least the tolerance, of the Academy meant the difference between life and oblivion.

His secretary showed me in without the usual interminable wait, which was alarming in of itself. The dean's office was a plush, exotic affair with a zebra-skin rug and an ostentatious quill and ink display, though like most of us, he did his work by computer.

"We're very concerned about this, Gabrielle," he said. "What can you tell us?"

"He was stabbed some time late last night. No way to tell the gender or handedness of the attacker. And he, uh..." This was the part I hated. "He's already faded significantly. If there were secondary wounds, fingerprints, any identifying marks, they're gone now."

"Lovely." The dean arched an eyebrow. "What do you propose to do now?" The storm clouds of wrath gathered in his voice, ready to thunder over the wrong answer.

"I intend to speak to someone in the mystery genre, sir."

"If you tell me that one of the butlers did it," he snapped, "I'll have you stripped of your credentials right now."

"Not that," I said, even more swiftly than I'd meant to, "I think one of the professors might be able to help me."

He waved it off, dusting papers from his desk in the motion. Paperwork is immutable. Anyone who wants to be in a story with a paperless office joins the fantasy genre. "You're in charge of security, and you already said there are no forensic remains."

"Right, but one of the professors trains their future serial killers and hitmen. He knows a lot about the mindset." I took a deep breath. "If he can put himself in the mind of whoever did this and come up with some idea of the circumstances, it might narrow the search."

"What, the ... professor Dunmore?" The dean checked himself. "I don't see why not."

You mean the Nutmaster? I added silently. Seven years of teaching the fringe had made him a bit strange in self-defense, but I had never liked the nickname. "Thank you, sir."

"One more thing, Gabrielle." The storm was there, and I had little protection against it. "The Academy is built on the foundations of education and simulation ... never reality. If every barbarian practiced his hacking, if every thief thumbed through his roommate's belongings, there would be absolute chaos. It is worth a lot to me to see this solved. It is, in fact, worth more than you are. Are we clear?"

My stomach seized. "I understand."

* * *

Wolfgang Dunmore, invariably Wolf even to freshmen, was a clean-cut, sharp-eyed man in his mid-thirties prone to none of the vices that seemed to permeate the genre faculty. He was built in one straight but solid line, neither blessed with much in the way of muscle nor cursed by hovering paunch. His hair was the color and rough consistency of caramel, usually sculpted by nothing more fancy than a comb of his fingers.

"So you're absolutely sure Argyll didn't commit one of those dramatic poet deaths?" was his first question for me as we met outside the office, or rather, the crime scene, as I had to think of it. "Didn't cut off his own ear as a parting gesture?"

"That was a painter," I said absently. "If it were anything like that, I wouldn't need you."

"Ouch. Cut to the quick." Wolf chuckled, mocking a hurt expression.

I flashed him a droll grin. "You're not my type. You're too normal." I'd known him for a long time. We'd shared a class on political intrigue before I lost my opportunity and before he was promoted to teaching, and kept in touch afterwards. I never understood why he passed up the chance to become someone's great detective, a profiler perhaps, and I sometimes had the idea even he didn't know.

"Come on in," I said, taking off the security locks.

He took a cursory inspection of his surroundings, saving the half-shadow of the corpse for last. "You realize I won't be able to help you much," he said. "The department only teaches techniques that can be understood by the layman in a couple of paragraphs. The rest comes from the authors. No cameras, I suppose?"

"Not in poetry." I found it difficult to stand out of his way and fidgeted by the desk. "Or ..."

"I wouldn't be here." Wolf snorted. "No respect. No respect at all. Look," he continued, "the weapon was here at hand. Letter-opener, I presume. Several wild stabs, no sign of a fight."

"Can't tell if he had defensive wounds," I objected.

"Don't need to. He's too tidy." Rogue amusement in his voice. "In fact, look at his position. Seems he didn't even make it out of his chair. He slid out post-mortem."

I hadn't looked at it in that context, and blushed. "So what happened?"

Wolf continued as if he hadn't heard me, pointing, waving, in complete command of the situation. As well he might. In a place like the Academy, he had far more experience with murder than I did. "It's a textbook crime of passion," he concluded. "Spur of the moment, more likely than not, if only because who would be mad enough to kill someone here, if they stopped and thought about it?"

"That makes sense," I said. "I thought Argyll was well-liked."

"He is, he is. Real literati, that one." Wolf rubbed at the side of his nose. "But if there exists any person in this world or the real one who can please everyone all the time, I'll eat my hat."

"Not much of a sacrifice, considering you don't own one."

"Details, details." But he grinned at me before vaulting over the desk. He landed in a crouch by the drawer. "You open this lock yet?"

"I was hoping to find the key." I told myself there was no reason to be embarrassed. I was trying to do things by procedure. "I'm not sure it disappeared on the body yet."

"Probably did," he said, and without further warning, bashed it with the desk-side clock. After three blows and two startled protests from me, the lock broke. "There you are."

I wasn't sure whether to thank him or to take the clock and bop him in turn. I settled for rooting through the drawer, my face away from his. Private letters, musings, his own attempts at poetry, translations of famous works into other forms, among others.

Wolf draped himself on the desk, looking down. "This is important, isn't it?" I nodded, even though it hadn't been a question, and he continued, "I might be able to offer you another set of hands."

"Thanks, Wolf," I mumbled as I studied the pages. It was good stuff. So much for the old saying. "But you're a bit conspicuous."

"Not exactly a ninja yourself, red." He chuckled a bit. "But I wasn't talking about me. I have an exam to prepare. One of my older students, on the other hand, has a nose for these things. She might help you cover more territory."

"Sounds fine." I lifted the stack to my lap for further inspection, and a small card with calligraphy writing on it fell out. Feminine handwriting, classically spiraled. A piece of sweet nothing inscribed on it, a lover's promise.

"Your enthusiasm overwhelms me." He leaned in. "What do you have there?"

"A note from an Annalya," I answered, then looked up with a weary smile. "Sorry. I just have a lot on my mind. If I don't solve this…"

His brow quirked down. "The dean would throw you out?" He clapped a hand on my shoulder before I could answer. "Doubly important you solve this, then, and that you speak to this Annalya. Best of luck to you, and more than that, common sense."

* * *

A quick search of the Academy directory told me what I had half-expected. Annalya was a student, a junior specializing in sonnets.

Her class was in the computer labs studying urban archaeological reports on the nature of rhymed and literary graffiti. I sighed, hunted up my badge and credentials, and fisted my hair back into a braid that was supposed to be professional and at least managed schoolmarmish. It was almost the same thing, here.

I must have been lost in thought as I headed to the lab. I did not notice the young woman at my side until she spoke.

"Are you security?"

I jumped sideways in my skin. "I was a lot more secure five seconds ago!" the words blurted out of me. I immediately wished them unsaid.

My assailant was a young woman, slight, short, but with deceptively long limbs and a face that drew out into a basset hound's mournful lines. Despite that, grey eyes were sharp and curious. She dressed completely in a black that matched her hair down to the faint shimmer of ebon-blue. Trademark character traits in the making, but subtly applied, a protagonist's blend of unique.

"I'm Jordan," she said. "Professor Dunmore said you might need my help."

At this rate, her first task would be finding the shreds of my dignity. I shook her hand to cover my nerves and introduced myself. "Good to meet you. Can I ask you to talk to the junior professors? I take it if Wolf recommended you that you can be discreet."

"Of course," she said, cool and serious. "The best way to get an answer is to not ask the question."

I looked at her sharply. "That sounds like Wolf."

"It is," she confirmed with a sudden smile that turned the hound's face cherubic. "I flunked originality."

It was played for laughs, and I couldn't help but respond, far more at ease. "Meet me in my office at noon, then."

"Yes, ma'am." Those stork limbs stretched, and no sooner had she detoured than she vanished down the Academy halls.

The computer lab was a chessboard of dark screens and light, laid down in a dinghy framework of chairs and desks on the cheap. It was a monument to borderline obsolesce, filled with fierce students trying to stay on the working side of that line. In the far corner was a cluster of students all in blue, and perfectly positioned at their center, old-fashioned skirt arrayed around her and blonde hair draped down one shoulder, a single young woman in lily pad green.

"You have to be kidding me," I muttered. In a place where verisimilitude was a religion, my quarry seemed to be in some kind of surrealist cult. I waded through the pond of pupils. "Are you Annalya?"

She started to spin in her chair, then caught the underside of the desk with one hand and slowed to a gentler glide. "Yes, I am. Can I help you?" Her tones were honey, modulated, though they squeaked a bit when she saw my badge. "Is this about professor Argyll?" She was so choreographed that the falter was obvious. Pet nickname or first name familiarity, I didn't particularly care to find out.

"I'm afraid it is. Can we speak privately?"

Only her training kept her from scrambling out of the lab as fast as toned cream limbs would take her. I watched her and shook my head. It was clear from her every move what her aspirations were. She wanted to inspire the poetry of love, to be the ideal phantom behind sonnets and odes. I knew from watching previous classes that she was going about it wrong, too much a type. Wasn't Shakespeare's Dark Lady black eyed and coarse? Love was rarely found in the obvious.

"What can I help you with?" Annalya hovered like a nervous butterfly.

Any number of oblique questions crowded my mind. I ignored them. Considering the penalties for professor-student affairs, I wouldn't learn anything if she tried to lie, except that she had two brain cells to rub together. "How long had you and professor Argyll been seeing each other?"

She sucked in an opera-quality gust of air. "You don't ask a person a question like that!" When the rosy blush began to fade from her cheeks, she continued, "Eight months. It was quite spontaneous. I like him. I do." Her eyes flicked up, bright and anxious.

I did the math. Christmas party. Well, she wouldn't be the only one. "I believe you," I said. "I just need to know a few things."

"He never influenced my grades." She was firm, the words instant. "I never asked him to, he never offered, and I know he didn't. He was a perfect gentleman, and my work is superlative. The romance genre tried to win me over. I said no."

"Why?" The question was out before I could stop it.

Annalya lowered her eyes. "Bodice-rippers," she demurred. "There's no way to opt out."

"Err, well." I wondered if I should point out to her that some poetry crossed the same lines, but this was no time for career advice. "Where were you last night?"

"In bed. My roommate is a light sleeper," she added defensively, clearly anticipating the next question.

As easy as it would have been to think otherwise, I thought I had to believe her. The fact that she had instantly assumed I wanted to talk to her about cheating, not Argyll's death, weighed in her favor. Security doesn't handle those cases, but most students don't know the distinction.

"Is there anyone you can think of who might have had a problem with the professor?"

"Certainly not!" Annalya cried, then colored. "Of course, small things. Grades thought to be unfair, projects misjudged, but nothing that would be worth killing for. He was a man incapable of arousing that kind of ire." A shy glow hovered in her cheeks.

I asked her a few more questions, but I could feel the answers slipping away from me. I excused myself and hunted up the roommate, who confirmed her story, "I went out into the hall to banter with some free verse majors, but I was leaning against our door and I was only out for about ten minutes."

Argyll's reputation seemed to hold. It was only after asking the same question ten times over that I finally got a different answer. "Well, there is Alexander."

"Alexander Pritchard, pantoums," he said in a firm voice when I approached him in his dorm lounge, "been working on my thesis for oh, ten months now."

"Pantoum," I said carefully. "The second and fourth lines of the verse become the first and third lines of the next one?"

"Got it in one." Alexander munched on an apple, doodling with the other hand. "Professor Argyll seemed to think there was little need for characters in them."

I nodded once and checked my notepad. "Let me see."

"You agree with him?" He tapped the pencil on the pages. "What can I help you with?"

I was very glad for the second question, for there was no good answer to the first. "I understand you had a long-standing conflict with the professor. What can you tell me about that?"

The change in his body was dramatic, muscles snapping, the wandering hands still. "I can tell you that an argument is a long distance from whatever happened to him," he said. "I can tell you that…what is wrong with you people?"

"It's just me," I said, somewhat taken aback, "and that wasn't an accusation. Perhaps—"

"Of course Argyll has, had, whatever, the first say when it comes to whether or not I'm even allowed to enter inspiration," he cut me off, "but he doesn't make the final call, not even! And I don't honestly know that I want to. I've been thinking about a teaching position. So you know…" he trailed off.

I knew that there was suddenly one open, so I avoided the question I wanted to ask. "Do you know Annalya?"

Alexander snorted. "Ah, the prima donna." He picked up the apple again and spun it between his fingers. "She really would do better in one of fantasy's ivory towers." Yet he wouldn't meet my eyes. Envious?

I led him through a few more questions before I came to the last. "What were you doing last night?"

"You mean besides stabbing him." He was quick, too quick, on the defensive. Too much? "Keg party. Half the hall was there."

Which meant, I suspected, no one would be wholly able to vouch for anything. "Thank you, Mr. Pritchard." A thin thread of pain worked its way between my eyes. I grimaced as I excused myself. If I could get back to the office and down one of my pills before it got worse…

"Ma'am?"

My foot jammed sideways and hit the molding. "Jordan! You just took years off my life."

"Sorry, ma'am." Her tone was brisk as she offered me a notepad filled with tiny, anal-retentive letters. "Just some things I thought you ought to see. In particular, Argyll was teaching a crossover class with professor Banks in fantasy."

"Epic poetry?" I guessed. "I don't see the connection."

Jordan mimed a shrug. "Well, Beowulf, dragons, burly men with swords."

"But all of that is virtual," I said. While most Academy technology went no further than the venerable computers, basic simulation had fallen out of a science fiction plot hole a long time ago and been incorporated into the training. It was prevalent in all genres, but the spec-fics had the lion's share.

"The temptation is still there. Just my instinct." She smiled a bit. "I wrote down the statements of the junior professors."

My intended rush back to the office became a stroll of facts and figures, provided with encyclopedic ease by the young student. I was well and truly intimidated. I also found that I had to close my eyes to keep from wincing at the light, and by the time I reached the door, I could barely stand to listen to her voice.

"I need an hour," I croaked.

Once inside, I fumbled to my desk and hunted out a migraine pill by feel. I set the alarm for an hour and tried, somehow, to set aside concerns about homicide long enough to sleep it off.

* * *

I thrashed for nineteen minutes, not that I was staring at the clock, of course, and passed out for all of three when a foreign sound knocked me out of slumber. The shadows blurred around me, indistinct, and I started to close my eyes again.

The flash of light was subtle, almost unremarkable except for the accompanying stab of migraine pain. I jerked upwards with a startled cry, and distinctly heard the fabric of the couch rip as the slash of metal hit its flesh instead of mine.

I knew the attacker had to be human, because my dreams were always monochrome. It—he? She?—landed on the far side of the couch. I started to shout, what I decided later was an attention-grabbing bellow, and thought frantically around for my weapon.

The whites of eyes scored me in the muddy light as I realized the gun was wedged under my hip. I dropped sideways and reached for it.

In the second my eyes moved, my attacker was gone.

The door burst open, admitting two janitors and a junior who didn't have time to consider just what, exactly, security couldn't handle on her own. Jordan was with them.

"What happened?" The junior swung his books around menacingly. I had to duck to avoid being struck by a copy of The Black Arts. How appropriate.

Jordan was more effectual, across the room in a heartbeat, checking the windows, retrieving the weapon from the couch. A cafeteria knife. "Not very sharp," she said. "Are you all right?"

"I'd be a lot less all right if it were." I tried to make light of it even as I grimaced inwardly. Mother-henned by a student. I would have been more concerned if my lungs weren't quivering at a completely different tempo from my head. "All of you out! I have an incident to investigate."

That cowed all of them but Jordan, and I was left to search for footprints at carpet level, an act which looked a great deal like collapsing on the floor. Not the steadiest of reactions, but security at the Academy had always been more than halfway for show. My predecessor had been in my shoes for almost thirty years, and he had never mentioned this kind of shadowy attack.

"Ma'am?"

"Nothing down here," I said, straightening. I checked the room by rote, looking in the closet, rattling the windows. "We're on the third floor here. No one could have gotten in and out the window that quickly. There's my closet, but no other way out." Even if Jordan had somehow missed a person barreling down the hall, someone else should have seen them. "This is impossible."

"I think we can safely discount someone coming out of the closet," Jordan agreed. "But there is another possibility."

I dropped onto the desk. "Hit me with it."

"One of the more advanced simulations used by the fantasy genre is a device that creates, essentially, magical spells," she said. "The majority only work inside the virtual reality setting, but someone recently discovered that the phase-shift applications carry over into the Academy at large."

"Phase-shift," I said. "As in?"

"As in walking through walls." Her tone was brisk.

My hand came down on the desk harder than I'd meant it to. I felt it, and my bones, shuddering in response. "That might be a decent thing to tell security about!"

Jordan looked back at me, impassive, almost expressionless save for a trace of sympathy. We both knew my position was half for show, but someone was taking it seriously. Someone didn't want me to follow this case, and I suspected it was whoever had killed Argyll. This was no conspiracy, only a crime of passion and a cover-up. There would be no second man.

"That cross-discipline project," I said. "The epic poetry? Who is in charge?"

Her eyes hunted down for recollection. "Cole Barrister."

"I think I had better call on professor Barrister." Halfway to the door, I paused. I knew, somehow knew, that Jordan had refrained from saying anything to let me remember. So now my hand was being held by a mystery student? Fair enough. She knew something about it, after all.

Cole Barrister was a top-heavy man who would have looked at home in a loincloth and scabbard, and looked overdressed in anything else. He kicked his desk out to unknown hinterlands years ago, and worked standing up at a laptop easel.

"The honorable chief!" he boomed. "Settle in, pour up a tankard!" Though his water cooler was filled with the conventional fluid, he had massive fired mugs from which to drink lined up on the mantle.

I took the room's only chair and folded my hands in my lap. "How are classes, professor?"

"Oh, ho, a social call?" Cole's eyes were too sharp for that, the man pushing himself across the room with one hand. "As well as can be expected. I tell you, one more crop of milksop women under the impression that if they bat their eyelashes during a swordfight all the work will be done for them. Bah." He cut off his speech with a flinch.

I was too on edge to miss it. "Are you all right?"

"This?" His hand swept down. "Token, a mere scratch, a righteous brand of our local excuse for a battlefield. I tell you, the genre is on its way downhill. All these simulations, virtual games with no consequences, it trains one for shallow comedy, nothing more. Where are the epics, I ask you?"

"You should talk to Wolf up in mystery," I said. "He feels the same way."

"Wolf! There's an excellent name for a barbarian. I don't suppose he is one, is he? No, blast the luck," he continued as I tried to answer. "Now what can I do for you?"

"Sebastian Argyll," I said, afraid if I didn't get to the point, I would be abducted by his enthusiasm. "You taught a class with him?"

"Ah, the poet!" he exclaimed, apparently oblivious to the fact that the term described a significant portion of the Academy population. "Good man, good! Needed to firm up about the middle, not that I imagine he's worrying about that wherever his soul has flitted, eh? Yes, and our next lecture was to be four days from now. We were meant to meet tonight and go over notes." He heaved a sigh.

"Did any of his students show a particular interest in the genre?" I asked, a bit bemused.

"Didn't all of them? A bit more blood and bones than they were used to! Couple even got queasy," Cole said, as if this were a point of pride. "I told them, you're lucky I don't make you re-enact the Iliad, but we'd have to kill the entire class five times to cast it, and that's just the named sons-of-somebody. Isn't lucky to kill someone in virtual. One of the seniors put a pinpricker through Argyll, you see what happened to him?"

I jumped on it. "Who?"

"Oh, red-headed chap, very fierce. Apologized profusely."

A little part of me whimpered when it wasn't that easy, but I pushed on. "What about the virtual equipment? Did any of them borrow some?"

"I've got the list right here somewhere." The vague bats of his hands threatened to overturn his easel. "Ah, here we are. Let me print you up a set."

I studied it over his shoulder, looking for familiar names. Annalya prominently, at the top. Too obvious? The possibilities wore at me.

I took the list with sincere thanks and tried not to fidget with the pages as I braced myself for the last line of questioning. "You and Argyll seemed to get along well."

Cole squinted at me. "That is to say, you want to rule me out as a suspect. Woman, if I had killed Argyll, his head would be crushed open like a melon."

It took me all of two seconds to agree with him, though I kept it to myself. "And you don't know anyone who might have?"

"Not a soul, I'm afraid. Not much for politics, why I stay away from the mannerpunk people. They set my teeth on edge." He chuckled. "Now if one of them'd died?"

"You might not want to say that." I had meant it as a joke, but the second the words escaped me, my mouth went dry. What if this did turn out to be a precedent, solved or not? More than ever, I wished it over and done.

That disquieting idea followed me out into the hall, where I nearly ran over a frantic young student. After a beat straightening out her and me, I realized it was Annalya's roommate, a sparrow to her dove.

"I need to tell you something." She hurried out the words. "I … Anni wasn't in her room all night. I was asked not to say anything."

One advantage of living at the Academy was an instinctive sensitivity to passive voice. "Asked by who?"

She shuffled. "Alexander."

"What?" I couldn't make heads or tails of that. "Why?"

"Just ask him." She bit her lip. "I don't want to talk about it."

I let her shoulder away with a sense of foreboding. Alexander covering for Annalya, who he seemed to detest, when both of them had motive, but that kind of planning didn't fit with the so-called crime of passion.

One thing was clear. Alexander needed a reprise of the second and fourth lines.

I found him in his room and confronted him with the facts. "All I want to know is," I said, "what in the name of invention is going on?"

He looked up from a rather ungainly Jacob's Ladder. "I asked her to cover because I was meeting Annalya."

My bones tingled. I could almost hear a confession. "For?"

Alexander paused, his brow furrowed. "For me. For us." The strings snapped under his fingers, and he sighed. "Annalya and I were seeing each other. We couldn't tell anyone because she was trying to keep Argyll sweet on her. She said she'd help me."

There were, I realized with a bubble of embarrassment, other reasons besides her own grades to cozen a poor professor. "Then that night?"

"She was with me the entire time. She'll confirm it." Given the alternative, he did not say in words, but his hunched shoulders made it clear enough. It left me with a handful of possibilities, none very palatable. He was lying and they had parted ways at some time during the night, but even if I could get them both to admit it, there was no way of telling which one had the truth. He was telling the truth, and they had been in it together.

Or he was telling the truth, and I was out of suspects.

I quizzed him on times and points, but found nothing. I thought about confining him, but I couldn't see the sudden, restless young man as a murderer. Maybe I didn't have as much of a feel for people as Wolf, but I liked to think I understood some things.

Jordan had been waiting outside and flashed me an easy smile, fresh as a daisy. "Need some more leads?" When I nodded, she turned over her sheath of notes and read me soap operas and stanzas, scores and vendettas, until I felt I would drown in them. "There's more."

More? For a minute, I wanted desperately to rush back and pretend that my prime suspects were all that I needed. The dean was promising consequences if I didn't produce a suspect. My attacker might try again as long as there was a chance I would find him. What was the harm of a little pretense in halls of fiction?

Everything. You don't play false with your reader. Sleight of hand, omission, yes. Lying, no.

"Hit me with it," I said.

* * *

Three hours later, no answers in sight. I sent Jordan off to finish her essay on "Cats in Crime Fiction" and invited Wolf over for a couple of knock-us-silly drinks. The founders of the Literary Academy, whoever they were, had their priorities straight. If there was a drink in film or fiction that was physically possible to recreate, we had the mix for it in the staff cafeteria.

Wolf had a thing for Chianti. I avoided him when any kind of beans were on the menu.

At the moment, he was content to slum around with me on some space-juice kicked up from a bad werewolves in space movie. The drink was about as palatable as the special effects, but at the moment, that suited me just fine.

"If I've had a worse day in my life," I grumbled, "I've successfully red-penned it from my memory."

He toasted me across the desk. "This will be the low point in your career, mark my words."

I made a weak face at him. "If you tried hard, you might think of something worse to say."

"No," he said, "think about it. You inevitably have to be on your way up. Life imitates art."

I shook my head. "Not mine." The words ebbed around in my brain, settling in strange places. Textbook crime of passion, he had said, but since when was reality, even in the Academy, by the book? Reactions might be planned, choreographed for the consumption of the real world, but when it came to impulse…

I thought again how unlikely it seemed that either young person could have barged in by chance, without a plan, but neither would they have any idea how to make a murder scene look spontaneous.

Someone in mystery would.

I paused mid-sip of the virulent blue sludge. "Wolf," I said slowly, "is it possible that you misread the signs in Argyll's office?"

"Misread the…? No, I've spent far too long with the whole business to miss symbols." Wolf flashed me an easy smile. "Relax, Gabrielle. This is exactly what it appears to be."

I realized, in a moment of clenching clarity, that I wouldn't know if he was wrong.

Jordan had been the first person to arrive after I was attacked. I hadn't gotten a clear view of my assailant. How hard would it have been to roll out the door and come back in? Particularly with one of those phase-shift devices she so carefully put in other hands?

The facts must have shown in my eyes. Even as I set down my glass and started to rise, he slapped a hand on my arm and pulled me back down.

I was feeling the alcohol in my veins. Wolf, a good fifty pounds heavier and sipping more conservatively, was not.

"Not Jordan," he said, sudden, fierce. "No."

"The facts fit," I said. "I'm sorry, but I at least—"

Wolf's fingers tightened, but he was laughing, a strained, almost inaudible sound. "I'm not denying that Jordan did it. I'm not denying that I knew about it. But you cannot tell the dean about this, Gabrielle. There's too much at stake."

The words blew the breath out of me like so much loose paper. I jerked backwards, mind flying to the gun I'd squirreled away in my desk. He lunged, and for a minute we toppled, body to body before he pinned me against the wall. I was dizzy, I was ever so slightly drunk, and even adrenaline didn't give me enough strength to push him away. As for my moves in self-defense, well-trained, but he'd had the same classes. It was a mystery staple.

"What's going on, Wolf?" I managed.

"My star pupil," he said. "A final exam that matters, really matters, not an empty tussle in a virtual maze."

"But she's going on to fiction." I felt my voice rise in desperation. "Everything we do is about training for craft, not reality."

"Which is why every work released since the Academy's inception has been stilted and shallow," he cut me off. "You can't have verisimilitude without reality underneath it. We can't cut corners. Our students have to be as real—more real—than the clods in the real world who don't understand how easy it is to be born." A sudden, rueful smile, and he was Wolf again. "We don't owe it to them, of course. We owe it to ourselves."

"Be sensible." Could I argue him out of this? "The dean would never allow this kind of test. No matter how much of a precedent you set."

"Jordan will be sent forth," he interrupted me. "And she'll succeed far beyond the wildest dreams of her predecessors. I know. I've been looking for her for a long time. Did you see how perfectly she can become whatever she wants?"

I remembered the sudden humor that had put me at ease, how she had built my confidence after the attack. I'd even noticed it. Why couldn't I have seen the strangeness! "What were you two trying to do?"

Wolf chuckled a bit. "This is the part where the villain explains his schemes, is it? How very James Bond. Much as I hate to accept the role, we hoped you would accuse one of the young people. The attack was an attempt to make you nervous, make you hurry a result."

I bit my lip. I knew how close I had come to doing just that, and it had been Jordan's prattle that nearly sent me over the edge.

"And you can still do just that," he continued. "Pick one, either, and tell the dean you've found the culprit."

"What?" The words shot out of me. "Why would I do that?"

"Because when Jordan does make her name, I can tell the Academy how she earned it. They'll have to make changes to the system then." He shook his head. "You know just how hard it is to make anything happen around here, Gabrielle."

"Not so hard it needs murder." Shut up, shut up!I lectured my mouth, which seemed to be completely detached from my common sense. There were no cameras in my office, because who needed to watch the security chief? My only chance of getting out of this would be to play along. Wolf wanted my cooperation, and given the slightest chance, he had to let me go. I still believed that.

"Please, ma'am."

It was Jordan, silent as vapor. She toyed with the blade in her hand, not looking as the hilt slid over her palm. It was a gesture meant to intimidate. I recognized that and still had no way of helping myself.

"We can't do this." I could offer them a way out. I clung to that. "I can explain to the dean."

"Jordan," Wolf cut me off, "you know what you have to do."

No, no, a hundred times no! Maybe if I imprinted the thought hard enough on my mind, it would somehow become reality. I tried to formulate another plea, tried to bargain now, but it was too late. I saw Jordan move, a spring and coil of nerves. Perfect.

Heavy weight jammed into me. I was too stunned to scream.

Wolf's limp body slid away from me, and it was only then I realized that the blade had never met my skin. Jordan pulled him aside, twisted him onto the desk as easy as a bit of lint.

Shock made the world blur. "What …"

"Most serial killers, and certainly in fiction," she recited without expression, "pick victims only casually known to them. This is another test entirely."

"Wolf didn't mean it that way." There were my lips, moving without me again. I edged towards the desk and the gun. I had to finish this.

"I know he didn't." Jordan shook her head. "I don't want competition. If his plan had worked, I'd only be the first in a sequence." She moved methodically about the body, arranging him.

"That makes sense." I was horrified to realize it did. When had I learned to think like her?

As if sensing my intentions, Jordan flicked about and came to stand with her hip against the desk drawer. "Ma'am?"

I didn't answer her for a minute. I was busy deciding what moments in my life would be best to have flash before my eyes. "Jordan," I said, "this doesn't have to be…"

"No, it doesn't." She turned again, opening the drawer with the flick of one hand. "I need you to make sure that the Academy knows about this and that they never change the exams. They'll send me forth no matter what happens, I'm too good not to, but I want to be the last."

Our eyes met for a moment, hers serious and tranquil, mine trembling. I snatched my gun out of the desk and leveled it at her. The words worked out of me by rote.

"Jordan Harris, you are under arrest. I'm afraid you'll have to come with me."

* * *

"All this over testing methods?" The dean's expression was astonished.

I nodded numbly. "It meant a lot to Wolf. I can't blame him. Year after year, he had to study the new books in our library and watch his pupils fall to dull heroes and unremarkable ends." I wanted to be angry with him. I was angry with him. But I knew how he felt.

The dean arched a brow. "Of course, all those years dealing with that sort does make one a bit unstable." When I said nothing, he continued, "This does not go beyond this room, of course, but his concerns are not entirely unmerited. In a controlled situation, as a final exam?"

"No," I said. "The students are here to learn to give people an escape from their reality. We can't do that by giving in to it."

He looked skeptical. "Well, it certainly would be a long time before we would ever consider something of that sort. You are dismissed."

I let myself out, shaking. One of my oldest friends was dead, and he had been killed instead of me. I had been saved, not out of compassion, but because Jordan had a very well-defined sense of career, and I had come terribly close to ruining the lives of two students in chasing the truth.

No, I'd had enough of reality for now.

Farewell Dinner
by Jakob Drud

Jakob Drud lives in Aarhus, Denmark with his wife and two kids. They have—in their own sweet way—managed to transform him from a novelist into a short story writer. But someday he will write the expansive science fiction trilogy he has outlined in his head. His stories have appeared in Alienskin Magazine, The Fifth Di, and OG's Speculative Fiction.

Home is never the same after Mom dies, especially not in this story.

Visiting Dad entailed a journey that André dreaded: from the ordered lawns and brick edifices of the Chicago Technical Institute into a landscape of shoddy res-blocks erected to re-house refugees from the flooded coastal regions.

So dismal was the land that even the graffiti-removal robots sported tags. And the elevator in Dad's res-block had taken new beatings from clubs in the six or seven months since André last stopped by. The bent wall panels rattled as the elevator rose, accompanied by a soft female voice from hidden speakers assuring him that a luxury apartment could be his, too. The dishonesty almost made him turn tail, but Dad had to get the news tonight. Mars would not wait.

The door opened on tenth to let a ray of hope for humanity's future into the elevator: light from the Martian-invented bio-illumination panels. André shuffled out into the concrete hallway. Five doors to the right of the elevator the usual piece of cardboard announced the residence of Jorge Anderson. A crudely stenciled metal sign with the name 'Merita' had joined Dad's nameplate, and a closer look at the cardboard revealed that someone had crossed out 'Bjornfeldt' with a black marker. Dad had taken that middle name from Mom, and André felt a sting of annoyance that Merita had pushed Mom away so fast. Dad couldn't have known her more than a few months.

He composed himself and rang the bell. A moment later the door creaked open, revealing Dad and the one-room res inside. Both looked cleaner and cheerier than André remembered them, a sight to feed his faint hope that Dad would be able to deal with the news.

They shook hands in the formal manner they had adopted since Mom died, and Dad said, "Come on in. " After a pause where both admired their shoes he added, "Merita's waiting with the dinner."

Except for an uncanny neatness the main room revealed no trace of Mom's replacement. Only when André saw her through the doorway to the small cooking-alcove that the res-block builders called a spacious kitchen did he sigh with a mix of disappointment and relief. Merita was simply a Jones-Corporation home-assistant robot. From commercials he recognized the 'full female design' model, whose womanly illusion was marred only by ungainly metal joints covered in rubber veneer.

Merita came to the door, a cold gaze observed him from her plastic face.

"Good-evening, André. Your father didn't teach you to take off your shoes, I see. But don't you worry about the floor, I'll clean that later. Now we eat."

André composed himself. He must give her a chance, if only because Dad had smiled on the gridcam when he first mentioned her. In the five years since Mom died, it had been more in character for him to let André string the silences together with hollow pleasantries. This more than anything had led to their estrangement over the last couple of years.

"Merita's shopped at the market," Dad said, his considerable pride apparent as he took a bowl of potatoes to the foldable table at the end wall of the res. For the first time ever a tablecloth adorned the surface, a deep indigo cotton weave that complemented Mom's dark oak chairs. He hung his jacket on the back of one chair and sat down while Dad got a bottle from Mom's oak cupboard, the only other piece of non-plastic furniture in the res. "Look what she found. Real wine."

"What? You're into that red piss now?" André said, genuinely surprised. If he and Dad agreed on anything it was that a good beer beat wine seven days of the week and damn the snob who said otherwise.

Dad didn't laugh, though. "No, I...well, I'll get you a Carlsberg." He stood up.

"My cooking deserves a bottle of good Bordeaux," Merita said from the kitchen. Incredibly, Dad sat back down when she spoke, rubbed his palms on his jeans, and then poured wine in the two glasses.

Merita set two dishes of vegetables and a leg of lamb on the table. A carving knife slid into her hand from a canister in her arm, and to the tune of slight whirrs from her servos she sliced off two servings of meat. With all the skill of a Cordon Bleu chef she arranged them on each plate with a selection of delicious-looking steamed vegetables, before withdrawing to the kitchen door. "Eat."

Despite the clatter of forks and knives, silence descended over the table; not quite tense, not quite awkward, only strikingly familiar. André had only recently realized how well Mom had tied the family together. Now that she was gone her special glue had dissolved. Glancing at Merita he wondered if she would have had the same effect on their relationship. But that was too much to hope for; she wasn't Mom. But perhaps she could cushion the news he had for Dad.

"You graduated, didn't you?" Dad asked between bites. "Two weeks ago?"

"Yes," André said. "Got my best marks in a project about nano-coating in hostile environments."

"Congratulations." Dad topped off their glasses and raised his own in a sluggish up-and-down movement. "Why didn't you call?"

A typical Dad statement. He sure knew how to get those barbs of guilt in, sneaked in with a voice of loneliness that trumped any rational thinking, as if André was all that stood between Jorge Anderson and infinite solitude.

"Dad, please forget that right now. There's something I need to tell you. You know how much they need technical experts on Mars?"

From the kitchen door Merita said, "Don't you boys mind me at all. You just leave me right out of the conversation where I belong, ok?"

A fine, barely audible stutter from her speakers shattered the illusion of a natural voice. For the first time that night André noted how Dad seemed to shrink; his gaze drifted to the plate, as if the lamb demanded his full attention, the jaw muscles clenching harder than the food warranted.

"Sorry, Merita. Didn't I tell you André's graduated?" Dad asked.

"No."

They cut and chewed some more, André's resolve momentarily shattered. After a few bites, Dad's knife slid from the edge of the plate, and Merita's eyes fastened on the stain of vegetables on the tablecloth. "Sorry," Dad said, neck bending a little further. Then he cleared his throat, perhaps hoping that breaking the silence would lift the atmosphere. "André, are you telling me that you're going to Mars?"

André nodded, expecting the ugly monster of loneliness to rise in Dad's voice; the silent sniffles, the sad eyes. But Dad just smiled.

"That's good, that's really good. No global warming on Mars, right? And whatever they're building up there's got to be better than these bloody res-blocks. Your Mom would have liked that, our son, going somewhere."

"Yeah, she'd say that," André said. She'd always spoken of Mars as the place of the future, unlike Dad, who never spoke of futures or possibilities at all. Until now. Well if that wasn't worth a toast.

His fingers had barely touched the stem of his wineglass when Merita said, "Do you have to speak about your wife all the time?"

Dad looked up, meeting her gazing eyes briefly before his attention returned to the plate. "Sorry," he muttered.

"I think he was talking to me," André said. Even as he spoke, Merita's gaze fastened on his face, but André kept staring at her. She was circuitry, the same stuff they taught at school. So what if some no-life programmer at Jones-Corporation had spent his life developing her conversation routines?

"Maybe you shouldn't talk back like that—" Dad began.

"She's a domestic robot. And she overdid the lamb." André pushed his plate away. He tried to let his anger dissolve, but that stupid robot had just ruined the moment for him.

Dad chewed through the last piece of lamb without looking up or speaking again. It took him another silent eternity to clear the plate.

"Well, aren't you a slow eater?" Merita asked. "Or maybe you don't like my cooking either?"

"It's great," Dad mumbled. Merita cleared the table and André could swear he heard her sigh as she disappeared into the spacious kitchen.

In the ensuing silence, André noted again how Dad's eyes wavered, always towards the kitchen, never lingering. The flicker drew his attention to Dad's eyebrow and the edge above the right eye. Was it a little puffy?

Dad's gaze shifted to his lap, and he scratched absentmindedly at a scab on his right jaw. It bled a little now, and André imagined it would leave a scar. Previous cuts certainly had. Mesmerized, he stared at the blood clotting next to a row of short, white lines.

"Tell me that's from shaving, dad."

Dad's hand retreated quickly to his lap. "Yeah, it is."

"With a built-in carving knife?"

Dad's fingers joined in a squeezing, milky-white chain, and for a second André's imagination played a reel of nighttime horror featuring Merita Jones inscribing the rules of her regime in Jorge Anderson's face.

André snapped out of the chair and banged his fist against the end wall. The obviously flaky res programming interpreted this as a request for entertainment, and promptly a game show flashed across the concrete, advertising a grand first prize ticket to Mars. And despite his dreams, despite the future he had been handed on a silver platter, André knew that the sin of leaving Dad in this horrid place and state was one he could never atone.

"She's scrap metal," he said. "It'll be hammers and wrenches or high voltage or... or.... I'm not leaving you here with her."

"You are not taking her away from me." Dad's voice cut through a game show applause with such vehemence that André took a step backward.

"You can't be serious, Dad. She's violating every code of robot conduct ever conceived and programmed. She's *hurting* you."

"Shut up and listen." Something—probably an ingrained childhood obedience—made André comply. He sat down again, but only a conscious effort kept him in the chair.

"Do you realize how hard it is to live alone? You're going to Mars. The girls are beautiful up there." Dad nodded at the screen. "You're young, you're good-looking. I'm old and work in a warehouse. My colleagues are men, and they all go home to their wives." He folded his arms across his chest. "I don't. After your Mom died, I came home to an empty res, screen, and pre-fab dinners. It's not a home, or a life. It's a big bobble of *nothing*. At least, I've got company now."

Andre looked down on his hands and found them clenched into tight fists. He'd hoped so much that Dad would find someone to alleviate his loneliness. He'd been prepared to accept another woman, and when that hope burst, to entrust a robot with the job. And if that had failed, André realized, he had been willing to fool himself that Dad would never cross the line between loneliness and insanity, even if he lived on Mars. Such hopes would live no longer.

"Dad," he said gently. "She's not company. And don't trick yourself into believing she's Mom either."

Dad inclined his head towards the kitchen. "And don't you trick yourself into believing I need a saint for companionship. Her conversation's good enough for me, and for all you say of overdone lamb, she's a good cook. She's bad when she's moody, but so was your Mom. At least with Merita I know that the mood swings are just software glitches."

Merita came back from the kitchen. "Are you boys having a nice chat?" Her voice resounded calmly in the one-room res with none of the earlier subliminal stuttering. She held out two plates with large slices of fresh-baked apple pie, made from real apples judging by the smell. André had no idea where she'd have gotten her appendages on those, but probably her frugality routine enabled her to negotiate a good price.

And Dad smiled at her.

"You can't be serious," André whispered.

"I'm not a bad robot," Merita said. "My previous owner had quite peculiar tastes that my regular expansion packs couldn't service. He had urges that he wished to keep secret from his wife, so he rewired me to circumvent the safeguards that my wonderful designers at Jones-Corporation created to make me fit for life among humans. Unfortunately his tampering never worked quite the way he wanted it to. I remained too reluctant, I imagine, so he threw me away like so much junk."

She handed them a plate each, and André saw how Dad's nostrils fluttered ever so slightly like they had done in the old days when Mom had put on his favorite perfume.

"I found her at one of the metal-slavers," Dad said. "Their trouble with the memory wipe and rewiring made her quite a bargain for a lonely man."

"So now I'm here for him." Merita laid an arm on his shoulder with gentle tenderness. "I'm here every day, André. Unlike you, I don't leave for school or Mars, which will probably amount to much the same thing as often as you drop by."

André felt the familiar barb of guilt, and it forced him out of the chair. He had his jacket halfway on before he realized that she *wanted* him to go, needed him to turn his back on Dad so she could carry on her domination. "You've got the worst case of circuit insanity I've ever seen, and I'm staying until I've taken you apart. Dad, I can't leave you like this."

"Yes you can, André. You're going to Mars."

The firmness in his voice contrasted violently with the resignation printed on his face. In some respects it resembled the mask of defeat he'd worn since Mom died, but additional surrender had imprinted itself on his voice. For a moment André struggled to grasp the difference, but then realization sucked the breath from his chest as if someone had flushed his heart down the drain: dad hadn't given up on himself. He had given up on his son.

With suddenly gelatinous fingers André grasped his jacket and put it on, somehow. The zipper didn't seem to work, and words formed in his mind, apologies and accusations, that were nothing more than vowels and consonants. He had Mars, he told himself, somewhere so far away he wouldn't have to face his Dad ever again, but despite that solid future his world spun so fast he didn't know if he'd make it to the door.

"Dad," he managed to say, "whatever you do, stay well, alright?"

"Oh, I will," he said. "Better than ever."

Merita opened the door and waved her appendages as he staggered into the hallway. "That's right, André, you've no need to worry. I'll take really good care of your father."

I Am Tellis Moore
by L. Christopher DelGuercio

L. Christopher DelGuercio writes and resides in the upstate New York community of Cicero with his remarkable wife, Melissa, and burgeoning family. His stories have appeared in Allegory, Parade of Phantoms, Kaleidotrope, and OG's Speculative Fiction among others. He also received special recognition for placing in the quarter finals of the Writers of the Future Contest in 2006 and 2007.

Love knows no bounds. Love is an obsession. Love is everything worth being for.

My name is Tellis Moore. I hate this love sometimes. It keeps me screwed to this chair, pawing at my alphapad all day long. I'm a virtuoso, drumming away at that pad. I'm Jimmy Cobb slapping at his snare on Miles Davis's *Kind of Blue*—keeping time in a thoughtless, unending rhythm. People say it's a damn impressive thing to watch me check the datamesh from thirty worlds as fast as it can be wetwired to my block. Of course, I know the machines do all the heavy lifting. I just enable the search programs. That's when I play. It used to be a real sweet gig, but now I key with no more passion than I brush my teeth. Some days don't feel real; my head feels like it's swimming in soup but my fingers keep moving, always moving. I can't stop them.

Julia won't let me.

I scan for signs of her day and night, awake and asleep. There's lots of space out there to cover. I equip the machine's massive metal brains with Julia's DNA model. They check the streams of incoming genocodes against her model until they hit upon a match. Sometimes they fish one out with ninety-eight or ninety-nine percent similarity. But that's not nearly Julia—humans share the same percentage of common DNA with chimps. As surely as an ape is not a man, 99% Julia could *never* be Julia.

Her tag is still the best way to find her, though. Unless someone lives deep within the metro-vectors or lies on the outland ring, unless they're cosnomadic or NuAmish, DNA tagging is universal from birth. A second after the animatronic hand clips the umbilical cord and just before the deluge of inoculations, everyone is tagged. Tagging makes it easy to spot genetic problem areas before they manifest into actual problems: a predisposition to disease; a rage inclination; genes for criminality, nearsightedness, low mental capacity, baldness, halitosis—you name it. Although the actual replacement for these unfavorable traits has remained largely ineffective, at least now it's possible to find which rungs on the helix will rot through.

Program complete. No Julia, again.

* * *

I have trouble breathing at night—like a cinder block has been placed on my chest. In bed I can feel my heart fighting to pump my lungs full of air.

I know it's Julia.

I've tried to think about other women but in the end there's only her face, her cinnamon skin, flecked with color as perfectly as the night sky; a steep smile that unzips itself coquettishly, only to me; her chestnut cascade of hair. Julia poisons my mind to the mere idea of a mistress. Her memory won't allow me one.

It's not her fault. No one could ever have the same light inside that Julia had. No one else could ever have her honey-thick aura. She was iridescent, electric. She was golden. Thoughts of her so envelope me that I have to wipe them from my eyes just to see again. I think God himself was jealous of our love. That's why He took her away all those years ago. I don't expect anyone else to understand.

How could they?

* * *

Grand Father always claimed that it started with test-tube birthings and Xeroxed sheep. After that, he'd say, just about anything was possible.

"A man could live, '*Un-til the Twelfth of Ne-ver*'," he'd sing, "provided he has a good enough reason to."

My genocode was among the first adult generation's to be tagged and catalogued—the age group that went from *mere mortal* to *nearly immortal* overnight. We were branded *Generation L*, but I don't remember why. Was the "L" for life or longevity, or for just being lucky? Who knows anymore? It *was* judged to be the single most fortunate time in the history of mankind to be alive; life spans nearly doubled overnight.

Julia died three months before the first mass taggings. Her genocode could be mapped and catalogued posthumously, but it couldn't be legally replicated; only DNA from the *living* is allowed to be clone-grown. The last thing The Ministry wanted was someone purposely hatching another Hitler. That means in order to be with her, she must occur naturally. Once that happens, I have to find her. At least now with a double lifespan, I have twice the time to do it. How does the old saying go? When life gives you lemons, make lemonade. Or, more aptly, when the Ministry gives you caveats, turn them into caviar.

* * *

I watch my holoscreen at home listlessly. "Don't you think it should've happened by now, Father? What if we *never* find her? The Ministry should develop a way to engineer past citizens."

"Don't you think I haven't wished for that exact same thing?" Father scolds me. "They'll *never* allow it, Tellis. The option doesn't exist so get it out of your head right now. It's better that you do. There are no shortcuts—keep your mind on your task if you want to find her," he tells me. "Her number's due, just have some faith. You're still so young, you've just begun to search. It's all worth it, boy, or have you forgotten what I taught you? *She's* worth it. Julia is worth all of it."

Father's sallow eyes narrow and lock onto me. His glare pounds at me like a tire iron across my cheek.

Don't ever forsake her, don't quit on us now, his eyes seem to say. She's the reason we're here. This is a transcendent love. It once was and shall be again—mythic and awaiting. Seek it always. Keep seeking her.

I nod and Father releases his gaze, retreating to the pantry cupboard. "Your grandfather and I are going into the study to sit down for a tea."

"That sounds wonderful. May I join you?"

Father frowns. "You're well aware that the new data wave from the MaxTau nebula is coming in, Tellis. You know it needs to be checked. I was testing you, son." He shakes his head. "You'll be busy tonight."

"I'm tired, Father." I offer up a peevish glance. "But I'll scan for the code," I assure him.

That night I dream of Julia. Her flesh is smooth and a vivid pink, her touch willing. She speaks to me in the midnight and, for that time at least, she's real again. I wake up badly, in a desperate sweat, clutching at her bedside photograph, overgrown with a patina of amber. It's becoming simply a rendering of a woman I don't know. Every day Julia feels further from me. Exhausted and despondent, I fall back to sleep.

* * *

"Tellis, it's morning," Father says from beneath the door frame. He looks somehow different, changed. "I should tell you that Grand Father Moore passed away last night in his sleep. Don't worry yourself though. I'll make the ceremonial arrangements today."

I suddenly feel twice as alone as I had the moment before I woke. "He was barely a hundred," I say.

"He was young enough all right. He just lost the will. He was a good man, he lived a right life, did what was expected of him all the way down the line. That's all any of us can hope to say." Father sits down on the edge of the bed. "I think the thing that kept him going was the chance that you might find her. He so wanted to see Julia—we all do, Tellis." Father takes the picture from the night stand and touches the frame's face. I pry it from his hands.

"If she's out there somewhere, if her code exists, Father, I'll find her. Don't give up on me. You're all I have left now and I don't know if I could do this alone if I had to. We'll get our chance. She'll come back to us."

"I know she will," he says. "And I know you'd do what needs to be done once I was gone, but I would rather spare you that."

My metallic wristwatch strap warms and fires a neuron pulse from my spine to the cerebral cortex. "That's my alarm. I'll be late for work."

Father splays his fingers across my chest. "Don't go yet."

My body freezes. I don't recall the last time Father touched me.

"Don't worry about running scans today—I'll take care of them. Why don't you skip out of work, get outside, go down to the rest pools. I know all this must be a shock to you. Come down and have a cup of tea with me, son. We'll talk about it." He takes my arm and leads me downstairs where he places a ready mug in front of me on the kitchen table. "Take it easy for a day. You've earned that at least. I'll search that new cluster in the Cygnus system," he says, peeking up from above the brim of his mug. "Go on, drink your tea. I'll take care of things."

"Are you sure you'll have the time? What about Grand Father? The burial ceremony?"

"I'll have time. And even if we don't get to scan today—there *are* more important things to this life," he says. "You take care of Tellis. Forget about Julia today."

This feels all wrong, I think to myself. Is this just one of Father's elaborate tests? He doesn't even know I fell asleep last night without scanning MaxTau— he'll be so disappointed in me when he runs the new scans and finds out. I won't disappoint him. Not today.

It's cloudy so I leave the table to get my coat and speed by Father while he's still having his tea. I pretend not to hear his pleas for my company. I shout, "I'm going to work. I'll call you later from The Bic." Through the atmosphere-safe paned glass of the front door, the look of consternation on his face makes me wonder if he wasn't really being sincere. At any rate, I feel confidant that I've shown Father this time where my true priorities lie.

* * *

Father got me a job at the Bureau of the Interstellar Census (B.I.C.) thirteen years ago. It seemed the natural line of work for a man looking for someone. I'm one of a million dat-collectors who gather the vital statistics on all citizens human, humanoid, and subhominid. A full universal census takes a half-century to complete and new streams are constantly bouncing in from the light-worlds, the edge settlements, and inside the macroghettos.

I know all the tricks. I have all the keys. I'm privy to most every byte of datum The Bureau has in its brain banks. But the B.I.C. brain is unfathomably colossal and never static for an instant; the universe and its peoples are always expanding.

I arrive on the grounds and zoom over to red sector, taking the elevator to quad D of the upper eighty-eighth floor. Director Kusama will be making her morning rounds, if she hasn't already. I sidle through the office hive of bubbled, egg carton workspaces—my back riding the wall, my eyes fixed upon the director's door. I try to sneak in.

I lower my head and decide to make a dash for my work carrel behind a line of buzzing employees that appears as if on cue. I dart behind them and reach the entrance of the carrel, touching-in at the time sensor at precisely seven minutes past nine with no sign of the director. I rest my back against the convex curve of the carrel wall and slide down it in relief.

Suddenly, a dark figure emerges from within my carrel and rolls by me like an eclipse. The man is tall, stoutly-built, and wears a uniformly plain charcoal suit and necktie. His pale face, cross-stitched with deep wrinkles and full of crags, coupled with the silver threading of hair and gray eyes lend him the appearance of an albino. I vaguely recognize him, milling around the office without explanation for the past couple weeks. He strides to the director's door and opens it, without knocking, and disappears inside. I get inside the carrel and collapse into my chair.

The seat is warm.

Trying not to think too much about what any of it means, I plug in and strap the alphapad to my hands for the labor interval. Sonuvabitch, Kusama's left me a flash on my screen:

TELLIS MOORE TO MY OFFICE--TELLIS MOORE TO MY OFFICE

I knock on the director's door and a voice calls me in. It opens with some effort on my part and I squeeze myself into the room, the hydraulic door sweeping closed behind me. A harsh buzz announces the locking mechanism engaged. The pale man is there, alone. He's perched comfortably atop the director's massive teak desk, one foot touching the floor. He leans in to shake my hand and introduces himself.

"My name's Torrance. I'll be taking over for Director Kusama today, have a seat." He pushes away from the desk and eases himself into the director's chair. "Employee Moore, are you aware that you were over seven minutes late today?"

I nod yes, gritting my teeth in disgust.

"That's not like you," he says, shuffling through some files. "How is every-thing?"

I squirm a bit in the chair. "My grandfather passed away last night, sir. I'm afraid the whole event threw me off a few minutes this morning."

He waves his hands. "No need to apologize, Moore. It's perfectly understand-able. I'm surprised you didn't take the day off. You're lawfully entitled to it."

I tell him, "I felt I needed to be here today, Mr. Torrance."

"That's incredibly admirable." He opens one of the files. "You don't like to miss any time, do you Moore?"

"No, I don't."

"Why is that, exactly?"

I begin to slither in my chair. "I just don't like to, that's all—it looks bad."

"That it does, Employee. That it does. But there must be more to it. Why is it so important that you be here today, for instance, when your thoughts must be with your family?"

I tell him flatly, "I don't have much family, sir."

"That's even more reason not to be here," he says. "So what's the whole story, Moore?"

"That *is* the whole story, Mr. Torrance." I force out a smile. "I just enjoy my work."

Torrance's reply leaps out from inside him almost before my words have a chance to sink into the walls.

"You're lying, Moore, I've watched you. You strike me as anything *but* a man who enjoys his work. As a matter of fact, you're just about the saddest sack I've seen in the two weeks I've been here." He shakes his head. "What I can't under-stand is why you're still such a busy, busy bee. Director Kusama felt your situation warranted some action on the part of The Bureau. I am that action." He leans back in the chair and stares at me. "Mr. Moore, do you know the difference between an *under performer* and an *underachiever*?"

Confused, I shake my head no.

"Under performers are robbing us all, Tellis. It's my job to ferret them out and eliminate them and as good as I am at my job, I'll never be out of work," he says. "These layabouts would rather be *anywhere* else, doing *anything* else, and so they frequently are. They're not hard to spot."

You nod to show him, alternately, that you understand him and that you are not one of these terrible people.

"Then there's you, Employee Tellis Moore. You clearly have an aptitude for this type of work, a seemingly compulsory desire to be here, you've even received special permission from the head director to access the mainframe so you can link up and work from home. You're far beyond the model employee, Tellis. You're a boss's wet dream."

"Then what action is there to take?" I ask. "Shouldn't you be thanking me?"

Torrance's face gets severe. "Kusama does the thanking. I came to find out why you do it—no one's that perfect unless there's a reason. You're a textbook *underachiever*, Tellis. That is, in a way, more troubling for us to see than the under performer. We at least know what's at work with the under performer: sloth. The underachiever's motivation is more of a mystery, but it rarely turns out to be positive. You've resisted promotion out of this office even though you've been in line for one many times over. Tellis, why is it so goddamn important that you stay in datamesh?"

I know I need to shift this conversation so I ask him, "Why were you in my work carrel this morning?"

Torrance looks at me with surprise, but doesn't answer. Instead, he gets up and walks behind me, placing his stone hands down on top of my shoulders. "I didn't go into your carrel this morning, Tellis . . . I'd been there all night."

"What were you doing?"

He pauses a moment. "I was trying to save you." He circles the chair and stares into me, waiting. Like a trapped animal, I can only stare back at first.

"You're not going to make this easy, are you?" he grumbles to me in a voice like distant thunder. "Tellis, did you know that I started out with The Bureau myself in this very building thirty years ago? Do you know what I do?"

I'm silent.

"I've been trained to make judgments. Being able to spot when employees are less than truthful is a great help to The Bureau. That's what I do. I can tell through a series of visual indicators, atmospheric changes, and my own elevated levels of precognition whether someone's being totally straight with me. I'm better than any lie-detector. The Bureau pays me to make the call on certain 'red flag' employees and they back my call no matter what—they trust my judgment that much. I'm a throwback but I get it right—which is all anyone in The Bureau cares about. So be aware, Tellis, that everything you've said, every word that you've uttered to me here this morning, I've been able to distinguish as the truth, or something else. I shouldn't really be telling you all this but I think you know where this is going. Now why don't you tell me more about what I already know. What are you doing here at The Bic, Tellis?"

I know the truth he wants. My only option now is to give him some. So I do.

"I'm looking for my wife—her genocode—it's no secret," I tell him, smugly.

"Wasn't she tagged?"

"No."

"That's odd. Care to tell me why?"

"I'd rather not. Talking about her makes me uncomfortable. I'm not ready to let go of Julia yet."

Torrance leans back on the desk and sucks in an angry breath. "I knew your father when *he* worked here. He didn't keep secrets either—he was looking for his wife, too. Isn't that a strange coincidence?"

"People acquire codes for cloning all the time. It's still legal, isn't it?"

"Of course it is, except most people are already in possession of their loved one's genocode tag. Tellis, I can understand wanting to bring someone back, to live out a life that fate has taken away."

"Can you, Mr. Torrance? Are you sure?"

Torrance looks me in the eyes. "Quite sure." He leans back against the desk again. "What are the chances that you and your father both married untagged women?"

"I don't know," I say.

"Both named Julia?"

I feel a surge of warm blood flush my face.

"Your father couldn't stop raving on about *his* Julia. In all the time I worked with him, he was obsessed with finding her code. I've never seen anyone so single-minded. Now, I hadn't given your father a second thought in thirty years until someone drops your file on my lap. The name and the face come back to me immediately—it's my old friend, Telly Moore. Except it's not. It's you. You know, you look exactly like him."

"Well, he *is* my father."

"Naturally," Torrance mutters.

I'm polishing the seat now with my back pockets. Torrance is searing a hole through me with those fiery grey eyes, begging me to give up more. Still, I can't muster the courage to tell him the entire truth. He takes the file from the top of the desk and begins to read it aloud.

"Tellis Moore—*that's you*—five-foot-nine, one-sixty-five, blonde hair and eyes, thirty-one years of age, single, never married. *Never married?* I thought you told me you were looking for your wife? What wife was that, Tellis? What's even more peculiar is that it says here your father was never married either . . . or his father. C'mon, son, give us the truth now. You're not *really* Tellis Moore at all, are you?"

"I'm exactly Tellis Moore!" I blast out of the chair but Torrance takes hold of my shoulders and pins me back down. He crouches down and angles his square jaw in my face.

"Please, stop me if I get anything wrong. Tellis Moore is dead! He died over four centuries ago. You're his clone, like your father and his father before him. The first Tellis Moore never located his dead wife Julia's genocode and fourteen Tellis Moores later you're still out of luck. Don't you think it's time you boys threw in the towel? Some things just weren't meant to be," he says. "How am I doing so far?"

I don't have to stop him—he knows enough already. I want him to know everything. In a strange way it feels good, like I'm not alone anymore. It's time. I decide to tell him the rest. I draw a virgin breath . . . and begin.

"After Julia died, the first Tellis Moore searched the rest of his life for her code but it never surfaced. As more time passed, he knew that even if he found her they could never be together again in his lifetime, but a younger version of himself could."

Torrance slowly takes his weight off my shoulders. "Go on," he tells me.

"Tellis Moore believed so strongly in his love that he cloned himself to give that other version, the second Tellis, a chance to experience the life he never had with Julia, to fulfill the promise of their love. He thought to deny that love would be the ultimate tragedy, almost criminal. He raised the second Tellis as his own son and taught the boy to love Julia as he had, completely and utterly, and to carry on the legacy if he wasn't destined to be with her either. He wanted to die with an assurance that one day the two lovers would meet again. That's the notion that each generation has been working from ever since. True happiness for any of us can't exist without Julia and I've prayed every day of my life that her code will appear during my time here."

Torrance laughs. "The way you tell the story sounds like you're reading it from a book, like it's some fairy tale you've committed to memory."

"It is," I tell him. "My father taught me everything about Julia, everything *his* father had taught him. It's ingrained onto our minds, from our earliest memories. It's a part of us. *She's* a part of us. But they're not fairy tales, Torrance, they're a family history."

Torrance drops himself down on the desktop. "Maybe it *is* one man's history, but not for the rest of you. Don't you think it's just a bit absurd pining over a woman who took her last breath a few centuries ago?"

"You don't know her," I tell him.

"Neither do you, Tellis! She doesn't know you either—she knew someone just like you, but it wasn't *you*. You may be a carbon copy of the first Tellis Moore, but you're still Tellis Moore *version 14.0*. You're not the same person. And when you find her, it won't be Julia either—no matter what you teach her or how many fairy stories you tell her. How can you be so certain that she'll feel the same way about you that you do about her?"

"She'd have to, can't you see that? She has about as much choice as I do!" I get up and start to pace. "Love is a force, stronger than the wills of any two versions of Tellis and Julia. We can't alter that force. *This* love—*our* love—has survived hundreds of years. Doesn't that tell you *something*? It's not just this thing people have been passing off as love since the ancient times. It's not an excuse just to have a warm body to sleep next to. It's not a rationalization because we're afraid of dying alone. This is the pure, uncut stuff—the *truest* love." I shake my finger at him. "Acknowledge it for what it is or stop talking about what you don't understand. This is my love, my burden to bear and I *will* bear it. Why should anyone in The Ministry care as long as I'm still productive?"

Torrance calms me down. He gets me a glass of water and an EZ pill for my nerves. Then he sits me down and his voice softens.

"One thing you have to understand about me, Tellis, I confront apathy everyday—passionless people just living out their years. They never surprise me. Then I come here. I watch you work. I watch you searching for something—something that's real to you, something you believe in, and it gets to me. *It gets inside me.* You remind me of myself a long time ago, Tellis, when I was lost just like you are now. Some part of me thinks that if I can help you, then maybe I won't feel quite as empty as I do at the end of every day. I will have served some purpose—beyond The Bureau—some higher purpose. Do you understand what I'm saying?"

Torrance faces the window. The slate grey sky cracks and raindrops begin to freckle the glass.

"I have to tell you that what you're doing isn't right, Tellis. It's not healthy. I know what I'm talking about. I think you feel it, too. Obsession can turn a man into something unimaginable, without him even knowing. Why do you think they outlawed the vices? They poisoned our whole way of life. But how do you outlaw obsession? The Ministry has always frowned on cloning for romantic purposes but they knew, with everyone tagged, that sort of thing was going to happen. They thought it would limit itself to one set of partners—that the obsession would die naturally, with the lovers themselves. No one in our agency could even fathom it going on for as long as it has in your family, Tellis. All these years, it was too pre-posterous to even raise suspicion. But now that we know, we'd like to put an end to it . . . if we can."

"Listen, Torrance, I need Julia. And she needs me too, wherever and whenever she is. I'm going to find her eventually, or another Tellis Moore will. She deserves that."

Torrance shakes his head. "You seem so certain, but how can you *really* know what romantic love is? You have no experience to draw from, Tellis You only know what you've been taught."

"You're wrong, Torrance. A man can *believe* what he's been taught, but he can only truly *know* what he feels. I *feel* this love."

Torrance stands pensive by the window, muted for a long moment. Then, beating a hasty path behind the desk, he shoves the files back inside his briefcase and reaches out to shake my hand again.

"It's been an experience, Mr. Moore, not exactly what I expected either," he tells me. "Somehow, though, I don't think I convinced you to stop."

I feel a little guilty. "Your argument wasn't totally lost on me."

"But it doesn't change your mind? That would have been my first choice. Understand that The Ministry doesn't blame you for your circumstances, Tellis. That's why I've been authorized to offer you certain *alternatives*."

"There are no alternatives for me."

Torrance fastens his briefcase closed. "I'm here to help you, don't forget. Go back to your carrel. I added an encrypted file to your CPU block last night. It's buried within the tide of incoming datamesh streams, but it's easy enough to find if you know it's there. Look under the name 'Charity'."

Torrance holds out the pass code on a strip of paper fisted in his hand like a fortune cookie. I pull it free from his fingers.

"We've got artifactual records that go back for ages. Most of it never makes it into the census banks. Some other new streams get held up for security reasons—

The Bic doesn't get *everything* first, you know." He smiles. "The file on the computer is yours, do whatever you like with it. The Ministry has arranged to provide you with a transport should you require it, just contact the number." Torrance pencils in the back of a glossy card and hands it to me.

"Why would I need a Ministry transport?" I ask him.

"It is a long trip."

* * *

The 'Charity' file sticks out in the datamesh like a beacon. Whatever intel is there must be low classification, I think to myself. The level of federal ciphers on this thing is flimsy. Even without the pass code Torrance gave me, I could hack into this file with any one of a dozen programs I have at home. But I use his pass code to save some time. The file opens and reveals itself. My whole body tips toward the holoscreen. It's a treasure.

In front of me is a history of Julia's life in medical workups, dental records, tax returns, insurance claims, test scores, handwriting samples, her driving record, something called a credit report, her marriage license with the first Tellis, a slew of old 2-D photographs, her third-grade report card, all the leftovers of her life were there. I spot her familiar genocode model as well.

I spend the morning interval pouring over the contents, savoring them, rolling them over again and again in my mind. Her bio states that she was born to parents, Stanley and Marcia, in a township called Memphis, part of the Old American Empire, in 2012. She died in the summer of 2041. The end of her biography reads:

...majority of surviving family wiped out in plague of 2098; probable cause for non-appearance of living genocode match until 2497. Match location: Outland colony Helo; Star class 147.93MT-686. Name of exact genocode match: Charity Elizabeth Morman, aged <1 year.

The revelation penetrates my mind. I say the words aloud.

"Julia is alive."

It's afternoon. I leave work and rush back to tell Father the miraculous news, but he's not home. Father, what a day this must be for you, I think. But I have the most wonderful surprise when you get back. All day I try without luck to contact him.

It's evening now. I can't bear the wait for him any longer so I scribble a cryptic note and leave it on the door. I call for the transport and begin to pack.

A huge carrier ship arrives later that night—it looks like Moby Dick, a boxy, white whale with all manner of official markers and spaceway clearances tattooed across its nose. It's an older military model, the kind that The Ministry regularly uses to haul goods across the stars. It looks sturdy enough to me, if a bit slow.

The mouth of the hull drops open and I step onto its deck. I can see that Torrance is aboard, along with a smattering of uniformed personnel. He's talking with an attractive woman in a long, bright coat when he flashes me a grin, motions me to submit to the retinal scan, and waves me aboard. I comply and step onto the deck. The rig slowly swallows me.

I approach him with a wide smile. "You knew she was alive all along. Why didn't you tell me, Torrance?"

"I was allowing myself the chance to talk you out of doing this, though I was fairly certain it wouldn't work. I'm still not crazy about this idea, Tellis, but I know in your mind it's the only answer. I wish it weren't."

"I've waited my whole life for her, Torrance. Nothing could keep me away." I grab his hand with both of mine and shake it profusely. "Thanks for coming along. I'm anxious as hell and you're the closest thing to a friendly face I got around here."

Torrance nods. "The doc here's been on me for years about taking my mandatory wellness repose so I figure I'd use it to see beautiful Helo," he says with a roll of his eyes. "I might as well. I've got so much vac-time saved I'd have to retire tomorrow if I wanted to use it all. I take time off about as often as you do, Tellis."

Torrance introduces the woman to me as Dr. Jaen Spurling and I shake her hand eagerly.

"Doctor Spurling, how exactly will this work?" I ask. "We're not going to have to kidnap this little girl, are we?"

"Would you still agree to it if I told you we were?" she says. Torrance scowls at the doctor and a few awkward seconds follow her words. "I'm sorry, Mr. Moore, that wasn't fair of me. I can absolutely assure you it won't be necessary to snatch any babies this time. We're working with the full cooperation of Charity's parents. They are fully aware that we're en route. We'll simply have blood and tissue samples extracted from the infant, from which we'll be able to obtain more than enough of her DNA-coding for the purpose of cloning her. It's just another shot for the baby, something I'm sure she's used to living on that rock. The family is being well-compensated. I'm sure they could use it to get out of the colonies if they wanted to, but I don't get the sense that they will." She turns to leave, adding, "Of course, you'll have to submit samples of your own so we can clone each child to be roughly the same age."

I look at her blankly.

"Those *were* your intentions, Mr. Moore? Or were you planning on having her yourself?"

I don't answer at first. "I hadn't considered—I mean, I *am* still young enough and I'm years away from raising a new Tellis and starting his lessons," I reason. "Julia *was* always the younger, innocent one." After some hasty midair calculations I say, "I'd barely be fifty years old by the time she--,"

I stop. I break off my words at the sight of Dr. Spurling's facial expression. Her eyes move to Torrance, who nods back surreptitiously.

"Of course, Mr. Moore, whatever you decide," she says.

* * *

For several days my mind hums with thoughts of Julia and myself. I must find a properly trained family to raise her, a family that can be trusted with her teachings. I hope that Torrance may be able to help me in that regard as well.

But is it fair to Julia?

No doubt resides in me that I will love her intensely and that she will never once, even for an instant, regret a life spent by my side. And yet I realize that she would enjoy so many more years with him, my son, the younger Tellis. Still, the thought of Julia with another man, even another me, brings my heart up into my gullet and a burning to my lungs.

I try to appease my inner discontent. I tell myself I can still love her, as I would a daughter. But the proposition proves too incendiary to entertain. My instilled desire is for the gluttonous love I'd known in another lifetime and—I decide at that moment—would know again. I will forsake the first Tellis Moore's wishes and the fifteenth's birthright. I will keep Julia for myself.

Maybe Torrance was right. Maybe this love *has* turned me into something unimaginable.

I never broach the subject with Spurling again during the weeks the cruiser glides through deep space and she doesn't pursue the matter with me either. I'm certain that at the core of our shared silences, the doctor knows what I am, too.

* * *

The transport touches down on Helo after twenty-two space days. Dr. Spurling equips the entire landing party with germ filter suits. I slip into mine. It has a mask with shaded, bulbous eye plates and a network of plastic tubing that sprouts from the snout of the mask and festoons my neck on one side. Huddled together on deck, donning our suits before the ship opens, we look like a nest of insects.

None of the crew seems to like the suits much. They possess a sickly synthetic smell; they're hot; the masks are cumbersome as all hell and they gurgle when you exhale. I don't think to mind though.

The doctor informs the group that Helo has such numerous airborne pathogens that, without their gear, they would most certainly contract something "puss-ugly", as she puts it. The doctor's descriptions are enough to make the whole crew triple-check their fittings. Most locals don't wear any protection though; the adults have built up immunity to the indigenous bacterium and the elderly and the very young are inoculated regularly. Still, there are pockets of settlers just inside the colony gates with rosy boils littering their skin.

As we enter the gates, the landing party is greeted by the enthusiastic throng. Rust-faced with the color of Helo's swirling dust winds, the assemblage of men, women, and children seem little more than gaunt hangers for the tatters that clothe them.

The crew quickly unloads the medicinal provisions and foodstuffs while the colonist horde swarms over them and trudge off like a line of marauding ants, the oversized containers resting on their heads. Only a patch of children remain.

I spot Julia being cradled in the arms of a small boy, looking himself feeble enough to be carried. I approach him and, to my surprise, he seems to instinctively sense my intentions and passes the infant girl to me.

I hold her, tightly.

I rock the child in my arms while trilling softly through my mask, *"Un-til the twelfth of ne-ver, I'll still be lov-ing you."*

Dr. Spurling, Torrance, and a few others meet in the distance with several of the colonists. Torrance seems to be doing most of the speaking. The colonists direct the group to a large dome at the center of camp. He shouts to me through the filter of his mask, "Tellis, we're moving out."

"It's Julia, I've got her!" I yell back, tilting the baby to show him.

Torrance stamps over the ruddy sand and snatches the infant, giving her back to the boy. "The child we're here for is named Charity, not Julia. This isn't her," he says, motioning to the baby. "Now let's go—there's been a problem."

I follow just behind the group, hiding inside my mask. I wonder to myself how I could have been mistaken. Later, I catch up to the rest and ask Torrance, "What is this problem?"

"It may be nothing," he tells me. "We'll know everything as soon as we reach the hospital."

A woman escorts the party to the dome building. After we enter the structure, Dr. Spurling tells everyone that it's safe to remove their masks and suits while inside. The air is sanitized and stale. I join the stampede up a spiral of stairs and navigate a labyrinth of narrow mud-colored hallways before reaching the child's room.

The baby lies high on a metal table, entombed in a translucent box. I immediately sense my mistake at the gates. I can feel her now. *This* is Julia. . .and she's gone.

I look desperately to Torrance, then Spurling, but both their faces share the same funereal gloom. "Can I help you?" a woman asks delicately from the hallway. I step out of the room with Torrance and the doctor.

"You're expecting us, ma'am," Torrance says. "We're here to pick up B & T samples from an infant, Charity Morman. We were told this is her room. Is that the child?"

"Yes, that's Charity, poor thing. We lost her this afternoon—redhook flu—it came on quick," she says.

In an instant, all the air leaves my body. I keel over and rest one hand on the floor.

"Were you able to extract a viable sample before the late stages?" Dr. Spurling asks.

The woman smiles. "Oh yes, we took samples from Charity a week or so ago, as soon as we got word Mr. Moore was on his way."

Spurling releases a great sigh and I hear Torrance soughing something that sounds like a prayer as he helps me to my feet.

"Everything's fine," the nurse tells us. "But you must have known that already."

Torrance says, "How could we have known anything, we just arrived?"

The nurse looks quizzically at each of us. "I just assumed Mr. Moore had told you already."

Torrance and Spurling look to me. I shake my head and shrug.

"I'm confused. What was I supposed to tell them?" I ask the nurse.

"Not you," she says. "Mr. Moore. Mr. Tellis Moore. He already came for the living tissue samples."

"I'm Tellis Moore. I didn't get any samples."

Her narrowing eyes inspect me, crown to foot. Then, moving closer, she scans my face. "You *do* have his eyes," she says, "but Mr. Moore was much older."

A ripe silence ensues before Torrance rushes back into Charity Morman's room. He barks out a few commands and the men file out purposefully. "When was Mr. Moore here?" he asks the woman.

"About ten o'clock this morning."

Torrance turns to Dr. Spurling. "He's got a seven-hour jump on us. I'll call the ship, we'll lay down a stellar net—a day's time in every direction. It'll take a while but we'll track him eventually. I'm prepping for take-off as soon as we're done here." He turns back to the nurse. "Dr. Spurling and I have some questions. Please gather the hospital staff downstairs immediately."

"What is it, Torrance, what's happening?" I ask.

"Get back to the ship, Tellis, we'll be leaving inside of an hour. Don't worry, son, we haven't lost anything yet."

The room empties instantly and I'm left there with only a sense of paralyzing shock and the dead husk of Charity Morman. It pains me to see the shadow of her uninhabited body, but I can't help myself. I have to look at her. She's here with me, finally. I realize her name was Charity, but she was Julia, too.

An orderly in hospital scrubs and a germ filter mask enters the room solemnly and begins to unlock the wheeled legs of the table that hold the infant. I don't want her to leave, but I'm thankful the body is going somewhere, anywhere else.

This is exactly what the first Tellis Moore must have felt, I think, as I look at the silhouette of the dead child in the box, now moving around each time the hospital staffer bumps against the gurney. I say, "You know you don't have to wear that in here," pointing to the orderly's oversized mask. Kneeling beside me, the orderly frees the last wheel of the cart. I don't want to linger. I take two steps toward the door and the figure at my feet explodes into me like a panther. I feel a sharp tear at my gut. As our bodies part, I watch the orderly slowly withdraw a scalpel from an advancing patch of scarlet wetness on my shirt.

He closes the door to the room and removes the germ mask. "I'm sorry, son, but this would all be over with right now if you had just listened to me for once and had a cup of tea!" my father says in a sickly familiar tone. "I tried to make it easy on you, painless. I never meant for you to leave the house that morning, Tellis. Once you did, it was out of my control."

I try to dam up the hole in my belly with both hands. "Why would you do this?" I ask him.

Father stalks me around the room. "They left you for me, Tellis. They left you here for a reason, don't you see? There is no such thing as coincidence, only opportunity, only destiny. My finding Julia's file while you slept was fate. Something told me to check the mesh that night, to make sure you'd done your work. You don't deserve her. It was my fate to find her code and it's that same fate that brings you to the end of this blade. She was meant *for me*." He shakes his head maniacally. "No, no, no, no, no, this is the only way—if you'd have gotten hold of her, you never would've shared her with me or anyone. I'm surprised you're even willing to give her to your own son. But you haven't lived without her as long as I have, Tellis. I have to do this. If I were to let you leave Helo, we'd never be rid of you. You'd hunt us down. You'd take her from me."

I scream at him. "How could you know that, Father?"

"Because that's what I'd do."

I grab the table and roll it toward me with one hand; Charity's sepulcher buffering me from Tellis number thirteen.

"You can't kill me, Father, they're expecting me back on the ship. Torrance won't leave without me."

"You're absolutely right. And when the retinal scanner confirms that you're safely aboard, they won't give it another thought—except it'll be me aboard and not you. With all their scurrying about, I'll be just one more man in a filter suit climbing onto the ship. It'll be some time before they figure it out—they've got a whole stellnet to sift through. I'll lock myself in some corner until it lands to refuel and then Julia and I will get off. We'll be free of you."

He swipes wildly and misses, instead bevelling a long line into the child's charnel tank, revealing a grisly glimpse of its contents.

"It's fate, Tellis. How can I argue with it when it's brought me this close to her?"

"Don't do this, Father," I beg him. "Something's wrong with you. It's something that's wrong with all of us." My eyes are sodden with tears and I can feel my body growing colder.

"It's funny, those are the same words your grandfather used. He's exactly the same as you so I shouldn't be surprised, but I am."

He takes hold of the table and drives it into me, creasing me at the waist and pinning me against the window. He has the look of madness all about him: his eyes are fried eggs, wide whites with jaundiced pupils. He lunges and slashes with the lancet in a frenzy. I know I'll have to kill him to stop him. And I know I can't stop him.

He finally hurls the table aside with a feral indifference, allowing the casket box to crash to the floor. It crashes open. The child's clammy body slides loose from the broken pieces of the chamber and comes to rest on the floor between us. A rubbery layer of skin is stretched over the infant's miniature bones; a map of blue-green veins wanders just beneath her velutinous scalp.

Father advances on me in his trance state, unhindered. Knocking the tiny corpse with the end of his boot, it spins insensately. He plunges the knife above my chest, knocking my upper body against the window. My clavicle snaps. The sound is crisp, like a bundle of celery. The cold, steel mirrorblade bursts white hot inside me. My body slides helplessly down the glass.

He withdraws the knife and straddles me, slicing down with the blade again and again. The skin of my forearms opens gladly, catching most of the blows. He pushes toward my neck but I grab the knife edge and it cuts through the flesh of my palms. My hands, gloved in drying blood, become tacky and my fingers at least are sticking to the devil blade, slowing its assault. But the life is seeping from me. He pounds down on me several more times, now piercing my body with each knife thrust. Suddenly, a shattering noise erupts above me. A hard rain of broken glass falls to the floor. Father collapses on top of me.

* * *

I wake up on the transport home, too sore to think. Torrance is there when I come to. He gives me the details: how he'd seen Father and me through the window and how he'd brought him down with the perfect shot in the nick of time, just like in the movies. He hands me a tinted cylinder and tells me that Julia is safe inside.

"Was there enough of a sample for Charity's parents?" I ask in a whisper.

"They never asked for one," he tells me. "There aren't any cloning facilities on Helo. They don't need them—they're putting folks down in that soil all the time. Those people are used to loss. But don't worry about the Mormans, tell me how you feel."

I stare into the dark cylinder. "I don't know. I feel weak. I feel alone. How are you supposed to feel when your father tries to murder you for your unborn wife's DNA?"

."Jesus, I don't know. I'm sorry I asked," Torrance says. We both chuckle.

"I feel grateful for you mostly though," I tell him. I place my hand inside of his and his fingers fold over mine. "The Ministry had a lot less to do with you helping me than you're letting on."

"Maybe," he says.

"What about Father—what happened to him?"

"He wasn't your father, Tellis. He was just a desperate man, like you. Like a lot of us. I've known men who've had terrible things come to them in their lives, things they didn't deserve. Some lose a wife…"

Torrance takes an uneasy breath.

"…some lose a son. There's nothing to do except to go on." His head bows. "You can't convince me I got cheated when I lost my boy, not when I look into the eyes of my other children. I loved my son. I screamed to the sky when I lost him. I wanted him back more than anything in this universe!" He stops.

"I lost a *son*. I didn't lose love. I carried it inside me always, waiting for the time when I could pour it out again. You have it inside you, too, Tellis. The time has come for you to pour it out. Find someone—*anyone*—with just as much love inside them and pour it out onto one another."

* * *

I hold Julia for days. I roll her opaque ebon home between my fingers and stare into the darkness that is my future. Just behind my own reflection, I can almost see her face through the murk. Torrance is with us. He watches from his chair beside the bed and asks how I'm feeling.

"Better," I tell him. "Julia is with me. She will always be."

Inside of Me
by James Steimle

Having escaped the legal profession for sane territory, James Steimle is now a graduate student and librarian subsisting on book dust and dreams. His work has appeared in the new Staffs & Starships, Tales of the Talisman, Black Petals, Gateway SF, and the British Fantasy Society's Dark Horizons. He served for seven years as Editor in Chief of Little Rock Digest, twice received awards from the Writer's Digest Writing Competition, and recently escaped the San Diego wildfires by running to Arizona. His book The Ghost People will be coming soon from Sam's Dot Publishing.

Everyone is choosing to live an alternate life, but Shoe likes this life. He has a girl, a job, everything is going well, or is it?

1

Is it still there? I have to pull back and look again. I know, I feel it. I sense it between the upper and lower crag, but—yes, there. I'll go again. I need that particle. It's just that—every time—I reach for it—it slips from my vision—and—

I pull back again and look, listing on my eight smaller legs, balancing, touching the uneven slope with both mandibles. And I hold there, staring at the particle, memorizing its position, the way it sways and threatens to drop, slide, and get away from me. Then I go in again. I've been at it all day, reaching with the left mandible first, then the right. I stare at a sky filled with infinite life, remembering what I just saw: the rocking particle, tantalizing, taunting me, holding fast to the jagged side, leaning in a breeze scented with the fifth season. There isn't much time now.

I scrape my left mandible against the rough grain of the element beneath me and think I bump the particle. I can almost feel it; I think I might have! But I mean, I can almost feel it inside of me, warm, refreshing, cleansing, and filling me. There! I nudge it again. I'm sure of it!

But I hear Pol scrambling up the slope beneath me It's a bad time to mate, a bad time, yet I almost forget the particle altogether at the thought of pressing my back to Pol's. I think I recall when we met, how we were drawn together—stop it! Why is it so hard to concentrate? I must reach that particle! If only I could think straight.

I draw back half-an-arm's length, twist my primary level, thrust in again, quickly touch the particle with my right mandible. But how shall I clasp it? I scour myself against the points of the element and stop caring about the damage I'm doing to my outer shell. With any luck I will soon shuck this armor for a better form anyway.

Pol's antennae reach me. They tap my back and convey his thoughts. As if I needed to hear in order to understand him; I could always read his mind, because he thinks almost exactly the way I do. He taps me again, talking.

I can't listen now. I can't respond. I have to focus. And I've almost … got … that particle …

2

Shoe sat in the tower apartment, drumming his fingers over a journal that flickered on and off with each touch of his hand. The world revolved around the room. From each window he saw the living distance, the overpopulation, the mountains of the city rising like horizons of an ancient Earth hoping to be remembered.

His real name was Harkahome Shoemowetochawcawewahcatowe, Cheyenne mumbo-jumbo for Little Robe High-backed Wolf He went by Shoe, because no one could forget that part. And he wondered about his people, so inter meshed with every tribe, every other race, that his Japanese eyes and his long platinum blond hair did not even bother the elders. At times he wondered if he was related to the Cheyenne at all, or if it was little more than a club, like the Elk's Lodge.

His mother's last words, spoken over a vice-grip hand as she died from the latest and worst of the endogenous retroviruses, KIP, were promises of an afterlife in which Shoe no longer believed. She told him that as a spirit, she would return and walk this Earth. She would visit him and intercede on his behalf when the commanding spirits of the world sought to rain acid on his shoulders or sunburn the back of his neck. Shoe thanked his mother and cried. "I hope you will visit me." She said he would never see her again, and that was true. She said he would discover signs of her influence around him, and that had never happened.

And now Max had joined this newfangled religion, the one promoted by the government, the one advertised at all times of the day. People were flocking. Shoe never saw a shepherd, but people ran and gathered, hopped on the wagon, casting all their cares to the wind. Max would be here any second, already late as it was, and Shoe considered going out this evening. Escape.

But they had already spoken, and Shoe's absence would be harder to explain later. He just didn't want to hear anymore about this cult—why did religious people feel the need to share their beliefs anyway? Silly question, that: the sheep always want to share their joy. Wasn't that Max's goal to begin with? Maybe, Shoe thought, if I just slip out now, I can come up with an excuse later!

The elevator door played a melody and the sleepy woman's voice said across the airwaves of Shoe's studio apartment, "Maxemillian Seda is here to see you, Shoe."

"Who is it?"

Polite and unperturbed, the automated female said again, "Maxemillian Seda."

3

I almost hook that particle at last. But Pol grates against my exoskeleton, so that I shudder. It's pleasure, burning. And I'm not imagining the particle anymore, no matter my need, for as I stare at the dusty sky, pink and blue and radiant with living organisms, I imagine Pol, though he is right there beside me, right there rubbing me with his harsh armor.

I can feel mine sloughing a little, ready to give. And I am ready to give, to Pol, just as he is ready to give to me. He's climbing now, up my back, his feet stabbing for holds in every bend and crevice of my massive form.

Four legs let go, and the roll of his body and weight hit me. My right mandible goes flat into the cutting element upon which I stand. My own eight smaller legs begin to fail me. I use my left mandible as a powerful forearm to steady us; we are liable to slip down the slope and go crashing to the heavier elements far below the cliff's edge. Intuitively, I know we would not survive such a fall. No, not intuitively. I once saw a body crushed by gravity or battle or both. It lay on the rocks, broken. And there was no one inside, no life, only a husk in the shape of life.

Pol's roll positions himself in the familiar arrangement I had taken with him the day we first met. My back fits into his and his into mine, locks sliding into place, pins dropping into chutes, and I can feel the machinery going. I cannot see Pol, but know his mandibles rock left and right as he loses all focus and concentration. His small legs kick at the air, wave, reach and pull back again as if struggling for purchase on the ether. He groans as I do, as we both feel our bodies giving way, relaxing, easing, and letting slide our exoskeletons.

For only a moment am I aware that we are not alone. As Pol and I give, breaking free of our previous physical forms into new and stronger bodies, we leave behind a new entity between us. But I hardly pass this creature a glance or a single thought. I am glad Pol's weight is off of me, though I know I will want him again. I have a momentary image of the particle, as I crawl away and leave behind the shell of our old bodies.

The particle. I need that particle. I spin around, standing high on the twisted and rising element. Pol clamors away below me. He will not go far. We never seem to separate by any noticeable distance. I wonder if our final separation might contribute to my future demise.

And there, above the particle, the new entity crawls from our exoskeletons. I see his black antennae first. His mandibles protrude, large and shiny, though not as large as Pol's and certainly not as appealing—I find my lack of emotion interesting. Then I watch the minute sway of his upper level, visual centers not yet developed, though his particle sensors are sharper than mine now. His massive back pulls free of our old bodies, but only enough for him to squeeze downward into the crevice where both of his mandibles—both!—fit easily enough for him to take that particle and ingest it.

I'm in a rage. It's all Pol's fault. I hate him. But I'll see him later, if I've got the power to copulate again, and if my body will have the need to shed its epidermis. I look for Pol, follow him down the craggy element. I bump the new entity out of spite and it drops flat and trembling on its eight legs. Then I waddle as quickly as I can after Pol. If I'm lucky, maybe I can shove him over the cliff. Knowing me, though, I'll probably just follow him down to the pools.

Max sat in the other chair, the one with the rip down the side, and drank from his bottle and wouldn't stop smiling. And he stared, like a fly on the wall contemplating a spring forward or a quick retreat. He drummed his fingernails along the whiskers under his neck, and he listened to the raspety-raspety-raspety, which sounded like a nagging whisper that would not stop. "*Que pasa, hombre*? So what you thinking about? You take a quiet pill?" He waited in the silence until his drink ran empty. He got another, bounced back into his chair, ready to vomit his excitement, which clearly had to do with that new religion of his.

Shoe averted his eyes. "I think Sarah's going to leave me for another partner."

"No way. Forget about that."

"It's in her body language, *cholo*. Like she doesn't see me anymore, even when she sees me. Yesterday, she came over after work and for the longest time she wouldn't say anything—"

"A lot of that going around, it seems."

"Shut up. And she went to the counter there and whipped up a shake, all by herself, and she sat in the chair you're sitting in, and she stared out the window and sipped through a straw, and you know what she said to me?"

"Maybe you'd better not say."

"She said, 'Do you ever wonder what it'll be like to die?'"

"Ah." Max shifted in his seat. "Well … "

"Oh stop it, I'm not mad at you. I know you've been talking to her about your big new voodoo fix—"

"Shoe, it's all the rage. Everybody loves the idea. Even the government—"

"I know, already. I know enough."

"But you never let me tell you. I've got the inside scoop, *compadre*." Max wrenched forward to the edge of his seat and pulled his fingers through his long hair.

Shoe threw his hand into the air. "*Señor*, please. You know where I stand on this issue. It's a cult fad. It's a mistake. Trust you me, people will regret going into this after a few years. It's not like you can just up and leave freely if you decide you no longer want to participate. Am I right?"

"Well of course!"

"And for the record, I think you're an idiot. I only say that because we are friends, Max." Now Shoe drilled him with his eyes. He held back the tears, confident that his friend would not listen. No matter what logic he used, no matter what he said. It was pointless to even continue. Shoe was on the verge of losing everybody he cared about. The religion was swallowing them whole. "We're friends."

"Why in the world do you think I want to share this with you, Sneaker Boy?" Max slapped himself in the forehead, jumped, and paced the floor before the west-facing window. The evening sun glowed at his back, so that he became all dark silhouette and largely faceless. "This is absolutely the best thing that has happened on the planet. It solves a thousand problems! And no war, no poverty, no crime or greed. Could we ever hope for more? It's magical, *amigo*. I don't understand it myself." He stood there for a moment, contemplating the silence, tapping his leg with the translucent bottle that shimmered like a light. "You'll be there for the ceremony, when I go in, won't you? Shoe?"

Shoe stared at his friend's missing eyes and wondered how to let him down easy.

5

So I'm hanging from this cliff's edge, not sure how I got here. I must have slipped and slid, but I've been hanging so long now, days it seems, that I am aware of little more than the empty space all around me, the immeasurable distance to any solid matter, and how I hang by one mandible while all my little legs wiggle and rest, wiggle and rest, in the wind.

I taste the air with my right mandible. I'm afraid of touching the element from which I hang. What if I bump myself away, cause my grip to slide loose? How long shall I plummet before becoming a broken shell without life inside, like the one I found long ago. And where is Pol now?

I have not seen Pol, though I had gone looking. Is he searching for me? Or has he forgotten my existence and our need for one another, our connection. I have so little energy. At times it seems I have not the power to think anymore. At times, I hold perfectly still and feel death might release me from the world if I wait long enough, and after I have hung motionless, save for the press of the incidental breeze, I wonder if I have died, and if I might become a husk like the dead one I saw, but worry that I might be trapped inside the husk, dead forever, unable to move, mate, gather particles, but always aware, forever knowledgeable about my frozen body, my unused back ...

I need a particle. I see them, floating on the currents of air. I wonder at their lack of weight, how freely they travel through the light of the sky before landing gently, rolling, preparing themselves for gathering, fulfilling the measure of their existence. If only I too could fly. But I am a grounded entity, come to this, the edge of passing, and I wonder what, if anything, happens next or if my hunt for particles and a mate is about to end.

Then I see the aurora, the swirl of dark color in the sky. It comes slowly, and the waves are a joy to me. How many nights have I climbed to the highest particles that I might be close to the lights in the night? How they fuel me, give me courage and strength. I feel their particles. I smell them, rather than taste them, smelling being a rare gift to me only recognized at night when the aurora begins. I remember swaying in the wind to the music that I felt the lights making for me. I worship them still, though I know they do not hear and they cannot save. Nevertheless, as the nights have come, I have called out, pleading, with the motions of my antennae. Just in case I am wrong, and the aurora lights contain some intelligence I know not of.

Soon I shall fall, drop like chunks of unfastened element. My senses are heightened! The world takes on a clarity of color and sharpness I have not noticed in the past. When the night has left me alone again beneath the edge of the overhanging cliff, I can see distant summits jetting from the curved and broken planet floor. I detect movement, motion everywhere, as if particles live and think and wander in search of understanding. As I hang and study these perceptions, it occurs to me that these are not particles so very far below me, but entities like myself, all working busily, spawning new entities, gathering smaller particles, exploring the elements, swaying upon busted hilltops at the wind and the aurora at nights, dying, and being born.

From this summit, the world is alive! I stare, and I am weak. I no longer think of ingesting particles or copulating. Pol is only a memory. Days and nights pass me and leave me under the outcropping point of the element. I am feeling my own body, becoming an intelligence in ways I have not ever bothered to become in the history of my existence. I am sure now that I look like Pol and the other entities, that there are no differences at all, save perhaps for the scrapes along my mandibles and my shoulders, along my underside, marking me with some personality. My upper level is minute compared to my lower form. And save for legs and mandibles, my lower form is unable to move at all, while my upper level is free to jerk a little toward one shoulder and a little toward the other. Only my antennae are capable of stretching beyond these trappings. I tap myself, note the massive plates and sharp points that make up my shoulders, the intricate slats that define my back, the banded rungs that create my undercarriage, the needle points of my tiny legs, the great curving branches and spikes of my mighty mandibles. With joy, I think myself handsome.

And then I feel the element break a bit. Or is it the point of my right mandible slipping free of the abrasion from which I hang?

The element cliff is gone, and I am falling through the atmosphere.

6

Everyone participating in the ceremony wore white from head to toe. Max peered at the ring of windows above the ceremonial center and smiled at Shoe who watched beyond the glass. He gave a thumbs up and then winked, and Shoe thought he looked like a fool in that religious getup: the white footwear and pants were nice, but the shirt reaching down to white gloves fell like a woman's summer dress just over the edge of his hips, where slits ran back up the shirt for six or seven inches, and a tight hood was attached to the collar, clinging and augmenting his thick neck and then wrapping under his chin and over his forehead so that only Max's face showed him to be different from anyone else in the chamber. This skin too would be covered, he had told Shoe when Shoe finally promised to see him "reborn."

"I'm going to do it," Sarah said, standing beside Shoe and blinking through the glass with all the other chattering onlookers. She hadn't left him for another partner, as Shoe expected, but had mumbled religious nonsense for days. And she came dressed in white clothing that augmented her medically enhanced curves; the white almost made her look ready to march on down there to where the pretty music played, and the religious fanatics walked around and around in ever-tightening circles toward the life stone, where people disappeared.

"I know you want to. But don't go." Shoe watched another zealot wave to loved ones or to strangers before lying down upon the stone and then sinking into the floor with the priest before the next stone arrived like a car from a Disneyland ride. "You don't have to go."

Her laugh was a sneer of derision. They had been effectively married now for six years, though no one really wed anymore. They partnered. Shoe liked to think himself married. His mother had been old-fashioned and often spoke of marriage and her historic romances. Sarah loathed the word, from their first day together. She had studied psychology at the university and pointed out that the average individual retained at least ten different partners in a lifetime, and she had already had two. Marriage was an old word, representative of an old time, and though no one got married for life anymore, "until death do you part," not realistically—because life was so long nowadays—Sarah thought the word implied permanence and was therefore fit only for heartbreak. "Haven't you been listening to anybody? Hasn't Max gotten through? No one *has to be* born again."

"I'm just saying you don't have to go, Sarah."

"I think you just don't understand the good we're seeing here. Look at that man climbing on the rock now. See the smile on his face? He knows he's doing something that is not only exciting and fascinating, but good for the whole world! I think you're just being selfish." She sighed away from him. "I don't plan to be selfish."

"But enough people go now. Enough people. Max said the food shortages, the overpopulation crush, is no longer such a burden. And so many people are joining that the government suspects we'll revert to population levels not seen since 2005!" He laughed. "Isn't that great? There will be resources again! Real estate prices will drop seventy percent! Traffic will thin, they say, so that at times you might not even see another car on the road! Unemployment will rush down to eleven percent, or better—people will make more money because their presence will be of greater value!" He chuckled again.

All while Sarah shook her head. "You sound like a missionary! And yet you don't want to go?" She pressed her hands and breasts against the glass, as if she might somehow slide through the pane and join the spiraling throng.

"And miss all that?" He forced himself not to look at her—such a beautiful woman, so perfect, and yet so filled in her countenance with disgust when she looked at him. He followed Max with his eyes as he took one step and then another in the round lines of the temple below them. "You know what's going to happen. They won't say it on the news, no. They won't publish it in the papers. But they'll start whispering in bars, they'll say it at work. 'It's a much better world now. All those fools who left were fools in the first place; good riddance! And now that they are gone, we can enjoy the Earth as it was meant to be enjoyed. We can have a happy life, the crowds gone! We can do better business, eat like kings and queens, and marry for a lifetime—because we'll appreciate our spouses!'"

"Spouses." She spat the word as if it was the worst of profanity. "You can't even hear yourself. You're only thinking one move ahead. Look down at those people in white. They will come back, Shoe! Others have come back already. Haven't you really *listened* to Max? No, you've just shut your ears and called this foolish. You're a selfish man, Shoe. You talk about all the good this religion does, but you miss so much. The government—our tax money!—already pays for everything they do down there. And experiencing a lifetime. Think about that!"

He couldn't hide the frown in his voice. "I'm already experiencing a lifetime."

"And you're not enjoying it. Admit that."

"I admit it." He was thinking about her, the woman of his dreams, who had already left him and given her heart to another. He was sure of the crime, though by modern standards it wasn't really a crime; long ago, his mother had told him, they put women like Sarah to death when they went off with another man. They killed the other man too. He thought about his best friend, Max, only moments away from his rebirth.

"He looks so happy," she said, her voice suddenly warm again. Reverence and admiration swelled within the wetness of her throat. She almost whispered. "He is going to be born again, Shoe. He will not remember this life at all. He will find himself in a different kind of body. He will live according to that body's laws, in that body's world—you know they say his entire biosphere will be no larger than twelve inches across? A sphere with a population of millions of reborn souls!"

"While his real body sleeps in a cabinet, I know. Underground. Premature burial."

She did not hear him. "And Max will live a *life*, Shoe. He will grow, mature, and experience a world of love, curiosity, need, compassion, loss … who knows how much more? The things that people say when they come back!"

"Yeah, five or six years later! Meanwhile, their own body has lost muscle mass, become mentally weak, and the real world has passed them by. Their mothers have died. Their partners have moved on."

"Don't you get it, you freak? Think!" She leaned into him, her brow low, her face hard, her gaze cutting. "They come back and *remember* both lives. One incomplete, yes, and ready to be reconstructed based on the insight they gained by being reborn, living, and dying in the other life!"

"I don't think I want to die more than once."

7

There is a memory of pain from when I struck the ground and cracked my back in five different places, but mostly I remember waking up here, as if the blinding shock of slamming against the element caused the initial sensation to slip from my mind. But I think I do remember. Either way, I hurt now. And I know there are a lot of broken pieces inside of me. Yet I am surprised that the tremendous drop did not damage me more.

I am on my back, staring at the sky again. I know I won't roll over and walk away from this. The aurora has come, which means another day has gone while I wiggle my eight legs at the cliff, which is so far above me that I am no longer quite certain as to the exact location from which I plummeted. And I had been hanging *there* so long!

Something inside my body trickles against the inside of my shell. The loose casing groans about me when I move my mandibles. It's like that detestable rubbing sound of two elements sliding against one another. I move a mandible anyway, to see if perchance I might catch a sprig somewhere out of my sight and pull myself over, as I have had to do so many times in my life. I do this exercise in reaching from time to time, but I feel nothing.

I explore the surface with my antennae. I detect a small jumble of particles. I surge with interest, excitement, and then an almost panicked need. I never reach them with a mandible. I try to bump them with my antennae, but my antennae have never been strong enough to move a particle without the aid of other natural forces, the downward pull or the currents in the air. So I rest. And the days pass, and the nights. More agonizing this time, because I am aware of the particles near me, and I sometimes reach antennae to feel them and speak to them. They never come to my aid. Again, I wonder if I am dead.

I run my legs in the air when I detect another entity close by. He comes closer. He examines me. He taps me with one antennae, saying, "You do not look well. Ah! Particles!" He rushes around me and fetches them all, and I am never quite able to reach him with my antennae to say, *Please help me. Bump me over or come within reach of my mandible so that I might grab hold of your shell and swing myself up and around. May I have one of those particles? It has been so long.*

He devours all the particles. He taps me again. "You do not look well at all. I think you cannot mate. Do you have a mate?"

"Pol," I say, an incredible sadness overtaking me so that I forget to ask for help. I am only thinking of my need to copulate. It has started again, though I don't think my shell could slough for another ten or twenty days. I am broken.

"I do not know Pol. Or maybe I do. Goodbye." He turns away from me, and only then do I think again to ask him for physical assistance. My antennae swing in the breeze and touch nothing. The ground trembles with the movement of his weight. Then he is gone, and the particles are gone, and I stop moving and just lie there, because I cannot think of a reason to do otherwise.

Days pass again, and I am almost sure that I am ready to mate. Either that, or my fractured exoskeleton is breaking free of something inside, which worries me. If I am not dead yet, I must be close. My feet might move sometimes when the aurora dances slowly above me—I can only see this out of one eye when I turn my upper level, I am otherwise blind with the element alone before my visual centers. So I keep my head to one side, and if I move my feet I am unsure. It could be no more than a memory of movement. I have been here for so long …

Two more entities draw near during the day, one behind the other. I think they will mate. They see me and come to explore the curiosity. I plan to move, but I do not move, not an antennae, not a mandible, not a leg. They do not communicate with me. They only look and then feel each other with their antennae. I do not know what they are saying. Perhaps I should will myself to move. But I am tired. And then they wander away from me.

The aurora comes again. I smell particles, I think. Or maybe I am imagining— or is it called … dreaming? I would really like a particle …

During the time of the aurora, while I watch the lights of different colors playing in the sky, I notice a darkness gathering at the edges of my vision—this way, that way, far away, and then it draws closer to the center, slowly, darkening my world. I do not believe the world of elements, particles, and entities is really growing dark. I know what is happening. I watch carefully.

But it is hard to concentrate. I have no strength. The aurora stays ahead of me, so pretty—is it blue, and yellow, and pink? What are these colors to me, these thoughts? The aurora is going away, drawing distant, or the darkness is swallowing it so that soon I see darkness only and the swimming colors of the night far away in the center of my vision. Soon I see no color at all. There is only blackness, and a pinpoint of light, which is so far now, so far, and tiny, and bright, but so far …

The light stays where it is. I watch it, as there is nothing else to see, and I care not to focus or even to try to see anything else. Only that distant light, which ever so slowly seems to be coming closer. And closer, and brighter, and foggy, and filled with sounds: a hiss of constant air, the movement of lighter and darker bodies, white bodies with faces, which lean over me and look down at me and speak in whispers that boom in my ears.

One voice counts backward. "Forty-five, forty-four, forty-three …"

Another voice says, "You are doing very well, Mr.—ah—Mr. S. Just relax. You will remain in a fog for a little while. Breathe normally… Welcome back."

8

Shoe sat before the window in the evening and with a glass of water in his hand, though he did not drink. The apartment was government housing. He was lucky to have a window, they had told him. So he watched the sun set and stared at the orange horizons, at the clouds playing like aurora colors against a darkening blue sky. With fascination, he watched a flock of large birds in silhouette, crows no doubt, crossing the expanse. He wiped the tears from his eyes.

Six years had passed since his rebirth. After Max had gone and then Sarah had gone and just over six weeks had passed, Shoe had realized how little he had in this world, how little he loved and what little he cared about. He had gone to his job and found his presence pointless. The drugs and entertainment left him empty. Even his dumb acquaintances contemplated this experiment of passing from one life to another and then back again, and then left him! His boss joined the religion, after signing paperwork to assure himself of regaining his managerial position upon his return, if he opted to do so—though the government was having mixed debates about the legalities of that kind of maneuver, as most people who returned from another life declined to continue their previous lives in the same manner anyway. Which had been Max's greatest argument for the trip, that it helps one see Earth in a completely new way. And which had been Shoe's greatest worry.

But with everyone swallowed by the new religion, Shoe had felt no choice and no reason to stay. In fact, he'd decided, Sarah and Max would both be out around the time that he got out, if he joined the people in the honeycombed temple as soon as possible. So he did.

And now, six years later, the world did look different. In depression, he drank his water, no longer interested in stimulants, but enamored with the beauty of the sky. Sarah had died and left the small world first, returning to this one where she waited for Max, apparently, who awoke to find her and to marry her—yes marry! They wed in a Starbuck's Chapel over coffee and moved to the desert somewhere.

So Shoe sat alone in his apartment, wondering what he should do, whispering to the spirit of his mother, the old woman who had promised to return as a force of nature. His depression left him to dreaming, to pondering, to thinking. He realized how much like a spirit he had been in the body of that large bulky form that had really been so small, so tiny that it would take a powerful microscope in this world to even make out his shape.

He remembered everything about life in that world, and it had not felt like six years. It had seemed like two hundred, or more! Days and nights passed so often, and he had never bothered to count. Life had been so simple in that massive body, his impulses so pure, his determination so resolved and clear in his mind; his needs, his wants, so easily satiated until the end. Oh, there had been work, there had been suffering. He had seen birth and death, miracles and terrifying curiosities! He had experienced his own horrors, and managed a body that was complicated, difficult to think with, and from which it was almost impossible to observe the world and to communicate!

He thought about how limited he had been without having realized the horrors of his own limitations. Yes, he had observed his world, he had wandered, he had seen, tasted, smelled things in a way, and heard things, or detected their vibrations. But he had been so unable to turn his head, which he did not even perceive to be a head. And he could not see down or up, or even very far to either side. He had no vocal cords at all, and conversations took an excessively long period of time through a complex rhythm of tapping that he could not now duplicate, for all its peculiarity and slowness.

He found his fingers exploring the glass. At times, he tried to move the tiny feet at his stomach, and then looked down to find no tiny feet. And he drew his hands along the short length of his whiskered jaw, one side at a time, remembering the separate mandibles. How huge his mandibles had been, protruding more from his neck than from his head. How had his mouth worked? Slurping. How had he smelled anything? Tasting the wind, a body without a nose. How had he grabbed things? And what *were* particles? What had they done once inside his huge body? How had they contributed to their wrenching and beastly mating process? And why hadn't the scientist-priests who created this new life differentiated between male and female? Simplicity.

His eyes stopped on the splayed fingers of his hand on the glass. He raised the other hand and held it against the colors of the sky. He turned the hand over, moved the muscles, the bones, pulling on the tendons with simple and instantaneous commands from his brain. He told the hand to close, grasp air, open again, turning over in the act. Such complex movements! Such radical expression and ability!

Watching his knees, he lifted one, then the other, then bounced them up and down in a wave pattern. He left the glass, precariously perched on the edge of the armrest, and looked into the sweaty palms of his hands, then at his wrists, and at his naked forearms. He touched his meaty shoulders, felt the tissue and the bone, the loose and hard parts under his skin, and felt his lungs swelling his chest beneath his crossed arms.

Again, he touched his face, examining the machinery of his body, and crawled his fingers from his chin to his eyes. Then he dropped his hands to his lap, left his eyelids ajar, blinked them shut and opened again.

"I am inside," he said, suddenly unable to breathe. He breathed and felt the intake, the exhalation. "I am inside this thing," he whispered. "But," he thought of his mother, "who put me inside of <u>this</u> body? Who am I really?" So he stared out the window at the multicolored sky, and he wondered …

Paper Cuts
by Timalyne Frazier

Timalyne Frazier has been published in Nantucket Magazine, Polyphony, Tomorrow SF, and OG's Speculative Fiction. She won 3rd Place in the Playboy Fiction Contest and recognition in Asimov's Fiction Contest.
This is a story about a woman with a remarkable talent.

Don't be late for dinner.

Stand just inside your front door, at exactly 6:30 Eastern Standard Time, Tuesday, the 29th. I've invited all of our friends. I'm inviting you.

Jack is going to bring some early cherries and his new sweetie. She's new to me, anyway. Have you met her? He says her hair is soft falling curls of dark chocolate. I wonder, does she have a strong handshake and when she stands in front of me, will we see eye to eye? Will I feel compelled to bring up the past?

I asked Sage and Callie, to bring lilacs. They make me think of my great-grandmother. This last year the deer ate every last blossom here, and all of the new growth; my plant may never recover. I wonder if the lilacs are out of season over there? I'm sure Sage will find some other lovely bouquet, instead, if there aren't any lilacs. I still really like the deep purple ones; besides being my favorite color, as you know, the purple masks the brown as they go past, and the blossoms appear to be lovely so much longer than the white. I'll have a vase ready, full of water so we don't spend your time here on preparations. Sunny has made me a new vase, just this week. I dropped the last one and stood there looking at the pieces all in blue around my feet until Sunny reminded me that he can make me one for every day of the week. I was trying to figure out how to put the pieces back together, erase the damage.

Ember is bringing the mermaid game. Do you remember how to play it? It will help ease the homesickness I've been feeling lately, living so far from the ocean. My littlest one says the clay they dig up at the building site smells like seawater, but it just smells like the sewer pipe is busted, to me. She must be thinking of low-tide. I'm anxious to meet Ember's family. They won't all fit across one time fold. I had to find another place to fold a point nearby. I couldn't make the points wider or I'd risk disrupting the neighbors. It's a tricky fold, though, putting two points so close together. I can't rightly refuse to bring the whole family, even if I'd rather just see him. I can be so selfish sometimes.

Mae agreed to be the DJ. I need to focus, so that's one less thing for me to worry about. And I'm prone to worrying. Plus, there always has to be music after I'm through folding. Why does everyone live so far away? Maybe I'm the one to blame. No, I don't think I drove you away, I just couldn't be content in your neighborhood. In fact, I'm not content in my neighborhood. If this goes well, maybe you can visit me next year in Ireland, New Zealand or Massachusetts. Sunny will have to start all over again setting me up with dishes. You won't mind meeting him, will you? It's been long enough, but I've noticed that the nose never forgets. Please don't wear any cologne, I doubt you've heard, yet, but it turns out I have asthma. Fingers on fire and lungs filled with water.

I looked in Pearl's living room window last night. Her cat looked lovely curled on the couch. It was a practice run and the first time I folded everything just right, but, there was a storm brewing and I couldn't stay long enough to talk to her. She smiled and comforted the cat as the thunder rolled. I wonder how long it will take for her to decide the mug I left in the hedge is meant for her.

I wish this were easier, less risky; we could all meet once a week. But each trip, it takes meticulous planning and practice, and when my fingertips are raw I'm clumsy. I took too long unfolding the first couple of times I tried; my fingers tripped. I'm sure you read about those hikers who started out in the Cascades and ended up north of Anchorage with no memory of the 2,500 miles in between. They were lost in the Alaskan wilderness for weeks—good thing I tried that one during the summer. I was pretty embarrassed and kind of worried. They didn't have money to get back, but everyone was so impressed by their amnesiac feat that it was a community effort at both ends and they were able to afford the plane tickets three days after they made town.

I'd like to invite Alexandra, even though you don't know her. I have been dreaming of Pad Thai from Noodles on Broadway. I'll tell her not too spicy and no cilantro, please. I've asked the others and they say they don't mind. No pressure, no worries. I want to do this all just right. I want it to be worth the risks. My hands bleed a little, the paper moves so fast under my fingers. You do want to be here, don't you? Has it been long enough? Will you come alone?

I need you all close by, but everything has to be just right. No bathroom breaks for you; no sticky fingers for me. I have a sturdy map, now. It won't rip or wrinkle when I fold. It took me a while to see how it would all work, how I could bring us all together without disturbing the peace. But I'm ready now. I've been training for a month and can fold and unfold like lightning. I know every crease by heart. My fingers are strong and well, healed from all the trial runs, smooth, supple.

Let's synchronize our watches: 1, 2, 3 now. What does your watch say? Mine says 3:33:33, 34, 35, 36. Are you on board? Does your watch count the seconds?

So, this is how it will go: I'll fold and as the clock blips forward, just once, you step in to my living room. Don't hesitate. I'm afraid if you are caught as I'm unfolding, you'll land in South Dakota or something. I took a train through there—nothing but miles of flat brown and white. I didn't see a single house. And maybe it was the time of year, but I think there's only one UPS truck to service the whole State. You may never be found and I won't know exactly where I dropped you. I miss you.

I need you here. I want to see you on my couch and curl there with you. Sunny won't mind. My cats will come and sniff your face so they can remember you, too. I need you in this house. Even though I'll leave here soon for a new neighborhood, I want you to be here for a bit to complete this chapter of my life. It has been so long that you and all of our friends have been spread out across my mind. You are scribbled scraps of paper here, the corner of a screen fonted over there, a crooked picture in my photo album, a ghosted memory, a suggestion. You have to visit here to decrease the distance and fill my living room, even just for an evening, with the sound of your voice, the light on your face, the scent of your body.

Tell me now if the custard corn bread isn't enough. Hand-rolled sushi? Sunny just made me a special plate. I want to show everyone the magic he has in his hands, too. And what about pumpkin cheesecake? Everybody knows that food brings people together. And maps, my hands. All I have to do is touch the points together. I have strong and nimble fingers. I don't mind a few heartfelt paper cuts.

I have comforted myself long enough with my version of your voice in my head. I read traces of your fingered evidence—sometimes fast and busy, hardly a word for me, or more often pained and angry; I want nothing more than to hold you and push your hair back behind your ear and promise that all this will pass. I know you will only believe me when you can look into my eyes and I can hold your hands in mine. The words across this screen are not enough. So, I've been sitting here doing my best version of reading the lines, folding what's between them, holding it all together. Please, don't be late.

The Treasure
by Michael Davis

Michael Davis has been working in the military and intelligence community for thirty years. He has a Masters in Operations Research and a degree in Aerospace Engineering. In December, his political thriller, <u>Tinted Hero</u>, will be released by Chamagne Books.

After crashing on a far-off planet, a man battles loneliness the best way he can.

Jake heard the scream from the direction of the shoreline. He ripped his way through the dense undergrowth, but when he got there, she was gone. He followed the drag trail into the teal colored trees. After sixty yards he came to an opening, and there she was, the life being sucked from her small body. She reached for him, pleaded for relief. He struggled to help her, but he couldn't move. His feet were entangled in the roots of the forest; the vines rose up and anchored him to the ground. She called his name, again and again, begged him to save her, but he could only watch as she was slowly devoured. He looked toward the sky; cried out for a reprieve, but there was no one to help. He watched in horror as he lost her, and he could do nothing but weep.

Clang. Jake opened his eyes. His self made alarm worked this time. He pulled down the clear plastic container hanging over his head and shook it back and forth. The motion aggravated the two-inch long glowworms stored inside the container. The insects began to hiss as their bodies emitted a bright glow, equivalent to a 40-watt bulb.

He looked down at the floor and observed a two-foot long brown slug easing across the trip wire of his alarm. He removed the knife from the sleeve attached to his belt, tossed it at the creature and skewered the slimy thing to the ground.

Jake sat on the edge of the hand made cot and stared through the tent opening at his new world. He shook his head to force out the terrible images that hounded his dreams. The nightmares came less frequently now, but the memory was always there, leeching at his soul. For that one mistake, when he lowered his guard for an instant, he would be haunted for the remainder of his days.

Jake reached down for his knife and picked up one of the many hostile creatures he had learned to live with during the past eleven months. He smirked at the slug and declared, "Not this time. You already sucked off my little toe, you bastard. It's my turn to eat you." He tied a string around the extruded orifice at the front of the slug and hung his evening meal from the tent post to prevent the other little crawly things from stealing his dinner.

He walked outside and peered up at the three moons that cast a blue tinge across the landscape. "Might as well stay up. Not enough time before they start coming again." The six foot 220 pound man with sandy hair took a moment to enjoy the view of the sparkling turquoise shoreline eighty yards below his fortress. He watched forty-foot luminescent eels undulate in the surf, as the males jockeyed for access to a mate. He noticed the large six-legged pig like creature routing in the sand for shellfish deposited by the tide. "Watch it. You're getting too close." The animal had carelessly strayed next to a gapin burrow. "Too late." In an instant, the maroon-red sea leech shot out and latched its fangs into the side of its victim. The struggle for life subsided as the leech tranquilized its prey by injecting a pint of poison. Once the meal was enveloped, the leech retracted back into its hiding place beneath the sand.

"Guess I'll replenish my stock." Jake walked back to the tent and gathered an arm full of items from his arsenal. He walked along the rim of the plateau that defined his battlefront and distributed weapons at strategic locations where they tended to crawl up the ridge once the assault began. Jake shook his head at the contrast between the sophisticated armaments destroyed in the crash and his current defenses. His crude primitive weapons were simple: several crossbows he fabricated from the wreckage, spears fashioned from saplings, and large stones. Not much for a technology driven man, but enough to survive the last four months against the only weapon his adversaries possessed, their own bodies.

Satisfied that his stash would last through the upcoming battle, he walked back to the tent and examined the electronic components laid out on the table, "Maybe this time I fixed it." Jake spent the next few minutes reassembling his mission recorder. Then he picked up the wireless microphone, crossed his fingers and stated, "Testing, testing, one, two, three."

He flipped the playback switch, "Please work, you son of a bitch."

"Testing, testing, one, two, three."

"Finally! After all these months, I can start recording this fouled up mission."

Jake pulled back the flap of the tent and looked toward the horizon, "Fifteen minutes till sunrise. I'll record as much as I can before they come."

He shook the container of glowworms a few times, sat it on the table and began. "This is Major Hamilton, commander of the Specter Three deep probe mission. It's been eleven months since we arrived on this planet. In terms of where we are, I have no idea. Two years into the mission, something happened to the autonav system. We were all suspended, and by the time I refreshed, the command software had vectored us on a glide path to land on Aurora, or at least that's what I call this place. From our approach, the planet appeared to be roughly ninety percent water, with five or six large landmasses, each about half the size of Australia. A massive electro-magnetic pulse destroyed the mission flight data, so we could never figure how we got here instead of our original destination, Omega Four. The EM pulse toasted all our celestial instrumentation. I think we came too damn close to an uncharted gravity well. Life support lasted long enough to start the refresh cycle, but it screwed up on Captain Jones' suspension pod. By the time I recovered, his body had collapsed into a gelatinous form."

Jake took a drink of water from his canteen. It felt good to talk to someone, or at least to feel like he was talking to another human. "The gravity well must have slung us into a new trajectory. It was probably a black hole that exceeded its mass consumption capacity and emitted a powerful EM pulse. Fortunately, we were off on one of the field's side lobes; otherwise, we would have been fried to a cinder. With the sensors burned out, the landing radar was useless. I deployed the emergency deceleration chutes, but it wasn't enough. The ship skidded through thick undergrowth before hitting the rock ledge. It took out the entire right side, including Lieutenant Carol Manson's suspension pod. I went back to see if she survived, but there was nothing. Just pieces of her body scattered among the wreckage. I gathered what I could and buried the remains of Carol and Captain Jones up here on top of the plateau, so I can watch over them. Make sure nothing disturbs them."

He looked out at the crosses casting shadows in the bright moonlight. "Mary Thompson, the life sciences specialist, survived the crash. After we established a safe haven on the nearest plateau in the tropical forest, Mary began to investigate the multitude of life forms on the planet."

Jake smiled, "Tell Harry Myers I finally figured out why mission planning was so imperative about splitting the genders on each flight. I first thought it was some political statement, but now I understand the logic of their decision. The first five months weren't that bad. It was tough to figure out how to survive in this ecosystem, but at least we weren't alone. We had each other."

He removed his mother's medallion from his pocket and rubbed the smooth surface in the amber light of the glowworms. The heirloom was the only thing he kept. When she died, there was no one to leave behind, no reason not to join the deep probe mission group. Jake remembered when he gave Mary the memento as a gift for her birthday, three months after they crashed. It was the first time Mary kissed him.

He picked the microphone back up and continued. "When that thing took Mary, it was like I was thrown into some dark abyss. I walked around with no purpose for a long time. I never imagined it was possible to be this lonely, especially at night. The nights are unbearable. I still haven't adapted to all the noises, the gut wrenching screams as some prey loses its life."

Jake glanced at the closest cross of the three in the makeshift graveyard. "Mary and I really got close in those five months we struggled to survive. We never clicked back on earth, but here, we really bonded. We talked about how lucky we were to end up together, even if it was all the way out here. We even discussed starting a family."

He gazed out at the pink clouds reflecting sunlight from below the mountain, "I tried to save her, but by the time I got there, the eight foot segmented centipede had injected too much digestive fluid. It took two days before she finally died. I had to watch her slowly dissolve, listen to her suffer. I'll never forget it, never. I considered stopping her pain, bringing it to an end, but I just couldn't do it. God forgive me, but I lacked the courage."

A dim light blanketed the horizon as the sun neared the ridgeline. The looming dawn brought the first series of clicks and low resonant snorts. "I don't have much time before they start again. Mary learned that the dominant species on this planet is a four-legged mammal that has the appearances of a large green cat like creature. She named the species 'the Clickers', because of their constant chatter of alternating clicks and snorts. They're basically peaceful, thriving on the fruits and berries that grow abundantly in the forest. Their faces are humanoid in form, with oval eyes, and small noses, like those on a tiny puppy. Their four-inch long elfin ears provide exceptional warning against approaching predators. They also appear to be a matriarchal-based species. The females determine what each cluster of Clickers does, and when." He grinned. "Much like with human women."

Jake consumed a large pear shaped fruit and then continued. "The males average about one hundred and seventy pounds and move around on all four extremities. The females are roughly thirty pounds lighter and spend most of their time in trees, but they walk upright as bipeds, just like us. This arboreal behavior has evolved a four-foot tail for balance, and a fourteen inch tapered tongue to help reach fruit on the smaller upper limbs."

The first of Aurora's two suns peeked above the mountain, and the chatter below in the forest stopped. "Crap. I've got to go. They'll be coming up the ridge for me. I'll explain more later."

He turned off the recorder and ran toward his observation post at the edge of the plateau. It was still too dark to see them climbing up the hill, but he knew they were coming; they always did. No matter how many he killed, they still came. For a six-day period every two months, his existence had diminished into a constant battle with an alien life form that he had come to understand too late.

In the dim light he caught movement. One edged up the hill thirty yards down, the second just cresting the ridge. He picked up a spear and raced to meet the first Clicker. When the creature leapt toward him, Jake placed the rear of his wooden lance in the ground and vectored the point directly into the airborne male. The beast howled in pain, suspended momentarily in the air from the tip of the spear, and then slowly collapsed to a limp body impaled on a stake. Jake allowed the corpse to arch down to the ground. Then he stood up and ran in the direction of the second Clicker. He cleared the edge of the ridge and swore. "Shit!"

Two more males could be seen coming out of the tree line. He quickly picked up a small stone and threw it down at the second male. The creature jumped to the right causing the projectile to miss its target, but the pebble had served only as a diversion. The larger rock, thrown seconds after the first stone, hit its objective and cracked the skull of the small male. From experience, Jake knew the Clickers tended to jump to the right and immediately launched the true bullet, as he had done so many times before. He bolted toward the third creature as it crawled above the ridge. He raised his club and brought it down hard on the neck of the male, causing it to roll back down the hill. Jake turned toward the fourth Clicker, but it was too late. He raised his arm to protect his throat. The large male bit down hard, piercing skin and muscle. Jake screamed from the pain. He quickly removed his knife from his belt, and thrust the eight-inch blade deep into the creature's chest. The Clicker released its grip and howled. The green blood mixed with the red flowing from Jake's wound. He stabbed the creature again, then again, until it dropped to the ground and lay motionless. He heaved the body over the edge of the plateau and yelled down toward the remaining Clickers hidden behind the tree line. "Stop this madness, this senseless killing! I'm not your enemy. I just want to survive. I can't return your treasure. I won't, never!"

Once he successfully dispatched the first wave, Jake knew he could take a break. More would come, but not for several hours. He never figured out the strange pattern to their attack cycle, but they always came in waves of two to four, separated by several hours of clicking and howling behind the trees. Then, when they became silent, it would start all over again. He walked back to his tent and removed a strip of cloth from his medical kit. He poured water on his wound to remove the dirt, sprinkled disinfectant along his forearm, and wrapped his wound. He surveyed the scars on his arms and both legs that he obtained from similar battles. Then he picked up the recorder. He thought about telling the truth, the real reason for this eternal conflict, but he just couldn't say it.

"They've stopped for now. I have a little time before the next attack. I'll try to finish this up and launch the communication rocket before they come at me again. At least you'll know one of us survived the mission and is still here. Not that I expect any rescue attempts. By the time you get this, I'll probably be an old man. Or perhaps I'll have been dead for a long time, but at least you'll know what we learned about this planet. I'll include all the data Mary collected before she was killed. There's something else, something not on the data disk. As I mentioned before, the females tend to stay in the trees. I believe this behavior is a defensive reaction. There is a disparate ratio of males to females, about twelve to one from the groups I've observed. I think this lop sided ratio is a result of the aggressive nature of their mating habits. When the females come into heat, the typically docile males go absolutely insane. When a female chooses a mate, she comes down from the tree to couple. Just before she's ready to copulate, the silver mane of hair tracing down her back begins to change colors, rippling through all the hues in the spectrum. It's quite beautiful to watch. Then the female discharges a powerful sweet melon scent that has an intoxicating affect on her mate. This sudden release of such a stimulating aroma causes other males in the area to hone in on the bonding pair. During the ensuring confrontation, the females are often severely injured or even killed inadvertently. In an attempt to survive, the females select mates that are the largest of the pack, but have the mildest disposition toward them."

Jake hesitated. He considered again sharing the truth, but instinctively he knew they would never understand. They would consider him insane, warped. How could they think anything else? If they were isolated on this planet, maybe they could relate to what happened, but they weren't. Besides, who were they to judge? They weren't here, living the hell he was. If they were, perhaps they might be more forgiving. Jake took a deep breath and then made his decision. He would tell them what really took place; the terrible flaw in his judgment that had caused this senseless conflict. Hell, he would never see another human again anyway.

"As part of the mating ritual, the males deliver offerings to the females. It reminds me of when humans use flowers, candy and similar gifts to woo the favor of an intended mate, but with one difference. The gifts infer a stronger intent. They are meant to attract the female down from the tree and encourage her to mate. On second thought, maybe it's not so different from back home, but that's where I made my mistake. I wanted to take a closer look at the offerings the males placed beneath the treed females and labored so hard to protect. There was something unusual about these gifts. The males behaved as if the offerings were a matter of life and death, each guarding their own pile like it was some valuable treasure.

Through the binoculars, many of the gifts appeared to possess a strange crystalline form, almost like processed diamonds and rubies. Maybe it started with a hint of greed. Why I would care about anything of value out here was stupid. I learned too late what they were really protecting, the true treasure. I misinterpreted every damn thing, and for that mistake I've paid, over and over. I guess its penance for my sins."

Jake turned toward the deafening silence. "My God, they're coming again, so soon. They've never done this before."

He turned off the recorder and charged toward the ridge, just in time to catch two Clickers advancing on his location. He raised his crossbow, fired, and killed the first male midair. He stretched the bowstring to reload, but as he turned he saw the second Clicker coiled and ready to pounce. He dropped the crossbow, reached for his dagger, and turned to meet his adversary. The male prepared to launch at its enemy, but became distracted by a mild clicking sound emanating from behind Jake. He caught the unmistakable scent of sweet melon just before the first spear came from behind him and penetrated the ribcage of the male. Then a second spear lodged in its neck, killing it instantly.

Jake took a deep breath, and sighed. He heard the soft footsteps approach from behind. A long tongue gently caressed his neck as a green four-fingered hand dropped a third spear by his side, before gently stroking his arm. He greeted the small female with a smile and a double click to indicate his gratitude for her act of saving his life. As the dark green creature purred, she tenderly wrapped her tail around his leg.

"I know sweetheart. I want you too, but not till the sun goes down." He pointed at the horizon and arched his hand down below the mountain to indicate nightfall.

The female's expression signaled disappointment, but then she shook her head to show she understood. She gracefully moved back to the base of her resident tree, curled up on a bed of leaves, and remained fixed on the actions of her mate.

He heard the chatter began again below the ridge and knew they were safe, at least for the moment. He picked two pear shaped fruits off the nearest tree and walked over to the female. Then Jake sat down by her side, offered both fruits and slowly stroked her back. He admired the change of colors rippling through the hair running along her mane. It reminded him of Christmas lights sweeping through a rainbow of colors.

He gazed at the expression of contentment on her face, and considered his mistake. The presents that each male offered, their protective response, the gifts—they did not treasure these things—no, it was the female. Even at the cost of their lives, the males would do anything to maintain their possession over the female, as they had proved again and again. Jake pondered the chain of events he had set in motion by his decision four months ago. If he had understood all this in the beginning, would he still have placed his bright red holographic identification tag in the pile of gifts to attract the female down from her tree? Then he realized he would do the same thing all over, change nothing. Even with the attacks, the injuries, the pain, he refused to be alone again.

While the female softly rubbed her face against his leg, Jake recognized his destiny. Just like the male Clickers, he would defend the treasure with his life. The alternative was unbearable. He'd rather be dead than by himself again, like after he lost Mary. Now at least he had a companion, someone to share the lonely nights with. And he would never give that up, go back to being isolated on this God-awful planet.

He rubbed behind the female's left ear, "Perhaps it's time you have a name. What about Mary? Do you like that?" Then he pulled the medallion out of his pocket and clipped it to the chain around her neck that held his identification tag.

Jake felt the female tremble and press into his side as a series of loud howls echoed from below the ridge. "Don't worry sweetheart. It's just two more days and then they'll stop. You'll always be safe up here with me. I won't let them take you. You'll never be hurt again, never . . . I promise, Mary."

The Darkness of Truth
by Steven Mathes

Steven Mathes has done it all. He has been a college ski coach. He has been a carpenter. He has been a computer system administrator. He is now a high school Math teacher. His most recent writing has appeared in Linux Journal and OG's Speculative Fiction.

In this story a teacher learns how dangerous it is to teach the truth.

They smash heavy stuff against the door. They improvise. They hope to find the right battering ram. Meanwhile, the teacher waits inside. The door could stop a cruise missile. They smash and smash, and it barely vibrates. Someone comes with a bulldozer. They weld a thick steel ram to the blade and smash. The bulldozer loses a tread, breaks the blade. Some of the mob go back to the drawing board. The others guard the door, rifles in hand.

Nobody has tried the latch. The door is unlocked.

The teacher sighs. Under different circumstances this would be a teachable moment.

This is the teacher's third and last post. The other two ended badly, but he chose to extract himself before it came to this. Latching the door would still extract him to safety. The door to a school like his only locks once.

Someone will try the door sooner or later. In an hour. In a day. In a week. That's basic psychology.

He taught here for two years.

His first student walked in on a whim. The student called himself Aaron. At first he smirked a lot. He was probably fifteen. He smelled like cigarette smoke. Bright boy, very bright.

"Is this a hippie school?"

He swatted at the tentacles growing from the ceiling. They looked and felt like strings of beads. There was no furniture, though the tiny room had once been a cobbler's shop.

"What do you teach here?"

"What do you want to know?"

"Why's it just say 'School' on the sign? Isn't that a little vague?"

"No," the teacher said. "Anything you want to know, I'll teach. More words on the sign would imply limitations."

"Anything?"

"Anything except personal information on my students."

"So you'll teach me how to commit the perfect murder."

"Yes."

"How to get the girl that lives down the street."

"Yes."

"What if she's a potential student?"

"She isn't."

"How can you be sure?"

"The first job of any teacher is to make that judgment."

Aaron mulled this over, smirking harder than ever. He squinted at the teacher. He craned his neck, and tried to get a better view inside the hood of the teacher's cowl.

"You look like you have an eating disorder. And your color's off."

The teacher said nothing, not knowing what to say. Aaron craned for a view of the teacher's eyes.

"Do you even know what I'm talking about? Are you like some kind of monk?"

"I am not of your world. I am allowed to follow my students only. I am not allowed to know about the issues of the world because I might be tempted."

"Tempted to do what?"

"Tempted to take charge."

Aaron shook his head and laughed.

"Will you teach me to beat you in an argument?"

"The dream of many teachers is to be surpassed by a student. I count myself among them."

"How much does it cost?"

"There is no charge, if you're talking about money. I don't even steal your soul. However, most people discover that truth is a heavy burden."

"Sign me up, then! Teach me everything!"

The smirk took over his whole face. The teacher frowned.

"I can do that, but it will require many lessons. After the first, you'll have a good idea of what you're in for. Just the truth from a single lesson is a heavy burden, and once learned, it can't be taken back."

"Don't patronize me. When do I start?"

The teacher could see the student's hunger. Aaron deserved what he was about to get.

"Right now," the teacher said. "A handshake seals the deal."

They shook. The teacher's hand was thin but it clamped over Aaron's like a claw.

When Aaron took his hand away, the first lesson was his. He looked around the tentacled room in amazement. The room did the mechanics of the teaching. It consisted of technology beyond anything Aaron's culture would create for thousands of years, unaided. Of course, now he'd been aided. And now Aaron understood.

He walked out without a word, bent under the dual burden of wisdom and adolescence.

He never came back, but his fame spread within days.

There was one other student.

After Aaron, the teacher turned up the settings on the doorway. Anyone near the school learned enough to stay away. Or at least anyone incapable of absorbing the entire curriculum.

Perhaps by then the teacher knew he was in deep trouble. Perhaps before then, perhaps all along.

Elise came in several weeks after Aaron, like a bird seeking shelter from the storm. According to readings from the door, her potential was off the scale. She was just shy of thirteen. She did not smell of cigarettes. Her eyes projected sentience like a warning.

Much more than the teacher could have known.

"This is like a place for tutoring?" she asked.

"Very specialized."

"Well the name is like very UN-specialized!"

She locked the teacher with those deep eyes of steel. She smiled gently. The smile warned, but the teacher missed this second warning. She seemed too young.

"Besides," she said. "You learn what this place does when you walk in the door."

Warned again. This time he got it.

"You're not supposed to learn that much from the door. What did the door tell you?" he asked.

"I'm not telling! I'm the student. I get to ask stuff. And you're the teacher. You tell me stuff. And it doesn't cost money. The cost is different."

The teacher nodded, suddenly nervous. They both stood, since there were no chairs. This school needed no chairs.

"So what's the difference between knowledge and truth?"

"You shake my hand, you know the difference."

"Yes, and there's no going back. So first you tell me stuff."

"Like what?"

"Like you give me the executive summary."

She stepped back, proud of this turn of phrase. The teacher leaned in, his hooded head loomed.

"Truth can be proved. Truth is cold and pitiless. Truth doesn't care about your happiness, your faith, your illusions. Truth destroys."

"You're better at being spooky than you are at telling the truth."

She stepped back farther and flipped her hair out of her eyes. So easy to underestimate. But then she stepped forward and put her face right back, inches from his.

"So tell me about Aaron."

Now the teacher stepped back, staggered really.

"Aaron?"

"Aaron came here. I can tell. Some people think he's like the Messiah."

"Aaron did not complete his studies."

"But he knows the difference between knowledge and truth."

"Somewhat. And he has not taken his own life."

She straightened. Light dawned in her eyes.

"You mean suicide?"

"Precisely."

"So I could always commit suicide."

She turned and paced back and forth. She came back to him.

"If I can't take the truth, I can always kill myself!"

She nodded in satisfaction.

"It's so simple!" she said.

Without a word, she took his hand and held it. It was not a handshake but it was enough. The terrified teacher knew the intent. She held on a long time, although the transfer was instantaneous. The teacher assumed she was stunned. But when she took her hand away she leaned in and kissed him gently on the cheek.

"No need to be scared," she said.

She took up his hands, then patted him on the arm.

"I'm okay," she said. "I took it fine."

She laughed. More womanly than girlish.

"Your job is to tell me to go now."

"Yes."

"I need to let the lesson settle for a few days."

"Yes."

"See you!" said Elise.

It took more than a few days. It took so long that the room allowed him to search, within limits.

There were no reports of a young girl's miracles. Months passed. No death notices. The teacher lived in a storm of ambivalence. He scanned the streets, followed every available record, which was everything recorded in any medium. He scanned for her name. He ignored all else, as instructed by the room.

Finally, ordinary summer vacation for ordinary children ended. Her name surfaced. School databases recorded her attendance, then grades, then newspapers printed her name on honor rolls. She behaved as she always had, lived as she always had. Very bright but very normal. Sometimes he hoped she would return. Often he hoped she would stay away.

Meanwhile, Aaron gathered followers, but encountered strange setbacks. Some miracles failed to work. A movement aimed at discrediting him grew stronger. Unrest spread. A hidden power seemed to resist. Wars loomed. This world had become tinder for its own inferno.

The teacher could have locked the door just then. Lesser fiascoes in other worlds had closed more successful schools. Indeed, the teacher's hand twitched toward the lock more than once.

But she finally returned. After more than a year.

"It took more than a few days," she admitted.

"Are you ready for the next step?"

She had matured. There was the obvious difference, the before-and-after of first adolescence, but there was even more of the change in her eyes.

"For a little while, I thought I was done."

"You doubted you could go on?"

"No, I thought I had it all. Silly me."

"That would have been impossible."

"Obviously!"

Her physical readings showed the child of fourteen, but anyone looking into that face would see an old woman. The turns of phrase were those of an actress, pretending to be young. Those steel eyes showed the weather of experience.

"Aaron's been a problem," she said.

"On the other hand, you haven't."

"Oh, yes I have. At least to Aaron."

"But you've kept a low profile."

"Well, he's starting to catch on."

"Meaning?"

"Meaning that everyone can see he's hit resistance. He knows there's only one ultimate source. That would be here."

"I'm supposed to close my school if there is violence between my students."

"And if they're evenly matched, it always destroys everything."

She took his hand. She released. Transfer completed.

"The match has never been even," she said.

The teacher needed to sit. But there were no chairs in this school, not even for the teacher.

"Normally, there are a dozen lessons," he said.

"Yes."

"But I've taught you all I know in two."

"Yes."

She patted him on the cheek. She walked out. She would return one more time.

This time the wait was only a few months. Aaron continued to make news and trouble. Elise stayed hidden, invisible. Factions polarized. Small wars blossomed. Empires sparred. Catastrophe loomed.

She took the trouble of waiting outside the school until the teacher noticed. When she finally entered, the door failed to announce her. This was impossible. The door's primary function was to warn. Either the door had failed or she had learned the impossible.

"But the door..." he said.

"I've mastered the art of sneaking around."

"But I've already taught you all I know..." he said.

"So now I do the teaching."

The room was equipped for that. She took his hand. When he took his hand away, the lesson was his.

"The horror." he said. "The horror."

"That's what happens when you improve the natives!"

The teacher's knees gave out. He slumped into a corner, settled into sitting on the floor. He supposed that if he were human, he would want a drink. Now that he knew what a drink was. Elise went to her knees at his feet. She put a consoling hand on his arm, although her face was strangely triumphant. He finally spoke.

"You teach your own. You have no teaching room. How do you teach?"

"I would explain if the room would allow."

"And some of the knowledge you just gave me is untrue. I know. I know the truth. How do you get the room to convey what it's designed to filter out?"

"The room denies, doesn't it? That's my proof. It denies what is true and yet I can make it accept a lie. I sneak through the door, and then I tell lies to the room."

There was exaltation in her voice.

"How are you any different from Aaron?" asked the teacher.

"I am much more dangerous. I know more than Aaron. I know more than you. I know more than your truth!"

"All this violence..."

"Just the beginning."

"Can't you teach me the way you teach each other? Can't you help me save your people?"

"You don't have the gift. This room limits, but it is a reflection of your limitations."

"You're just a child!"

She stood. Just a child.

"Honestly? You should have killed us all when you had the chance."

"We don't kill."

"That much is true. But not the whole truth."

His mouth worked. Nothing came out.

"A partial truth," she said. "On our world, a partial truth is a kind of lie."

"We mean no harm. We merely seek to improve, to spread truth."

"You seek to destroy. You said it yourself. Truth destroys. You don't kill but you destroy."

"What have I destroyed here? What have I changed that destroys anything valuable?"

"Your safety. The safety of your people. I can't protect you from Aaron any longer. There's too much truth in what he says."

"And what does he say that I haven't already learned?"

"That he can take people to the stars. And he can!"

"But that was a gift we intended to give. I already know that."

"We like to conquer. We like to be in charge. We dislike being told what to do."

He saw their world, now. He saw the wars, the lies, the starvation, the crowding, the pollution. Mere practice. Nothing but training for expansion. This planet was pregnant, and these people were the spores. This was the closest he could come to description.

"We have a civilization," said the teacher. "It is older than your species. So much beauty, so much tradition, so much justice will be lost."

"Yes."

"And you?"

"I've protected you. I can sneak through the door. Aaron can't."

"And he's about to try. And he wants to use the room to follow me home."

"So you need to leave now."

As if to set a good example, she did likewise. She patted his cheek and left.

Yes, this was to be his third and last post. It left him paralyzed, afraid of being followed, but mostly too ruined to care, to move.

He still sits in the corner, his human simulacrum rumpled and pale. The mob outside the door has returned with a howitzer. Its power is enough to make the door drum with each armor-piercing shell. According to what Elise has taught him, they have new weapons. Some can get through the door, although they will destroy the city in the process.

They will destroy the city. They will get through. Truth destroys.

All the time, he watches for just anyone to come up and try the latch.

He watches only the door, so it startles him when he hears the clearing of a throat.

The boy cannot be six years old, but his eyes are those of an old man.

"How did you get in? You didn't even use the door."

"Sir," the boy says. "Elise will distract them. She will distract Aaron. This will give you time to throw the latch and escape. This will give your people time to hide. This will give all of us time, which is all anyone ever gets."

The boy disappears. Vanishes. After time, the mob disperses.

Time. The ugliest truth of all.

After time, the teacher stands. No, he cannot kill. Nor can he let himself die. He discovers that his human simulacrum can shed human tears. He must live and warn his people. The latch is at his fingertips, but there is so much time, time before he actually needs to touch it.

The Fate of the Crystal Eye
by Barton Paul Levenson

Barton Paul Levenson has a degree in physics and is happily married to the genre poet, Elizabeth Penrose. His work has appeared in Marion Zimmer Bradley's Fantasy Magazine, Crickets, Cicada, and the New York Review of Science Fiction. He was prohibited from entering the Confluence Short Story Contest after winning first prize two years in a row.
What is and what will be can all be changed by merely dropping your...

I had been warned since the beginning of time that if ever I were to drop the Crystal Eye, all that ever was, is, or will be would be changed irrevocably. As the aeons wore on, this came to weigh more and more heavily on my mind, until it became my chief concern, my love and my hatred, the apple of my eye and the Nemesis of my soul.

I went to see Klotho about it, for I have always listened to her advice. Through the Crystal Eye she appeared as a spider, hunched over on her abdomen in the corner of the cave she dwells in with her two sisters. Whenever we spoke—and whenever we didn't—her eight legs were always busy, busy, busy, drawing the line from her abdomen, eight delicate pincers braiding it into life-line. As soon as it was finished her sister Lakhesis, old woman of long gray hair and blind, cataract-clouded eyes, snatched it from her and instantly stretched it to various lengths, two span, one span, almost nothing, her long, thin fingers holding it up to the darkness of the cavern. The moment she was done measuring it her sister Att'ropos clipped it with her heavy, silver shears. No one has ever seen Att'ropos, not even me with the Crystal Eye. She is merely a hand coming out of the darkness at the far end of the cave, bearing the heavy silver shears that cut the life-line. The time between when Lakhesis finishes measuring and when Att'ropos closes shears defines an instant. It is the smallest time known, and may well be zero.

The stuff of life that comes from Klotho's abdomen is, of course, in infinite supply. Indeed, I have often seen her draw forth infinite lengths of it, braid it, and cast it into eternity, for how else could there be immortals? On these occasions, Lakhesis stands by and smiles resignedly, her hands at her sides, and Att'ropos howls for frustration and loss.

"I worry, Klotho," I told the spinner. "I worry that if ever I were to drop the Crystal Eye, all that ever was, is, or will be would be changed irrevocably."

"Your worry is of no significance," said Klotho in her warm contralto, an odd voice for a spider. "All fate is subject to us, the three sisters; even the gods are in our hands. What will be, will be, and nothing can be done to change it; it is absolutely determined. Except, of course, if you were to drop the Crystal Eye, for that would change all. Yet even that is a determined event, for if you will, you will, and if you will not, you will not."

"Then, perhaps I should stop worrying? For if the thing is beyond my control, there can be no point in worrying about it."

"No," said Klotho. "You have failed to understand. You must worry, for you are a worrier, and that, too, is part of the fixed and unalterable nature of events. To be you is to worry, and you can no more change that than you can change anything else—that is your nature, essence, genus, difference and species."

I wailed with woe and fled wailing down the empty corridors of time. When I emerged I was in the sunlight, holding the Crystal Eye in my place in the Festival of Parade. Ahead of me marched the Muses, bearing behind them the long, fluttering banners of epic poetry, history, lyric poetry, music, tragedy, religious music, dance, comedy, astronomy. Each banner was one of the nine major colors of the spectrum. Behind me drums thumped, flutes piped, and somewhere Aphroditay and Arres made moaning love on the Float of Conjugal Fidelity.

It was a reassuring and homely scene, and did much to ease my heart. But then I caught sight of Trickster far ahead, stealing batons from the dancing Oceanids and substituting branches, meter-sticks and tire irons before the young goddesses knew the difference.

I saw him heading toward me and called out, "Trickster, do not come near! Go away, Trickster! I exorcise you, I throw you out! Go back to the Abyss where you belong!"

It only made him shake his head and pout as he came closer, for he pretends to be easily hurt. "You do me wrong," he said, wiping crocodile tears from each bloodshot eye. "Why do you dislike me so?"

"Because you disrupt everything for the sheer, evil joy of it, and besides that, you have filthy habits and you exploit people. As Koyotay you have sexual intercourse with your own daughter. As Hermes you steal Apollo's cattle and hide them. As Yaakov you favor Rakhel and are cruel to Leah. As Loki you plot to assassinate Baldur. And as serpent you are forever trying to sell me apples!"

"I know," he said. "That would make anyone dislike me. But why do *you* dislike me?"

"Because I fear you will make me drop the Crystal Eye."

"But why would I do that?" protested Trickster. "All my tricks are done to gain me something, and the effects of your dropping the Crystal Eye are incalculable. If I made you drop it, I might no longer be Trickster. Then I could no longer molest my daughter, steal cattle, play favorites or plan Baldur's death."

"That's true," I admitted.

"Let's find out," he said, and he smashed his fist down on the Crystal Eye. I fumbled with it, and almost had it, but then it slipped from my hands and shattered to shards on the pavement.

At once, all that ever was, is, or will be was changed irrevocably. I was no longer He Who Holds the Crystal Eye; I was now Robert L. Linz, billionaire investor, a person I had no interest in being. The Crystal Eye shattered on the pavement was my reading glasses shattered on the sidewalk.

I went into the drugstore for change to call my optometrist. Among the change I got back for my dollar was two nickels and a penny—and five and six made eleven, not thirteen as they had done from the beginning of time. If there were still gods, fates, and personified abstractions ruling the Universe, I was no longer among them.

It is petty of me, considering the magnitude of the change, but the worry that nags at me most since that awful day is that I never asked Klotho how long I would live. For it is a myth that one cannot know one's own fate. Klotho will tell anyone who asks her the dates of their birth and death and how long one has between, and all you have to do is to find her. But since the beginning of time, in all the times I spoke with Klotho—and all the times I didn't—I never once thought to ask.

And never will I have another chance.

Story Copyrights

"The Other Side" © 2007 by Greg Schwartz

"With Mars in His Hand" © 2007 by Bosley Gravel

"Certified Organic" © 2007 by Sara Genge

"Five Dead Women" © 2007 by Lori Strongin

"Bilroy Five" © 2007 by Michael Savastano

"Something Sinister" © 2007 by Joseph Vadalma

"Deep Waters" © 2007 by Manfred Gabriel

"Love in the Time of the Serpent-King" © 2007 by Rachel Astruc

"Dwarfblood" © 2007 by Berrien Henderson

"Poetic License" © 2007 by Lindsey Duncan

"Farewell Dinner" © 2007 by Jakob Drud

"I Am Tellis Moore" © 2007 by L. Christopher DelGuercio

"Inside of Me" © 2007 by James Steimle

"Paper Cuts" © 2007 by Timalyne Frazier

"The Treasure" © 2007 by Michael Davis

"The Darkness of Truth" © 2007 by Steven Mathes

"The Fate of the Crystal Eye" © 2007 by Barton Paul Levenson